Praise for **Kate Bateman**

A DARING PURSUIT

"The ambitious, intelligent leads are admirable and easy to root for, and their erotic spark is undeniable. The fast-paced romance and undercurrent of suspense keeps the pages flying." —*Publishers Weekly*

"*A Daring Pursuit* is a winsome enemies-to-lovers tale."
—*Romance Junkies*

A RECKLESS MATCH

"Bateman launches a Regency trilogy with this pitch-perfect enemies-to-lovers romance centered on the feuding Montgomery and Davies families . . . Brimming with intrigue, passion, and humor, this is sure to win the author new fans."
—*Publishers Weekly* (starred review)

"*A Reckless Match* is sexy, sassy and distinctly divine. Explosive!" —*Romance Junkies*

THIS EARL OF MINE

"Bateman's scintillating first Bow Street Bachelors Regency is full of intense emotions and dramatic twists. Intelligent, affable characters make this fast-paced novel shine, especially for fans of clever women and the men who sincerely admire them. Future installments will be eagerly anticipated by Regency readers."
—*Publishers Weekly* (starred review)

ALSO BY KATE BATEMAN

Ruthless Rivals

A Reckless Match
A Daring Pursuit

Bow Street Bachelors

This Earl of Mine
To Catch an Earl
The Princess and the Rogue

A Wicked Game

Kate Bateman

St. Martin's Paperbacks

This is a work of fiction. All of the characters, organizations, and events portrayed in this novel are either products of the author's imagination or are used fictitiously.

First published in the United States by St. Martin's Paperbacks, an imprint of St. Martin's Publishing Group

A WICKED GAME

For information, address St. Martin's Publishing Group, 120 Broadway, New York, NY 10271.

www.stmartins.com

ISBN 978-1-250-80158-6

Our books may be purchased in bulk for promotional, educational, or business use. Please contact your local bookseller or the Macmillan Corporate and Premium Sales Department at 1-800-221-7945, ext. 5442, or by email at MacmillanSpecialMarkets@macmillan.com.

Printed in the United States of America

St. Martin's Paperbacks edition / January 2023

10 9 8 7 6 5 4 3 2 1

Prologue

June 1813

If there was one thing impossible for a Davies to resist, it was a challenge from a Montgomery.

Harriet Montgomery knew this in the same way she knew the earth revolved around the sun. She also knew, with aggravating certainty, that her life would be infinitely less exciting if Morgan Davies managed to get himself killed while off fighting against Napoleon. The man was insufferable, but their gleeful mutual animosity had been a constant in her existence for as long as she could remember.

Who would torment her if he were dead? Who would she delight in infuriating as much?

No one.

It simply wouldn't do.

One solution, of course, would be to tell him she hoped he never came back. Generations of Davieses had made it their primary goal to thwart their Montgomery rivals, and Morgan wasn't one to flout tradition. He would stay alive just to spite her.

But Harriet couldn't bring herself to utter those particular words. She *did* want him to come back—as annoying as that was to admit—and she preferred not to lie unless absolutely necessary.

The best way to ensure that he returned safely, therefore, was to offer him the chance to get the upper hand in their never-ending battle of one-upmanship. At least temporarily. He would do everything in his power to make it back to England simply for the chance to gloat. Or to claim his prize.

He was leaving tomorrow. Which was precisely why she'd saved her most outrageous dare for tonight. Why she'd allowed him to corner her in Lady Glencoe's ballroom.

She had to give him something worth living for.

"I suppose you've heard I'm off in the morning?"

Morgan kept his tone studiously carefree. It had taken him twenty minutes to maneuver Harriet Montgomery into a quiet corner of Lady Glencoe's ballroom, and he relished the hectic flush that rose to her cheeks when she realized she'd been trapped into a private conversation with him.

"Yes, I'd heard."

Harriet's gray eyes clashed with his and his gut tightened in response, but he kept his face as inscrutable as ever. It would be a cold day in hell before he revealed the effect she had on him.

He tilted his head and sent her a mocking glance. "What, no tears to send me on my way? No wistful good-byes? Perhaps you're hoping I'll meet a watery end out there in the Atlantic?"

Her cheeks reddened even more. It could have been with embarrassment, or merely irritation. It was too much to hope for both.

"My commiserations would be for the fishes, for having to endure your eternal company," she said pertly. "Now step aside."

He grinned at her acerbic wit and stayed right where

he was. "Come now. Aren't you the least bit worried that I might come to grief? Who will you aim your barbs at if I'm not here to be your target?"

She raised her brows. "As much as your presence irks me, Davies, I'm not so mean-spirited as to wish you *serious* harm."

Her overly sweet tone indicated that a small degree of injury—a bloody nose or a slapped face, for example—would be perfectly acceptable. Morgan fought the urge to laugh. He'd take a slap from Harriet over a kiss from another woman any day. He sent her a mocking bow. "I'm touched by your concern."

"I *am* concerned, actually. You've had the devil's own luck up until now. You've managed to wriggle, fight, or charm your way out of every sticky situation you've been in. But luck runs out—especially in wartime." She shook her head. "You men are all so foolishly heroic, I bet you'll do something stupid and end up dead."

Morgan's grin turned wolfish as he pounced on her careless wording. "You'll *bet me*, eh? Very well. I accept."

"Accept what?"

"Your bet."

Harriet blinked. "It was a figure of speech! I—"

"No, no. You said, '*I bet you'll end up dead*,' and I'll take that bet. Nothing would give me greater pleasure than to disoblige you."

"Oh, for goodness' sake." Harriet gave a huff of disapproval, but Morgan was sure her lips twitched with the slightest hint of amusement too. His gut tightened in response. She really did have the most tempting lips.

"So what are we playing for?" he pressed.

Her cool gray eyes studied his face with such intensity that for a brief moment he lost the thread of the conversation.

"Fine. I'll play. If you return alive, Morgan Davies, I'll give you . . ."

His brain snapped back to attention. "Three wishes? Like a genie in one of those Eastern fairy tales?"

She scowled at his cheeky suggestion. "No! You'd make me do something illegal, or dangerous. Or something that would ruin my reputation."

He clapped his hand to his chest in faux distress. "You wound me, Miss Montgomery! But all right, think of something else. Something good. If I lose, I'll be dead, remember. And you'll be celebrating."

"If you win, I'll declare *in public* that you're my favorite Davies."

"Pfft. That's like saying I'm your favorite strain of cholera. Try again."

"Very well." Her gaze dropped to his lips and a flash of naughty amusement lit her face. His cock twitched in his breeches.

"If you win, and return home unscathed, I'll grant you three . . . kisses."

Morgan blinked. In all their previous interactions, they'd never bet with anything so physical.

So intimate.

With anything he'd wanted more.

Harriet's cheeks were scarlet and he could see from the panicked rise and fall of her chest that she'd surprised *herself* with her provocative response, but she forced her gaze back up to his and their eyes clashed again.

The gauntlet had been thrown down.

The game was on.

He leaned in, enjoying the way she backed against the wall to try to maintain a chaste distance. He caught a tantalizing whiff of her floral perfume, and bent his head until his lips hovered near her ear.

"Enduring three kisses from me is the worst forfeit you can think of?"

"It is." She sounded rather breathless.

"Worse than attending a ball without a corset, or accepting a dance from Lord Litchfield?"

He pulled back just a fraction, until they were nose to nose, and tilted his head to indicate the aging, lecherous aristocrat to their right. The man was as renowned for his lack of bathing as he was for his wandering hands.

A flash of defiance lit Harriet's gray eyes. "A hundred times worse."

He sent her a cynical, mocking look. "What did Shakespeare say about ladies who protest too much? I'm starting to think you'd *like* me to kiss you."

"I'd rather kiss a frog," she said quickly. "A frog would have a chance of turning into a handsome prince."

"Whereas I'll never be anything other than an ugly rogue, is that it?" he finished, amused.

"Precisely."

"Ah well. Since I *am* a rogue—although I disagree with you about the ugly part—I can't refuse your suggestion. Three kisses if I come back alive? Done."

He let his gaze linger for a long moment on her lips. God, if only he could give her a brief sample of what she'd let herself in for. His blood surged at the thought of pressing his mouth to hers. He'd dreamed of it forever. She would taste of disapproval and desire: a heady, irresistible combination.

She'd slap his face, of course, or knee him in the groin, and there would be one hell of a scandal. He was tempted to do it anyway and then sail away, leaving her blustering to make the necessary explanations.

But he wasn't such a cad as to ruin her in public. She might be a Montgomery, but she was still a lady.

"Would you like me to enter it in White's betting book? Make it official?" he teased, just to be perverse.

"What? No! The whole world would see it! This is between you and me, Davies. A private wager."

"Can a Montgomery be trusted to keep their word?"

She sent him an outraged glare, just as he'd known she would. "Of course!"

"All right then." He reached out and pinched her chin, forcing her to meet his eyes again. "You know I'll hold you to it, don't you?"

Her throat dipped as she swallowed. "Yes."

"Even if—by some miracle—you find a man fool enough to marry you while I'm gone, you'll still have to grant me those kisses."

"I know," she breathed.

"Good." With a final nod he forced himself to take a cooling step back.

God, they were ridiculous. Why couldn't they simply admit to wanting to kiss each other? But things had gone too far to backtrack now. They were stuck in this cycle of provocative teasing, even though there was no question that Harriet looked at him with a combination of irritation and reluctant desire.

She might be too innocent to realize what it was, but he was not. Unfortunately, there was nothing he could do about it now. Not when he was about to leave.

He sent her a mocking bow. "I'll bid you adieu, then, Miss Montgomery."

She caught his wrist as he straightened, surprising him. She rarely touched him voluntarily. His skin tingled at the unexpected contact, even though she was wearing evening gloves.

"Don't say adieu. Say *au revoir,*" she scolded. "We have to meet again if you want those kisses."

"Very well. *Au revoir*." He tried to lighten his tone, to leave her with a laugh, but a crushing sensation was squeezing his chest and a knot of emotion was forming in his throat. Leaving her was harder than he'd imagined, damn it.

She released his wrist and lifted her chin to that haughty angle that made him want to grab her and kiss her senseless. "Stay alive, Davies. If I hear that you've died, I will be *seriously displeased*."

Chapter One

As he strode along Whitehall, Morgan repressed the urge to whistle a jaunty sea shanty. The sky was blue, the birds were singing, and the world was, in general, rather excellent.

There was nothing like a brief spell in prison to put one's life in perspective, and he'd done a great deal of thinking while locked in his cell on Martinique. He'd returned to England with two specific goals: seduction, and revenge.

Although not necessarily in that order.

After almost two years traveling the globe with His Majesty's Royal Navy, he was back in London and buoyed by the fact that the revenge part of his plan was about to take a significant step forward. Robert Dundas—Viscount Melville and First Lord of the Admiralty—had finally agreed to disclose the identity of the mapmaker whose incorrect chart had been the cause of Morgan's shipwreck and subsequent detention six months ago.

Falsely accused of being an English spy by the island's sadistic French governor, Morgan had spent each and every day of his incarceration vowing to exact sweet revenge on the cartographer responsible for his suffering.

The error suggested a shocking lack of competence.

Sandbars, it was true, could shift position over time. *Entire bloody island chains* could not.

The defective map had borne the name of an engraver, "R. Crusoe" of Bury Street, Bloomsbury, but no mapmaker of that name existed in London. The pseudonym—employing the name of Daniel Defoe's fictional castaway—was clearly someone's idea of a joke.

Morgan hadn't found it remotely amusing.

But now, as he approached the Admiralty offices, a smile curved his lips. Today he would finally get some answers. And when he discovered the man behind that dangerously inaccurate map, he would track the bastard down and make him suffer.

He had no intention of subjecting the culprit to the same brutal hardships he himself had faced—starvation, beatings, unbearable thirst. He was nothing like General Jean-Luc De Caen, his captor, who'd treated Morgan and his crew with the utmost cruelty.

He just wanted an explanation. And an apology.

And then he'd punch the idiot in the face.

He'd lost weeks of his life in that sweaty, stinking hellhole of a prison. The least he could do was give the man a broken nose or a couple of cracked ribs, a few weeks of painful discomfort in return. That would be justice.

Morgan's fingers curled into an anticipatory fist.

Yes, such a revenge was rather petty, but he didn't care. It was the principle of the thing. Maps were supposed to be trustworthy. The Admiralty had no right using someone so lackadaisical, nor sending their fleet out with sub-par navigational aids. Men's lives had been put at risk.

His *own* life had been put at risk, and he would have been very cross indeed if he hadn't made it back to London in one piece to fulfill the other promise he'd made to himself.

This second part of his plan—the seduction—might well prove the more difficult, but he'd always relished a challenge.

It wouldn't have been a problem if he'd wanted just *any* woman in his bed. His dark good looks and cheeky smile had always made him a favorite with the ladies. Coupled with the resplendent blue and gold of his captain's uniform and the whisper of his heroics against Bonaparte, and he was well-nigh irresistible.

To every woman except one.

The one he wanted.

The one who'd haunted his nights and invaded his dreams for years: prickly, studious Harriet Jane Montgomery.

His sharp-tongued, lifelong obsession.

The rivalry between their two families had shaped their interactions ever since they were children. Over the years it had developed into a kind of gleeful antipathy, a never-ending game of one-upmanship that neither side would ever consider abandoning.

They'd teased each other with challenges and foolish bets, and the words "Go on, I *dare* you!" had been a constant refrain throughout his boyhood.

Sometimes they'd been uttered by one of his brothers, or by Carys, his sister. But when they'd been thrown at him by a Montgomery, especially in Harriet's prim-yet-mocking tones, the challenge had been impossible to ignore.

I dare you.

Those three words were the reason he'd broken his wrist the summer he was ten, why he'd almost drowned in Trellech's moat, and fallen from countless trees, ledges, and battlements. They were the reason he'd been scratched while trying to pet a leopard, and pecked while trying to pluck a feather from Geoffrey the peacock's tail.

There had always been a prize to play for—the literal spoils of war. His brother Gryff had stolen Maddie Montgomery's shawl and flown it in triumph from the battlements of Trellech Court. Morgan had filched Harriet's favorite drawing pen, the one with her initials engraved in the silver, and thrown it in the stream.

But then Harriet had punched him on the arm, her eyes suspiciously bright with tears, and Morgan's chest had tightened with something he rather feared was guilt. Because while he thoroughly enjoyed seeing her angry and irritated, he hated to see her genuinely upset.

When he heard Harriet's deceased mother had given it to her, he'd felt like the lowest heel. He'd scoffed that he'd lost his own mother too, and *he* didn't place such import on stupid pens . . . but his hitherto-dormant conscience had pricked at him.

He'd felt so bad, in fact, that he'd slipped out at dawn the next morning and waded into the freezing water to retrieve the damn thing, courting pneumonia, and cursing the bollock-shriveling cold with every step.

Since Harriet was one of the hated Montgomerys, he couldn't simply send it back to her with a note of apology. A Davies *never* apologized to a Montgomery. So he'd been in a quandary as to how to return it.

In the end he'd done it anonymously. He bribed two of the village boys a shilling to say they'd caught it in their net when landing a trout, and sworn them to secrecy on pain of a good thrashing if they ever revealed they'd been given it by him.

He shook his head wryly at the memory. Their sparring had continued right up until Morgan had left for war.

It would not be an exaggeration to say that the thought of claiming those three kisses was the reason he was still alive. He'd been determined to return to London and make Harriet keep her end of the bargain.

He knew she wouldn't have forgotten their parting words. And while he was desperate to claim his prize, the chance to torture her, *just a little longer*, had been impossible to pass up.

Racing to her doorstep the moment his boots had touched dry land would have betrayed his eagerness to a humiliating degree, and so he'd forced himself to bide his time. To that end, he'd been back in England—clearly alive and well—for a month now, and although he'd finally seen Harriet at Gryff and Maddie's house party in Wales a few weeks ago, he'd studiously avoided any mention of their scandalous bet.

He hadn't mentioned it when he'd seen her at Carys's wedding to Tristan either, and the omission had driven her mad. He'd watched her bite her tongue a hundred times, clearly on the verge of broaching the topic, and then losing her nerve.

It had buoyed his spirits immeasurably.

Still, he couldn't tease her forever—as much fun as that might be. They were both back in London now, and it was time to stop playing childish games and end the torment. For both of them.

Because imprisonment had granted him a shocking epiphany: He needed Harriet Montgomery.

In his bed.

In his life.

Permanently.

True, they rubbed each other the wrong way, but that constant friction created a delicious kind of heat—a heat he planned to kindle until it burst into flame. He knew perfectly well how good the two of them could be together. Not just physically, but intellectually too. They shared a quick wit, a love of the absurd, a thirst for knowledge and adventure.

Harriet, of course, would need convincing of their compatibility. They'd been enemies for so long that irritating each other had become a habit, but the glint of attraction in her eyes whenever they spoke was undeniable. He would show her they could be more than adversaries. Much more.

Their three kisses would be just the beginning. He wanted all of her; body and soul. Nothing less than total surrender would do.

But first, the matter of that misleading map.

The steps of the Admiralty loomed in front of him, and Morgan took them two at a time. His brisk knock was answered by a grizzled old seaman in the uniform of a midshipman, who lent him a friendly smile.

"Captain Davies? His Lordship is expecting you."

Morgan removed his hat, tucked it under one arm, and followed the man along a series of sumptuously appointed corridors until he was ushered into a small private room.

Viscount Melville, a stately man in his early forties, stood behind a vast leather-topped desk, but it was the unexpected second occupant of the room who garnered Morgan's immediate attention.

His heart stilled in his chest.

Lord Melville cast him a smile of welcome.

"Ah, there you are, Davies. You're acquainted with Miss Harriet Montgomery?"

Chapter Two

It took every ounce of Harriet's poise not to laugh at the expression of shock on Morgan's face when he saw her across the room.

To his credit, he recovered with admirable speed. He sent Lord Melville an easy smile and treated her to a polite bow.

"Acquainted? Yes, indeed. It's a pleasure to see you again, Miss Montgomery. Although I admit I'm surprised by your presence. Lord Melville and I have an important matter to discuss."

Harriet sent him a sweet smile, even though her heart was pounding as if she'd run a race.

"Yes, I'm aware of that. It was Lord Melville who invited me here, actually. You've been asking after a particular mapmaker. As a cartographer myself, I have some information relevant to your request."

"Quite so." Lord Melville indicated an ornate gilt chair to his left. "Please, Miss Montgomery, do take a seat. You too, Davies."

Harriet sat gratefully. The sight of Morgan in full naval regalia was enough to make her weak at the knees. Some men looked ill at ease in a uniform, but Morgan looked as if he commanded the world and everything in it.

He took the chair on the opposite side of the desk to Melville.

"Captain Davies, you wanted to know the identity of the mapmaker Crusoe."

A muscle tightened in Morgan's jaw. "I do, sir. I have unfinished business with the man."

Melville nodded. "In that case, I must let you in on a secret. I trust I can rely on your discretion?"

"Of course."

"That name was a nom de guerre to protect the identity of one of the Admiralty's most valuable assets."

Morgan's brows lowered. "Asset? Forgive me, but your trust was grossly misplaced. The map of the Caribbean that man produced was so inaccurate it caused my ship to run aground on a reef that shouldn't have existed. My men and I were captured by the French and held on Martinique for six miserable weeks as prisoners of war because of it."

Melville nodded. "Yes. I heard that was the case and I offer you my sincere condolences. I quite understand why you might bear a grudge against the mapmaker. But what if I told you that it was not a mistake? Or rather, it was a *deliberate* mistake."

"What?"

"The Admiralty is well aware of the misleading nature of that particular map, Captain Davies. We did, in fact, order Mister Crusoe to make the amendments."

Morgan didn't bother to hide his astonishment. "Why?"

Melville turned to Harriet. "Perhaps you'd be so kind as to explain, my dear?"

"Of course."

Harriet fixed her gaze on Morgan and adopted a prim,

businesslike tone. She'd never had the opportunity to display the full extent of her expertise in front of him before and a tiny, vain part of her was thrilled at the prospect of impressing him.

"Cartographic disinformation—the altering of maps to disguise or mislead the enemy—has been a weapon deployed in wartime for centuries."

Melville nodded. "Back in the fourteen hundreds the German cartographer Martellus distorted the southern coast of Africa on the orders of King John of Portugal to pretend that the eastern sea route to Asia was longer than it actually is. They wanted to discourage foreign interlopers from profiting from Portuguese discoveries."

"The Russians did the same thing fifty years ago," Harriet continued. "They extended Siberia by thirty degrees eastward to exaggerate the difficulty of the Northeast Passage, so European merchants wouldn't attempt that route to China."

"In more recent times," Melville said, "the Admiralty ordered Captain Cook to amend his maps of the places he encountered in the Pacific to conceal any strategic discoveries. We told him to omit any naturally deep harbors where ships could be anchored, and we even employed a second mapmaker, a Doctor Hawkesworth, to amend Cook's charts even more, before they were printed as the official account of his voyages."

Melville chuckled. "That was back when the Earl of Sandwich was First Lord of the Admiralty. We've been misleading our rivals for decades."

Morgan's expression was one of pained frustration, and Harriet tried to conceal her smile.

"As fascinating as the impromptu history lesson is," he said tersely, "I fail to see what it has to do with my predicament. The Admiralty hasn't been providing misleading maps to its *own* men, surely?"

Melville sent him a sympathetic glance. "Of course not. But I'm afraid, Captain Davies, that you and your crew were the unfortunate victims of a ruse by our government to play havoc with the French. May I ask where you found the map that led you astray? Because I can assure you, it was *not* issued to our own sailors."

Harriet saw the exact moment Morgan realized how the error had occurred. His eyes narrowed and he raked his hand through his dark hair with a groan.

"It was taken from the *Brilliant*—a French ship we'd captured the week before and taken to St. Lucia." He shook his head, clearly lost in memory. "The governor of the island, General Delaval, ordered us to continue harassing the French around Martinique, and since my own map was in a sad state, I confiscated the charts from the *Brilliant* to use instead."

Melville steepled his fingers on the desk. "Well, that explains it, I'm afraid. Our spies went to a great deal of trouble to make sure the French received those falsified maps. Your shipwreck was exactly the result we intended—only for the enemy, not one of our own."

Morgan's cheeks reddened with an angry flush. "I see."

Melville shrugged. "A regrettable and quite unforeseen accident, I'm afraid. Who could have imagined you'd end up using that particular map? The odds of it happening are staggering."

"Indeed."

Harriet was sure Morgan was grinding his teeth. And she was absolutely certain he was hating the fact that she was present to witness his mortification. If he hadn't been a Davies, she might have felt sorry for him. As it was, it was hard not to enjoy the moment.

Just a little.

"So you see, there really is no need for you to know the mapmaker's identity."

Morgan opened his mouth to argue, but Melville wasn't finished.

"*However.* In light of the high esteem with which you are held by the Admiralty—not least for the capture of the *Brilliant*—I shall tell you. Provided, of course, that you swear not to exact any form of retribution. Your shipwreck was beyond his control."

"Fine," Morgan growled, and Harriet almost snorted at his obvious reluctance. "No retribution. You have my word."

Melville shot her a satisfied glance and Harriet returned it with a smile of her own. Morgan's eyes narrowed in sudden suspicion.

"In that case," Melville said happily, "the mapmaker known as Mister Crusoe is none other than Miss Montgomery here."

Harriet's heart was pounding so fast she could barely breathe, but she inclined her head in serene acknowledgment. An unholy glee bubbled up inside her, even as she waited for the explosion that was sure to follow Melville's shocking pronouncement.

Oh, she'd been both dreading and dreaming of this moment for months!

Morgan's brows shot toward his hairline. "I beg your pardon?" His gaze speared her own as he turned to her. "You? *You're* 'R. Crusoe'?"

Harriet nodded again and relished the wave of triumph that threatened to sweep her away.

"I am indeed."

Chapter Three

Morgan didn't know whether to laugh or cry. This, surely, was some bizarre nightmare. He waited, willing himself to jerk awake, but Harriet and Melville remained stubbornly corporeal in front of him.

A clock ticked loudly on the mantelpiece. He cleared his throat and tried to ignore the thunderous beat of his own pulse in his ears.

"Explain. If you please."

Harriet's impish expression clearly showed how much she was enjoying his discomfiture.

"My father's provided maps to the Admiralty for over thirty years, but his eyesight began to fail a couple of years ago."

"That's when Miss Montgomery took over." Melville beamed, sending her an affectionate look. "She's just as skilled as her father."

A becoming pink stained Harriet's cheekbones and Morgan quashed a flash of irritation at the admiring way Melville was looking at her. *The man had a wife, for God's sake.*

Harriet shrugged, as if embarrassed by the praise. "I'm just glad the Admiralty recognized the quality of my work and agreed to keep me on in his place."

"We asked Miss Montgomery to provide falsified maps to annoy the French," Melville continued, blissfully unaware of Morgan's irritation.

"And issued them under the name of Crusoe to keep my identity a secret," Harriet said. "Not merely because I'm a woman—and most men seem stubbornly inclined to disbelieve anything produced by a female, however competent it may be—"

Morgan hid a wince at her shamefully accurate observation.

"—but to also stop any disgruntled Frenchmen from tracking me down and exacting revenge. In precisely the same manner as *you* have done today."

She lifted her brows in a way that reminded him of Nanny Maude, his old nursemaid in Wales, scolding him for some heinous infraction.

A sweep of dread chilled Morgan's blood at the thought of anyone ever threatening Harriet. He shot an angry glare at Melville. "*Did* any French ships come to grief because of her charts?"

"Oh, yes indeed. Our sources suggest at least three floundered or wrecked."

Harriet sucked in a breath. This, apparently, was news to her. The color leached from her cheeks. "Were any men killed? Or drowned?"

Melville shook his head. "Not that we're aware of. One ship ran aground off Crete. Another got stuck on a reef while trying to dock in Mauritius. And the third hit rocks close to the Isle of Wight. All three crews surrendered without bloodshed."

"Oh, good," Harriet said faintly. "I wouldn't have wanted anyone to *die* because of me."

"That's not counting your own ship either, Davies," Melville added cheerfully. "I suppose we should add that to Miss Montgomery's tally. Even if it was one of ours."

But Morgan didn't care about that. "So the French never realized the maps were fake?"

Harriet shrugged. "A few of them might have suspected, of course, when they ran aground. Just as you did. But even if they *did* realize they were duped, the war is over. Bonaparte's about to be exiled for good. I can't imagine anyone would bother coming all this way to track me down simply for revenge."

Morgan sent her a simmering glance. "Oh, you'd be amazed, Miss Montgomery, at how obsessed a man can become. Thoughts of getting even, of *winning*, can consume his every waking moment."

Harriet's lips parted as she caught the double meaning of his words and he suppressed a triumphant grin. He wasn't just talking about revenge for the map, but also about his promise to return and claim those kisses.

He dropped his gaze to her mouth, so she'd be in no doubt. The pink rushed back into her cheeks, and his mood lightened considerably.

He slapped his palms on his thighs and stood. Melville did the same.

"Well then, it seems there's nothing more for me to discover here." Morgan kept his tone amiable. "My dreams of exacting vengeance on Mister Crusoe lie in tatters. Miss Montgomery, you are a credit to our nation."

He shot her a mocking look.

Melville sent her a kind, regretful smile. "Indeed. It's a shame your involvement can never be made public. But we must think of your safety. And that of your father."

Harriet gave a small laugh as she, too, rose to her feet. "Oh, I'm quite happy to remain anonymous, my lord. I'm just glad I had a chance to do my small bit for my country." She sent Morgan a droll look of her own. "Especially since we women can't show our patriotism by joining the navy and sailing about getting suntanned."

"Getting shot at, shipwrecked, and unjustly imprisoned," Morgan amended tersely. "It wasn't all sunshine and rum."

Melville chuckled. "Quite so."

Morgan placed his hat back on his head and offered his arm to Harriet, maintaining a polite façade for the benefit of their audience.

"Miss Montgomery, may I escort you out? I trust you have no other secret matters to discuss with Lord Melville this afternoon?"

Her eyes widened at the edge in his voice and Morgan cursed himself for showing the flash of jealousy. Harriet must have heard it too, because she sent him an amused glance.

"I do *not* have more business with His Lordship today. So yes, you may show me out." She nodded in a familiar way to Melville. "Goodbye, sir. Please tell Anne that I'll have finished the map she asked for in about a week. I shall send her a note when it's done."

"Thank you."

Morgan sucked in a breath as Harriet placed her ungloved fingers on his forearm and allowed him to escort her from the room.

They hadn't been this physically close for weeks, not since they'd danced together back at Trellech, and his blood surged as he caught a waft of her floral fragrance. She always smelled of roses and something deeper, something uniquely her that made his stomach twist into knots.

The moment the door to the briefing room closed behind them she dropped his arm as if it were made of burning coals and took a step away from him.

Morgan suppressed a smile.

They walked in silence down the long, echoing marble hallway, the sound of his top boots combining with the faster staccato click of her ankle boots. He sneaked a glance sideways at her. Her pelisse and gown were a lilac silk that complemented her pale skin and brought out the lavender gray of her eyes.

She must have been aware of his gaze, but she kept her face stubbornly in profile until they reached the front door.

The same midshipman as before opened it and sent them a jaunty salute. "Good day, miss, Captain, sir."

A carriage was waiting at the bottom of the steps. Morgan turned to Harriet more fully, forcing her to stop.

"Is that yours?" he asked.

"It is."

"Would you give me a lift?"

Her brows rose in surprise and she finally looked at him directly. "You didn't ride here?"

"I walked, since the day was so fine. But the shock of discovering Mister Crusoe's identity has left me too exhausted to repeat the task."

She rolled her eyes at his mockery. "Oh, very well. Although Hanover Square is in the opposite direction to Bloomsbury. You *do* still reside in Hanover Square, I assume?"

Morgan hid another grin. He'd bet every penny he owned that Harriet knew the exact details of his living arrangements. Just as he knew hers.

Know Thine Enemy, and all that.

He only wished he knew the color of her bedroom.

"With Rhys? Yes, I do." Carys, his sister, had moved out after her wedding to Harriet's cousin Tristan just a few weeks ago.

Harriet glanced up at her driver, perched on the seat above, to confirm that he'd heard the change of route. He nodded in acknowledgment.

Morgan swung open the carriage door, let down the step, and handed her up into the interior. He followed, settling himself on the bench opposite her with a lusty sigh.

She sat up very straight, fussing with her skirts so they didn't touch his boots.

It was vastly improper for them to be together like this, unchaperoned, in a closed conveyance. Anyone who chanced to see them would be amazed.

A year ago the sight of a Davies and a Montgomery voluntarily sharing a carriage would have been the social equivalent of seeing Lord Wellington playing cards with Bonaparte, impossible to comprehend. And just as likely to end in bloodshed.

But now the idea wasn't quite so preposterous. Ever since Gryff had married Maddie and Carys had succumbed to the inexplicable charm of Tristan Montgomery, the very foundations of the Davies-Montgomery feud had been shaken.

Morgan and Rhys were the only Davieses left standing— and Morgan planned to do everything in his power to forge a Davies-Montgomery alliance of his own.

Chapter Four

Morgan watched Harriet rap on the ceiling to tell the driver to move on, then place her hands neatly in her lap.

He caught her eye. "I'm sorry to hear about your father's illness. I had no idea his sight was failing."

She looked surprised by his solicitousness. "Thank you. He has what the doctors call cataracts. His vision has grown steadily worse. Now he can't see much at all, just patches of dark and light."

"Is there no medicine that can improve the quality of his life? What about eye drops?"

She let out an exasperated laugh. "Oh, there are several treatments, although some sound utterly nonsensical. I've researched the condition extensively. The most promising is a new type of surgery, performed on the eye, that removes the cloudy lens and restores the vision almost completely. But Father's refused to contemplate it."

"I don't blame him," Morgan said stoutly. "I'd be terrified of having some old sawbones poking about in my eyeball. What if you lost whatever vision you had? You'd be completely in the dark."

She frowned. "Modern medicine has made enormous strides in recent years. Yes, there is an element of risk—

as there is with any medical procedure—but I've been trying to convince him to at least *speak* to an eye surgeon for months. He won't hear of it."

"Perhaps I should try to convince him."

Morgan tried not to laugh at her expression of horror.

"As if he'd take advice from a Davies! He'd sooner listen to the devil. The only way that would work is if you told him not to attempt it under any circumstances. Then he'd probably do it, just to be perverse."

Morgan chuckled. "Just like your uncle, Baron Lucas. He loved nothing better than taking the opposite course to the one suggested by my father."

Harriet's lips curved in a reluctant smile. "Well, yes. But you have to admit they both enjoyed the rivalry." She slid him another wary glance. "You took the news of my being Mister Crusoe surprisingly well."

"*For a Davies*, you mean," Morgan snorted. "What did you expect me to do? Leap across the desk and strangle Melville with his own cravat?"

He let his gaze drop to her throat, as if imagining his hands there, and enjoyed the way her muscles contracted as she swallowed.

"What I mean," she said, a little breathlessly, "is that it sounded as if you'd planned an extremely unpleasant punishment for Mister Crusoe."

Morgan smiled. "Oh, you're right about that. I spent *months* fantasizing about all the things I would do when I finally got my hands on him."

She sucked in a breath.

"Being told to abandon my vengeance was extremely disappointing."

Harriet looked as if she couldn't decide whether he was joking or not. Morgan sank farther back in his seat and allowed himself the sinful pleasure of inspecting her at such unexpectedly close quarters.

In truth, although he *was* annoyed that his dreams of a painful payback had been thwarted, he couldn't deny a certain crushing sense of inevitability at learning Harriet was the culprit.

Of course she was.

Because no matter what they did, they seemed destined to vex and complicate each other's lives. He should have expected it, really. Fate had a warped sense of humor.

"How did you plan to punish him?" Harriet asked, and Morgan's attention snapped back to the coach. "Since you're a man, I assume it involved some kind of oafish physical retribution."

He feigned affront, naturally. "You women aren't the only ones allowed to think up fiendish ways to torture men, you know. Mister Crusoe caused me weeks of discomfort and frustration. I was going to return the compliment."

"Well, that isn't an option, now you know it was me. You promised Melville."

He sent her a simmering glance. "I would never abuse you physically, Miss Montgomery."

"Only verbally," she finished drily.

"That's different. You give as good as you get. It's an even playing field."

She tilted her head in wry acknowledgment of the compliment.

Seized by the need to provoke her, he stretched and added, "I suppose I'm just going to have to find some *other* way of ridding myself of all this pent-up frustration . . . Boxing, perhaps. Or fencing. Or some other form of enjoyable physical exertion."

Her cheeks colored at the subtle innuendo, but she rallied gamely. "I'm sure you'll have no difficulty in finding a partner willing to punch you. Or stab you."

Or lie with you.

The words she'd left unspoken hung heavy in the air between them and a new idea struck him. He might not be able to punish "Mister Crusoe" using violent means, but there was no reason he couldn't exact a little sensual retribution while coaxing Harriet toward the altar.

Her map had led to his hunger, thirst, and exhaustion. He could make her suffer the same torments, but with a decidedly carnal twist; she would hunger for his touch, thirst for his kisses, and emerge exhausted from his lovemaking.

It would be a mutually enjoyable revenge. She'd come to realize she couldn't live without him—just as he couldn't live without her.

The smile that curved his lips was impossible to hide, and Harriet eyed him with distinct suspicion.

Oh, this was going to be fun.

For years he'd attended every social event, every ball, every soiree, with the anticipation of seeing her, gleefully waiting to cross verbal swords. Her quick wit and ability to return his barbs delighted him. Sparring with her was a pleasure he never wanted to end.

He'd thought about bedding her countless times before he'd left for war, but the risks had been too great. A liaison between a Davies and a Montgomery, however discreetly conducted, was so scandalous that it would never have stayed a secret for long. Someone, somewhere, would have found out. He would have been expected to marry her, or been branded a despoiler of innocents. And if Harriet had refused his suit—which he was certain she would have—she'd have been ostracized by society as a soiled dove.

But things were different now. *He* was different now.

Two years ago he'd been too young and too restless to consider settling down. He'd wanted to see the world and have adventures. Now his seafaring days were done. He was lucky to be alive, and the only new adventure he wanted was the challenge of having Harriet as his wife.

His desire for her hadn't decreased in the slightest. What *had* changed was his willingness to make their situation permanent.

He couldn't imagine a future without her in it. She was the only woman of his acquaintance who could make him instantly hard with just a look, a sly smile. She flayed him alive with her withering scorn, and he loved it.

If his constant thoughts of her when he was in prison hadn't been enough to convince him that she was the one he wanted to spend the rest of his life with, the recent weddings of his siblings—first Gryff, and then Carys— had impressed upon him the importance of committing to a permanent relationship and seizing happiness wherever it was found.

Even if that happiness came in the form of a woman he'd provoked for most of his life.

A woman who disapproved of him as much as she fought their mutual attraction.

He sent Harriet another furtive look across the carriage. Convincing her that he was serious was going to be his greatest task. How could he show her that what had started out as teasing rivalry had turned into something deeper?

As contrary as their relationship had become, simply *asking* her to marry him was out of the question. Any declaration of love would be greeted with disbelief, derision, or scorn. Possibly all three.

But neither of them was getting any younger, and he

took heart from the fact that she hadn't married anyone else while he was away.

She had feelings for him, he was sure. She kept them deeply hidden, like a seam of gold buried beneath the earth, and since he was far too impatient to chip away at the rock face, something more drastic was in order. Something *explosive*, to jolt them both free of the rut they were in.

That something would be to demonstrate how exceptional—and combustible—their physical attraction could be. Their kissing bet would give him that chance.

"Why are you looking at me like that?"

Harriet's clipped demand snapped Morgan out of his reverie yet again.

"Like what?"

"As if you'd like to wring my neck."

"I'd never intentionally hurt you, Montgomery. Which is more than *you* can say." He raised his chin and pointed to the pale scar visible where his neck just met his jawbone.

Harriet's eyes widened in recognition. "That was an accident!"

He sent her a skeptical look. "With a rusty sword too."

"Because you and Rhys had stolen it from the armory at Trellech," she countered hotly. "Along with breastplates and helmets so you could play castles and knights. It was your own fault. You shouldn't have taken me hostage."

That was probably true—it had been one of the many times he'd underestimated her core of steel. He'd commanded her to kneel and swear fealty to House Davies, as medieval vassals had once pledged allegiance to their Sovereign Lord in times of old.

Harriet, of course, had flatly refused. And while he'd

been momentarily distracted by how pretty she looked with her eyes flashing daggers and her cheeks all flushed with furious indignation, she'd reached out, grabbed a stout branch from the ground, and swung it at him.

He'd lurched back, taken by surprise. The bough had struck the sword, knocked it backward, and the blade had nicked him beneath the chin. He'd heard her gasp, felt the sting and hot trickle of blood that coated his fingers when he'd dabbed at the cut, and for a moment all he'd felt was outrage.

Bested by a *girl*! The indignity!

Rhys, however, had dispelled his stunned disbelief with a crow of delight. "Oho! First blood to House Montgomery! Bravo, Harry!"

Morgan's natural levity had reasserted itself. He'd sent Harriet a jaunty grin, satisfied that she looked suitably appalled by what she'd done. Her face had gone as white as a sheet.

"Oh, God!" she croaked. "You're bleeding."

"A lucky hit." He'd shrugged, feigning insouciance when the damned thing hurt like the devil. "Want to kiss it better?"

That had done the trick. The color returned to her cheeks in a rush. "Never!"

She'd scrambled to her feet and raced away through the forest, and Morgan had let her go. But not before he shouted after her, "You'll kiss me one day, Harriet Montgomery!"

He'd never known if she'd heard him or not.

The carriage gave a jolt, and Morgan caught her eye again, certain she was recalling the same incident. Her hands tightened on her skirt.

"My business with Mister Crusoe might be done," he said softly. "But there's another matter between you and

I that needs to be resolved. I seem to remember a certain bet we made, before I left for war."

He made sure to hold her stare. "Since I'm here, safe and well in London, I think it's fair to say that you owe me three kisses."

Chapter Five

Harriet's heart was pounding with a strange mixture of dread and relief.

At last.

She hadn't stopped thinking about their foolish wager since the moment she'd heard Morgan was back in England. Or for any of the months before that, if she was being honest.

The secret, scandalous part of her had fantasized that he'd come to her immediately on his return. That he'd be so desperate for her kisses that he'd gallop up to Bloomsbury on his fastest horse, hammer on her door or clamber in through her window, and claim his prize.

That, of course, hadn't happened. She didn't live in a fairy tale.

Morgan had been back for weeks now, and this was the first time he'd even *mentioned* the blasted subject.

She knew he hadn't forgotten—no Davies would ever forget such a prime opportunity to get the upper hand over a Montgomery, or to flaunt their victory in the most humiliating way—so the omission was deliberate. It was a fiendish way to torture her and keep her on edge.

And it had worked.

She'd been a jittery mess when she'd seen him at Gryff and Maddie's house party a few weeks ago. She'd tried to escape his notice by lurking at the perimeter of the ballroom, but he'd singled her out with unerring precision, just as he always did.

He'd asked her to dance. Well, *demanded* that she dance was more accurate. He'd simply held out his hand and said, "My dance," and then swept her out onto the dance floor without waiting for an answer.

Not that she'd minded. The wicked thrill of being in his arms, even at a perfectly respectable distance, had warmed her entire body.

She was a hopeless case. Morgan Davies was a bounder. An irreverent tease who flirted with every woman in skirts. There was no man in London more unsuitable for her to be attracted to, but passion, apparently, paid no heed to logic. He'd held her heart hostage for years.

She'd been *absolutely certain* that he'd mention their scandalous bet during their waltz, but he'd merely made mocking comments about the other guests and told her that her dress looked like seaweed.

She'd been oddly . . . disappointed? Filled with a sense of anticlimax, certainly.

This, she suspected, was the same feeling a battle-hungry army might feel at arriving at the designated field of combat only to discover the enemy had decamped overnight.

She'd been eager for battle to commence.

And he hadn't obliged, the swine.

His goal, clearly, was to rouse her to a fever pitch of anticipation, obsessing over when he might call in his winnings. Which meant she'd spent weeks and weeks imagining what it would be like when he finally kissed her.

She'd never been kissed.

Not by him.

Not by anyone.

A hot flash of jealousy streaked through her. *He'd* probably been kissed hundreds of times. It wasn't fair.

He was still looking at her from across the carriage, and Harriet realized she'd been silent for an unreasonably long time. Words, however, failed her. Morgan's masculine presence was almost overwhelming in the close confines, and she was aware of every detail of his appearance, from the glint of the golden buttons on his navy coat to the way the muscles of his thighs shifted and flexed beneath his snowy-white breeches.

She dragged her gaze back upward.

Well, since he was studying her, she would return the favor. She would not be cowed or flustered by his regard. But her pulse fluttered in her throat as she let her eyes rove over his face—so familiar and yet subtly different from her memory.

Morgan at twenty-one had been unbearably handsome. This Morgan, the one who'd returned from war, was a different, more thrilling creature entirely. Two years of dangerous living had left their marks on his face. New lines crinkled the corner of his eyes: from laughter, or from squinting against the tropical sun. His face was tanned, his hair longer than it had been. A little too long for fashion, but the wild, windswept look suited him. Her fingers itched to touch the dark, rolling waves.

She clenched her hands into fists and forced her throat to work.

"Very well. I owe you three kisses." She was pleased with how cool she sounded. "Never let it be said that a Montgomery reneges on a bet."

At least they were somewhere private. There would be no chance of anyone witnessing her humiliation.

She sent him what she hoped was a challenging look, eyebrows slightly raised, and let out a long-suffering sigh. "Come on then. Let's get this over with."

She closed her eyes, pursed her lips, and leaned forward.

And waited, breath held, for her first kiss.

What she got was a rumble of laughter.

Her eyes popped open and she glared at him in indignation.

"What's the matter? Have you changed your mind?"

His eyes danced with merriment, even as he shook his head. "Oh, Harriet. You don't honestly think I'll let you off the hook *that* easily, do you?"

Her stomach did a strange little flip. His wicked expression suggested he was about to do something outrageous. Something quintessentially *Davies*.

"If I remember rightly," he said, "the original wording of our bet was that you'd grant me three kisses, correct?"

She nodded.

"Which infers that I'm the one who gets to do the kissing."

"Agreed," she croaked.

His gaze roved over her face, from nose, to lips, to chin, then slid lower. Heat flashed over her skin as his attention lingered on the swell of her bosom. Her corset seemed inordinately tight.

"There was no stipulation about where those kisses would take place."

She frowned. "You mean like in a ballroom? What's wrong with here?"

He sent her a pitying look. "I don't mean geographically. I mean physically. As in, '*where on your body*?'"

Harriet's mouth dropped open in shock.

"Where on my *body*?" she repeated hoarsely.

Morgan's eyes were bright with amusement, and something else, something hotter she was afraid to identify.

He nodded. "Three kisses on the lips isn't much of a prize. Not when there are so many other, more interesting places I could put my mouth."

"But—I—" Harriet could barely form a coherent thought. Her heart rate seemed to have tripled.

Where else was he thinking of kissing her?

Damn it all. When she'd conceived of this bet, she'd done so with the delightful expectation of kissing Morgan on the *lips*. She was desperate to know how his mouth would feel against her own. But now she might never get the experience. She wanted to punch him, the perverse creature.

"Can't you *start* with my mouth?" she managed. "For the first one?"

His gaze dropped to her lips, as if he was considering the idea, and she bit the lower one in nervous response. He expelled an audible breath that sounded suspiciously like a groan.

"No, I'm afraid not. That would be too easy."

"So where—? When—?"

His expression turned wicked. "I'm not going to *tell* you. It will be a surprise. Anticipation is half the fun in cases such as this, believe me."

Harriet suppressed a growl of frustration. She should have expected something like this. She'd been a fool to underestimate the fiendish ways a Davies could twist a bet. Still, she had no doubt she was equal to whatever new challenge he presented.

"It can't be anywhere public," she said quickly. "You'll ruin me."

He flashed her an unapologetic grin. "It *might* be in a public place. There's something especially thrilling about the risk of being caught."

Harriet frowned, torn between irritation and insult. Was the thought of kissing her so boring that he needed to spice it up by adding an element of danger?

He spoke again before she could ask.

"But I *do* promise we won't be seen. I think we can both agree that we don't want this"—he swirled his finger between the two of them—"to get out."

She shuddered at the thought. "Definitely not. But you can't possibly guarantee we won't be seen. No matter how careful you are, someone might come along and—"

"Are you refusing to pay?"

She glared at the accusation. "Of course not. But—"

"Then allow me some credit for greater experience. We won't be seen."

Harriet let out a disgruntled huff. This was not how she'd expected this conversation to go *at all*.

Morgan sat back and straightened his cuffs, then glanced out of the carriage window. "Ah, here we are. Hanover Square." He glanced back at her. "Will you be attending Maddie's soiree on Tuesday evening?"

"I've been invited, yes."

He sent her another wicked smile as the carriage rocked to a stop. "In that case, I'll see you there."

He pushed the handle to release the door and swung it wide.

"Will it be *there*?"

His smile was diabolical. "Maybe. Maybe not. You'll just have to wait and see."

Harriet could only stare after him in speechless frustration. The man was a born tease.

She watched him mount the steps of his handsome town house—the one he shared with his unmarried brother, Rhys—and disappear behind the shiny black-painted door.

Good Lord, what a morning!

Chapter Six

Madeline Davies, née Montgomery, the new Countess of Powys—a title she'd acquired on her recent marriage to Morgan's oldest brother, Gryff—looked radiant as she ushered Harriet into their new town house in Grosvenor Square.

"Harry, you look divine! Is that one of the dresses we ordered from Madame de Tourville?"

Harriet returned her cousin's hug with a warm smile. "It is."

Maddie had badgered her into visiting the modiste favored by Morgan's sister, Carys, who was infamous for her stylish, flamboyant outfits.

The dress was certainly more daring than anything Harriet had ever worn before: a dark blue taffeta with a sheen like wet ink on a freshly printed page. The color made her eyes look deep and mysterious—instead of muddy, like the Thames—and the cut was flattering in the extreme, with a daringly low neckline.

Harriet forced herself not to hoist it higher.

It felt strange to be wearing something so expensive. Last year she'd alternated between the same five dresses, forced to be endlessly creative with hats, gloves, and shawls to disguise the paucity of her wardrobe. She still hadn't adjusted to the sudden improvement in their finances.

The Montgomery fortunes had been precarious for years. Maddie's father, her uncle William, might be Baron Lucas of Newstead Park, but Harriet and her father had always lived in the shabby-genteel area of Bloomsbury, making a steady, if not luxurious, living as mapmakers. Her mother had died of a fever when Harriet was nine.

When her father's eyesight had begun to fail, the burden of running the printshop had fallen to Harriet, but she didn't begrudge it in the slightest. She loved mapmaking, and she'd relished the chance to prove her skills and continue his cartographic legacy.

The discovery of a new seam of gold beneath their ancestral lands in Wales—lands jointly owned with their dastardly Davies neighbors—had eased their financial burdens considerably. Uncle William had gifted them such a generous sum that they didn't really need the income from the shop anymore, and for a brief, glimmering moment Harriet had imagined visiting all the places she'd only ever drawn on maps. But no amount of money could restore her father's sight; he needed her here in London, so she'd pushed her dreams aside.

"Lord John Copeley's been asking about you," Maddie whispered, linking her arm through Harriet's. "And Eugene FitzGibbon has been clamoring for an introduction all week." She shot her a congratulatory look. "They say he owns half of Shropshire."

Harriet rolled her eyes. "Society's so fickle. They're only paying me attention now because our fortunes have improved. Neither of them gave me a second look last season, when I was just your poor relation. Do they really think my memory's so bad?"

Maddie chuckled. "I'm afraid so. Still, it's nice to be wanted."

Harriet shrugged. She tried to quell her nerves at the thought of seeing Morgan again, and, as if summoned, caught sight of him across the ballroom, standing with her two great-aunts, Constance and Prudence.

She quashed a groan of dismay. The Aunts were shameless gossips who delighted in meddling in everyone's affairs. Their deceptively sweet appearance—Constance regularly brought her knitting to evening entertainments—belied two razor-sharp wits and a propensity to wheedle information out of absolutely anybody. Harriet had often thought that the war against Bonaparte would have been over a lot quicker if Wellington had employed the two of them as spies.

Morgan, however, seemed to be enjoying their company. As she watched, he threw back his head and let out a laugh that had the gaggle of women hovering at his periphery, all hoping for an introduction, murmuring and fluttering their fans.

Harriet rolled her eyes.

"I have to welcome the other guests," Maddie sighed. "Will you be all right on your own?"

"Of course." Harriet smiled. "You go."

When Maddie drifted away Harriet slid into the ballroom, trying not to attract attention, and threaded her way through the crowd toward Morgan.

As if he weren't handsome enough in regular evening dress, tonight he was wearing full dress uniform, all gold braiding and broad epaulettes, and her heart gave a little twist in her chest. It was no wonder he had women fawning all over him.

Would he kiss her tonight, as he'd threatened? The thought made her palms sweaty.

Using a potted fern on a pedestal as cover, she edged closer to a group of young matrons who were loitering nearby, intrigued to hear what they were saying.

"Do you think he has a mistress?"

Harriet's eyes widened at Lady Brassey's throaty whisper.

"I haven't heard any rumors," Caroline Thurlow replied, equally sotto voce. "But he must have. A man like that can't go without a woman for long. He was deprived of female company for *weeks* when he was held prisoner, don't forget. And then he endured a month at sea. I bet he went straight to the nearest brothel the moment his ship sailed into port."

"Lucky tarts." Louise Huntley sighed wistfully behind her fan. "Just think how desperate he would have been. How passionate."

All three of them shivered in lurid delight.

"I'd give my eyeteeth for a night with him," Lady Brassey admitted. "Brassey's so *dull*. He only ever visits me when he's drunk. Captain Davies is divine."

Harriet shook her head, torn between amusement and dismay. Such bawdy topics were never discussed in front of unmarried women like her.

But it was hard to disagree with their assessment. Morgan *was* irritatingly good-looking, in a vibrant, masculine way that made every other male in the ballroom look somehow less imposing. As shaming as it was to be so shallow, she couldn't deny that she, too, lusted after him to an unhealthy degree.

Accustomed to noting the smallest details on her maps, she knew the topography of his face as if it were her own. He might have the same features as other men—eyes and nose and mouth—but the way they were put together was more aesthetically pleasing.

God, the number of times she'd mentally traced those contours: the hollow of his cheek, the straight ridge of his nose, the luscious dip in his upper lip that made her own lips tingle in response.

Unlike the women in front of her, however, she appreciated Morgan for more than just the physical. His cynical wit, while cutting, always made her laugh, and beneath that handsome exterior beat a deeply loyal heart. A black, treacherous, *Davies* heart, to be sure, but loyal nonetheless.

Whenever she was with him, she felt wickedly, prickingly alive.

Nobody else had the same effect.

It was extremely vexing.

"Whoever would have thought we'd get half a dozen Davieses and the same number of Montgomerys in the same room without someone drawing a blade?"

Harriet smiled as Aunt Prudence's quavering tones reached her ears.

"We've entered a new age, Constance," Prudence continued. "A lessening of hostilities, to go with the new peace on the Continent."

Aunt Constance nodded benignly. "A détente, as the French would say."

"That scoundrel Bonaparte still has a lot to answer for, though. Fancy forcing all the handsome young men to sail away and fight? I tell you, Captain Davies, London has been quite devoid of company for two seasons at least."

"All those poor debutantes languishing at the side of the dance floor," Constance added.

Harriet bit back a snort. *She* hadn't languished. Not much, anyway.

Morgan seemed to hear her thoughts. His head lifted

and his gaze clashed with hers and she swallowed a gasp of shock.

How long had he known she was there?

"Oh, I don't think you can blame Bonaparte for *every* male absence," he said drily, making sure his words carried to her. "There are some women who make a man want to sail very far away, and stay there for a very long time."

His eyes twinkled with devilry and Harriet sent him a scowl for implying that *she* was one of those women.

"And I'm sure some young ladies were celebrating my absence," he continued. "Your niece Harriet, for example, probably spent the entire time writing my eulogy."

He shot her another amused look over Prudence's shoulder.

Prudence, unaware of their byplay, merely shrugged. "Yes, well, all this means there's now a glut of unmarried young ladies wafting around London, all desperate to catch a newly returned officer."

Constance raised her eyebrows. "You, young man, might think you're the hunter, but believe me, you're the *hunted*."

Morgan laughed. "I stand forewarned, ma'am."

"It's going to be a bloodbath! I can't wait." Prudence chuckled with undisguised delight.

"You sound like a spectator at the Roman Colosseum, watching gladiators fight to the death."

"You can't deny the similarity. The matchmaking mamas are quite as determined to catch their quarry. All they lack is tridents, nets, and swords."

Prudence shot Morgan a sly, speculative look. "You're still unwed, Captain Davies. Will *you* be looking for a wife now you've returned to these shores?"

Harriet heard a collective gasp from the gaggle of

women on the opposite side of the fern as they strained to hear his answer.

And then her heart stopped in her chest as Morgan's gaze slashed back to hers.

"As it happens, I *have* decided to look for a bride now that I'm back, Miss Prudence."

Shock held Harriet immobile. She couldn't have been more surprised if Morgan had declared himself Tzar of Russia.

Aunt Constance gave a triumphant little crow, but Morgan wasn't finished.

"But I'm sure many women would scorn to be a sailor's wife, only seeing their husband every few months during shore leave."

"Some might *prefer* an absentee husband," Prudence countered drily. "They'd get financial support without the inconvenience of actually having to live with a man. Messy, careless creatures, the lot of you."

Morgan, laughing, didn't take offense.

"You do have your occasional uses too." Constance twinkled naughtily. "I'm sure you'll make some lucky young woman an excellent husband, Captain Davies."

Morgan raised his voice. "Do you think that's true, Miss Montgomery?"

Prudence and Constance both turned and caught sight of her lurking behind her fern. They beamed in welcome and with a reluctant sigh Harriet stepped out from its protection and joined them.

"Do I think what's true?" she asked, just to be perverse.

"That any woman would be pleased to be a sailor's wife?"

"I do not." She sent Morgan a superior glare. "An arrangement like that would not be my idea of a happy marriage."

He lifted his brows in challenge. "And what *is* your idea of a happy marriage, Miss Montgomery? Do tell."

Put on the spot, the only thing Harriet could come up with was the truth.

"I'd want to be necessary to someone. As necessary as a map to a sailor. I'd want him to be lost without me."

Aunt Constance cocked her head to the side. "I say, that's a lovely idea, Harriet."

Harriet sent her a grateful smile, even as her cheeks heated in embarrassment. "My own parents were like that, according to Father. He and my mother shared a passion for numerous subjects, as well as for each other."

"You should be considering marriage too," Aunt Prudence commanded, with all the tact and subtlety of a sledgehammer. "You have plenty of choice." She turned to Morgan. "Every fortune-hunting cad in London's after her now she's rumored to have an inheritance."

Was there anything so mortifying as one's relatives? Harriet prayed for the floor to open up and swallow her whole. Sadly, fate did not oblige.

She risked a glance at Morgan and found him trying, unsuccessfully, to hide his mirth at her discomfiture.

The beast.

"There's no denying my dance card is fuller than in previous seasons," she said stiffly. "But I'm quite aware of the reason for my sudden popularity. Most of those gentlemen never gave me a second glance before news of the gold came out."

Morgan's lips twitched. "Oh, they gave you a second glance, Miss Montgomery. And a third. But they were looking at you as someone to bed, not wed."

Harriet's mouth dropped open at the impropriety of his words, but Prudence and Constance just chuckled indulgently.

Morgan raked her with a head-to-toe glance that made her blood heat to a slow simmer. "*Now,* however, you're the winning lottery ticket. Beautiful, rich, *and* unmarried. I'm surprised there hasn't been a stampede."

Her heart did a funny little jolt at his compliment, even though he was only putting on a show for the Aunts' entertainment.

"Of course, some chaps might have been put off by the fact that you're clever," Morgan continued. "Or by that wickedly sharp tongue of yours. But not all." He tilted his head. "In fact, the only way to be *completely* sure a man isn't after your money now would be to remember who spoke to you before you were rich."

"You spoke to me," she countered tartly. "Is that a *proposal,* Captain Davies?"

His eyes glittered in appreciation of her calling his bluff, but his lips curved into that devilish smile that haunted her dreams.

"Would you like it to be, Miss Montgomery?"

Chapter Seven

Harriet was still trying to frame a reply to Morgan's provocative question when Lord Melville and his wife joined them. They exchanged pleasantries, and when Anne engaged the Aunts in conversation, Melville turned to Morgan and Harriet.

"Evening, Captain Davies. Miss Montgomery. A word with you both, if you please? Is there somewhere we can go where we shan't be overheard?"

Morgan lifted his brows, intrigued.

"The gardens?" Harriet suggested. "Maddie's put lanterns near the house, but if we go toward the stables, near the back, we shouldn't be interrupted."

"Unless there are any would-be lovers out there in the shrubbery," Morgan murmured. "Then we'll be the ones doing the interrupting."

Harriet sent him a quelling glare. *Trust him to think of such things.*

"This way."

Slipping easily through the crowd, she led them out onto the flagstone terrace, down the steps, and along one of the formal paths. As the shadows lengthened, she indicated a wisteria-draped walkway, one of Maddie's favorite places in the grounds. Thankfully, it was devoid of amorous couples.

Morgan strode halfway along the tunnel and turned to Melville. "What's all this about?"

"I had a report today that your old friend De Caen has been spotted in London."

Morgan stilled. "Who saw him? Where? Are they sure?"

The older man sighed. "A shipmate of yours, one Thomas Cowper, claims he saw De Caen at Deptford, alighting from a clipper just in from Trinidad. De Caen's limp drew his attention; then he recognized his face. Cowper tried to follow him, but he lost him in the crowd."

Morgan muttered a curse.

"Damn it. Cowper was imprisoned with me. He definitely wouldn't mistake De Caen. You don't forget the man who tortured you."

Harriet winced. It was hard to see Morgan's features in the shadows, but his tone was grim.

"Why in God's name would he be here, in London?" Morgan demanded. "Surely not for revenge against me? The man's unhinged, no doubt about it, but that's excessive, even for him."

"Why would he want revenge?" Harriet asked. "I thought you were his prisoner?"

Morgan let out a sound that was half laugh, half snort. "*I'm* the reason he walks with a limp. I'm sure he'd love the opportunity to return the favor." He paused, thinking. "But if he wanted me, he could have found me quite easily. Half the *ton* knows where I live. It's no secret."

Melville cleared his throat. "Precisely. Which is why we have to assume he's up to something else. Something that may well be related to Miss Montgomery here. Or rather, with our mapmaker Crusoe."

Harriet stiffened in shock. "What?"

"Someone broke into the Admiralty offices last night. They entered the map room and went through every drawer, made a shocking mess. When we did an inventory of what had been taken, the only things missing were some maps drawn by Crusoe."

Harriet's heart began to pound. "But why would someone want those?" She felt a little light-headed.

"And why would you assume it was De Caen?" Morgan added.

"De Caen fled Martinique when he heard of Bonaparte's defeat at Waterloo. The French government expected him to return to France, and planned to arrest him as soon as he set foot in the country."

Morgan raised his brows. "Why?"

"According to them, he's a traitor. Bonaparte's brother Joseph sent a shipment of gold and other valuables to Martinique on Napoleon's orders around six months ago. An insurance policy for the Emperor to collect if he ever had to leave France. De Caen was put in charge of guarding it."

"But Bonaparte's a prisoner on the *Bellerophon* now, is he not?"

Melville nodded. "He is. Moored off the coast of Torbay, until the government decides where to send him. Elba, clearly, was too close to the Continent. I've heard they're considering an island named St. Helena, way out in the middle of the Atlantic."

"I know where that is," Harriet said absently.

Morgan shot her an amused glance in the shadows. "Of course you do, Madame Map."

She tried not to wince at the resurrection of one of his many teasing childhood nicknames for her. Cartography Kate had been another favorite.

Melville shook his head at their byplay.

"We took control of Martinique when the French withdrew, but agreed to return the gold as part of the peace settlement. General Delaval and his men searched the entire island but found no trace of it. We think De Caen hid it somewhere else, maybe on one of the other islands nearby."

He turned to Morgan. "While you were there, did you hear any rumors about it?"

"No. But then, we were working in the fields or locked up for most of the time. De Caen had a deputy, though, a Lieutenant Garonne. I don't know if that was his real name, or just a nickname based on the part of France he came from, but he did a lot of De Caen's dirty work. I bet he knows where it is."

"Garonne's dead," Melville said. "His body was found shortly after De Caen left the island. Shot himself, apparently."

"Or was made to look like he did," Morgan said darkly. "De Caen's a madman. I'd bet he killed Garonne to keep the location of the treasure to himself."

Melville grunted his agreement.

"There are hundreds of islands within a few days' sail of Martinique," Morgan continued. "Some are barely more than atolls dotted in the ocean. Without knowing which one to search, and without an accurate map, it would be like looking for a needle in a haystack."

Harriet let out a crow of triumph. "*Finally!* An appreciation of cartographers and all we do!"

"The Admiralty have always appreciated your skills, Harriet," Melville said smoothly.

Morgan merely rolled his eyes. "If De Caen had already retrieved the treasure, he wouldn't be here in London. He'd be under a palm tree somewhere, sipping rum."

Harriet snorted. "That's what you'd do, I suppose?"

"There are worse ways to spend one's days."

"Precisely," Melville said. "Which is why we *don't* think he has it. Not yet, at least."

Harriet took a few steps along the tree-lined tunnel, then swung back in the opposite direction, her skirts swirling around her legs. Pacing always helped her think.

"I have an idea."

"Always dangerous," Morgan muttered.

She ignored him. "There must be a reason why De Caen would want Crusoe's maps specifically."

"Explain."

"Well, there are hundreds of maps of Martinique in existence. De Caen could have bought one from any map-maker anywhere in the world. But perhaps he can't *use* any of those maps to find the treasure."

"Go on," Melville prompted.

"What if he used one of Crusoe's maps when he hid the gold? If that was the case, then the only way he could find it again would be by using the same map."

She nodded, sure she was on the right track. "If he tried to use an *accurate* map to navigate back to the gold, the island he wanted might not have been marked. Or he would have found more islands than he was expecting. I added islands where none existed, deleted others, and moved real ones miles away from where they should have been."

Morgan sent her a congratulatory grin and Harriet tried to ignore the warm flush of pride that impressing him provoked.

"You could be right," he said. "I bet he went looking for the gold as soon as he heard Bonaparte had surrendered, but failed to find it." His brow furrowed in thought; then he let out a huff of amusement. "He *could* have been using a Crusoe map too. When I ran aground in the *Briseis* he confiscated everything on board—including the maps I'd taken from the *Brilliant*."

"That would be rather poetic justice, wouldn't it?" Melville chuckled. "Hoist with his own petard, so to speak. But if that's true, why wouldn't he use that same map to relocate the treasure?"

"Maybe it got destroyed?" Morgan shrugged. "Or maybe he thought any map would do, and used another."

"He probably thinks Crusoe's version is more accurate than the one he was using." Harriet chuckled.

"And since he couldn't return to Martinique or to France without being arrested," Morgan said, effortlessly catching her line of reasoning, "and since he thinks our navy uses Crusoe's maps, he must have decided to come here to London and get one for himself."

He shot Harriet another smile at their joint deductions and her heart gave a funny little twist in her chest. Working with Morgan, instead of against him, was a heady, unfamiliar sensation.

"That would certainly explain why he went after the maps at the Admiralty last night," Melville murmured.

"Was a map of the Caribbean among those he stole?" Harriet asked.

"Couldn't say." Melville shrugged. "I'll have to go back and look at the list of what was taken." He nodded briskly, clearly glad to have a plan. "I'll keep you both updated. Meanwhile, Captain Davies, you should be on your guard. If De Caen's here in London he may well create some unpleasantness for you. Men like him can always find time for revenge."

"Thank you, sir. I'll keep an eye out."

Melville inclined his head. "Well, I'd better get back to the ballroom. Anne will be wondering where I am."

He patted his pockets absentmindedly. "Probably thinks I've sneaked outside for a cheroot—even though she made me stop six months ago." He snorted in wry amusement. "She refuses to believe I've done it. There's love for you, eh?"

Harriet sent him a fond smile. "Good evening, sir."

Melville peered out of the arched tunnel, scanning left and right to be sure there was nobody there, then strode back across the shadowed garden. Harriet let out a long, incredulous exhale.

"Well, what an adventure! This is the most exciting thing that's happened to me in *years*."

Morgan shook his head. "You seem delighted at the prospect that a murderous Frenchman with a grudge might be looking for me."

"Pfft. You're more than capable of looking after yourself, Morgan Davies." She stepped forward, ready to follow Melville back to the house, but Morgan caught her wrist.

"A moment more of your time, Miss Montgomery," he purred. "I have a question. About . . . cartography."

Chapter Eight

Harriet's pulse began to pound with the sudden, belated realization that she was alone with Morgan. Pale purple wisteria fronds dripped from the arches above, swaying slightly in the breeze, while the twisted trunks writhed like sea serpents in the flickering light cast from the house.

"I'm sure you're the only person who can give me a satisfactory answer," he said.

His face was indistinct in the dappled shadows, but there was no missing the laughter in his voice. He knew just how unacceptable such behavior was, detaining her like this, and he did it anyway.

Typical Davies.

She turned with what she hoped was an exasperated sigh. "You do not have a question about maps."

"I might."

"You don't."

"I never know which way to hold them. Is north up or down?"

She sent him a withering glare.

"Very well, you've caught me," he admitted, utterly unrepentant. "I just wanted to get you alone."

Her heart gave a panicked little thud against her ribs.

"We should *not* be out here, together, in the dark," she

scolded. "What if someone sees? We should get back to the ball before we're missed."

His teeth flashed white in the darkness. "Tsk. Where's your sense of adventure? I thought mapmakers were consumed by the desire to explore. To push the boundaries of knowledge, to find out what lies beyond the blank spaces at the edge of the page. I *assumed* they'd be brave enough to venture to the places where it says 'Here Be Dragons.'"

The challenge in his tone was unmistakable, and Harriet shivered. She'd always wanted to be that bold, adventurous person, thumbing her nose at convention, unafraid to take risks. Real life, however, didn't always give one the chance.

She frowned up at him. *He* was the dragon, the sea monster. A kraken, merciless and irresistible, just waiting to drag her down to the depths.

And oh, how she wanted to go.

Music and laughter spilled from the house and across the grounds, and her body thrummed with awareness as he took a slow step closer. He still hadn't released her wrist. His thumb slid lazily over the pulse that hammered under the skin and her breath hitched as she caught the scent of him: masculine spice. Her toes curled in her silk dancing slippers.

"Are you ready for another adventure, Harry?"

Her stomach swooped in terror. Was he about to claim that first kiss *now*?

She wasn't ready. She might never be ready.

Flustered, she pointed through a gap in the leaves toward the house. Lights shone from every window, but the building next door was dark.

"Do you know who owns that place? I've always wondered. I've driven past it a hundred times but never seen it occupied. The knocker's never on the door."

Morgan let out a snort of amusement at her painfully obvious attempt at diversion. "I do know, as it happens. It's the Duke of Evesham. He's famously reclusive. Never comes to town."

"What a waste! A place like that shouldn't be shut up. He ought to sell it and let someone else enjoy it."

"I don't suppose he needs the money." Morgan shrugged.

A high redbrick wall separated the duke's garden from Maddie's, and Harriet craned her neck in a vain attempt to see over. "Aren't you curious to see what's on the other side of that wall? There's clearly a garden or a courtyard."

"It's probably just stables and mews. I'll give you a leg up if you want to take a look."

Heat warmed her skin at his teasing suggestion. She imagined him picking her up around the waist, his face level with her cleavage, or worse, around the thighs, which would press his face against her stomach.

"No, thank you," she managed faintly.

He lifted his free hand and stroked a stray wisp of hair back from her face.

"I, ah, actually used that courtyard to copyright one of my maps, you know." Her voice had risen an octave in panic.

His lips quirked. "And you can tell me all about it some other time. Stop stalling."

Her stomach twisted, but she lifted her chin and met his gaze. "Stalling? I don't know what you mean."

"Oh, I think you do."

He finally released her wrist and used both hands to cup her face. "I'm going to claim my first kiss now."

Harriet was sure her heart was beating so loudly it could be heard across Grosvenor Square. Morgan's face was in shadow, his broad shoulders blocking out the light, but she could feel the force of his gaze on her skin like a brand. Her whole body swayed toward him, caught in an undertow impossible to resist.

She didn't really want to resist. This was precisely why she'd maneuvered him into their stupid bet in the first place. And she'd waited *two years* for its fruition.

"I've been thinking about what I said about not kissing you on the mouth." Morgan's breath skated over her cheek. "And I've decided it's unfair to throw you overboard if you can't even swim."

"You *are* going to kiss me on the mouth?" Harriet could scarcely believe she was saying those words out loud.

The rough pad of his thumb idly stroked her jaw. "I am."

She cast around for a little fortitude. "Oh. Well. All right then. Go ahead."

His chuckle sloughed against her lips. "You look like you're awaiting your own execution."

"Just take your stupid kiss, Davies."

"Very well. But there are certain stipulations. It has to last for at least ten seconds. And you have to kiss me back."

"All right."

Her stomach somersaulted as he leaned in. This close she could see the dark tangle of his lashes, the fine grain of his skin. His green eyes were dark, brimming with challenge, but she held his stare defiantly. To look away would be to admit defeat.

"Do you remember playing hide-and-seek in the woods?"

Harriet blinked at the unexpected question.

Of course she remembered. The incident—and the nagging sense of having missed a golden opportunity—had haunted her for years.

The Davieses and Montgomerys had played together

as children on numerous occasions back in Wales, despite their traditional enmity. Most of the games had, admittedly, been combative in nature, and almost all had included an element of goading and challenge, but this particular day all seven of them—the four Davies siblings, plus Harriet, Maddie, and Tristan, had agreed to an impromptu game of hide-and-seek in the woods.

Harriet had been fifteen or so, Morgan a year older—too old, really, for childish games, but when Gryff had been chosen as the seeker, and started to count to a hundred, they'd all scattered into the trees.

Harriet had known just where she would hide: the half-ruined folly near the river. She hitched up her skirts and scrambled through the woods, her heart racing with the primitive thrill of being hunted.

The folly was a shambolic maze of half-tumbled walls and moss-covered stairwells. Some long-dead Davies had built it as an architectural joke, a "castle" left deliberately unfinished as a picturesque setting for picnics and a talking point for guests. Only one tower still had a roof. Huge ferns sprouted from between chunks of masonry as nature slowly reclaimed the ruins.

Panting and out of breath, Harriet ducked beneath an arched cornice and squeezed into the narrow gap between two parallel walls. The leaf-strewn tunnel was dark, and she almost screamed when a scrabbling noise sounded above her, and a rain of pebbles pattered on her head.

She glanced up, expecting to see an animal, but Morgan dropped into her hiding place. He landed in front of her with the easy grace of a panther and she pressed back against the moss-covered wall in alarm.

"Get out of here!" she hissed furiously. "Go and find your own hiding place."

He raised his forefinger to his lips with an infuriating smile. "Shh. Gryff will hear. He's coming." He stepped closer. "Move over."

"There isn't room for two, you idiot."

"Of course there is. We just have to squeeze together." His eyes glinted with wicked humor as he slid his body into the gap behind her, deftly wedging himself into the narrow space between her and the wall.

Harriet gasped in outrage. Her front was crushed against the cool, mossy stones, and Morgan's chest was hot and hard against her back. She could feel his ribs rising and falling as he breathed.

Her cheeks burned, despite the coolness of the shadows. They were sandwiched together like two sardines in a tin, and she was excruciatingly aware of the way her bottom fitted perfectly into the lee of his thighs.

The crunch of approaching footsteps made her catch back her scold.

"Come out, come out, wherever you are!"

Gryff's singsong voice echoed round the clearing.

Harriet clapped her hand over her mouth so she wouldn't give away their hiding place, but still almost squeaked in surprise when Morgan slid his arm around her waist. He tugged her against his body, silently drawing them even farther into the shadows.

She'd never dared venture so deeply down this tunnel—she'd always been afraid of disturbing a badger, or bats, or some other dreadful thing, but Morgan had no such compunction. He'd always been braver than her.

Gryff's footsteps rustled the fallen leaves outside and Harriet squinted along the narrow tunnel. Would he see them back here in the darkness? She caught a glimpse of his blue jacket as he passed their hiding place and tried to stay completely still, but her pulse was pounding at the feel of Morgan's arm banded around her waist.

They'd never been this physically close before. His left hand rested on her hip and the heat of him burned through the layers of her clothes. He smelled of pine resin; he must have leaned against a tree and crushed the sap into his hands. The pleasant, woodsy smell tickled her nose and made her go weak at the knees.

When his chin brushed her shoulder, her heart almost seized as his steady exhale fanned the tiny hairs at the nape of her neck.

"Shh!" he breathed again, right in her ear, and her stomach somersaulted in wicked delight.

Oh, this was so *wrong*, so completely forbidden, to be crushed against her enemy like this and *enjoying it*, but there was no denying the breathless excitement she was feeling.

She turned her head sideways, just a fraction.

He moved his head at the same time.

His chin brushed her neck and then—*oh, heavens!*—was that the touch of his lips on the sensitive skin behind her ear?

Harriet almost groaned, then remembered she had to stay quiet. She bit her lip instead, and tilted her head, suddenly bold in the cocoon provided by the darkness.

Morgan's cheek slid against hers. Dear God, if she turned her head just a fraction, he'd be kissing the corner of her mouth!

Was he teasing her? *Testing* her? Trying to make her embarrass herself by inviting a kiss only to have him laugh in her face?

Her pulse was pounding in her ears. The urge to capture his mouth was almost unbearable, but there was no space to turn around. Frustration and lust simmered in her blood, even as she acknowledged that it was probably for the best. Kissing Morgan Davies would be a mistake of epic proportions. He'd never let her hear the end of it; he'd brag about it in front of the others and shame her mercilessly forevermore.

Out in the clearing, Gryff gave a frustrated curse. His footsteps retreated and Harriet slid sideways, disengaging herself from Morgan's embrace.

He made no murmur of protest, and she didn't know whether to be disappointed or relieved. She stepped between the stones, peering left and right to make sure Gryff really had gone, then ran off through the trees without a backward glance.

It was only later, as she'd lain in her bed, that she wished she'd been brave enough to claim that kiss for herself.

Chapter Nine

"*Do* you remember?" the adult Morgan purred, jolting Harriet back to the present.

His mouth was hovering tantalizingly close to hers, his breath tickling her lips, as he deliberately played out the moment to torture her.

"Yes."

"I should have kissed you. I've thought about it a thousand times since. How your lips would feel on mine." His voice was a dreamy whisper, reaching into her chest, curling around her heart and squeezing. "Admit it. You've thought about it too."

His shocking admission made her heart pound, but she rallied gamely. "Not once."

"Liar."

He was still watching her. The corners of his eyes crinkled. She could almost feel his smile against her lips.

"I *know* you, Harry. You're desperate to know. It's killing you. You thirst for knowledge the same way I thirsted for water in that cell on Martinique. You need to know what's missing off the edges of the map."

Pride made her snippy. "I could have kissed a hundred men while you've been away."

For a split second he paused, and she congratulated

herself on a direct hit. And then his big hand slid to the side of her neck and she sucked in a breath as he found her pulse beating an erratic betrayal.

"You haven't." His certainty was breathtaking. "But even if you had, this won't be the same. You've been waiting for this, Harry. Been waiting for *me*."

She ought to kick him for his monumental arrogance, but it was hard to argue with facts.

And then his lips touched hers and she forgot what she'd been about to say.

She was kissing Morgan Davies! Or, rather, he was kissing her.

His lips were a diabolical combination of soft and hard—*how could they be both?*—but she kept her own lips firmly closed. Yes, she'd dreamed about this for years, but to react now would be the worst sort of capitulation. He was only using the opportunity to tease her, or to satisfy some perverse childhood curiosity. Or maybe to punish her for being the mapmaker who'd run him aground.

One . . . two . . .

He pulled away. "You're not kissing me back."

"I was counting to ten."

He paused, and she could sense his exasperation. "Well, I don't trust you to keep an accurate count."

He reached into the pocket of his waistcoat, withdrew a silver pocket watch, and pressed it into her hand. "There. You can use that."

Harriet closed her fingers around the watch. The metal was warm from the heat of his body and a tiny mechanical vibration pulsed against her palm with every tick of the second hand. She was about to object to the absurdity of the suggestion when he slid his fingers into the hair at her nape, tilted her head to the perfect angle, and kissed her again.

There was nothing patient or respectful about *this* kiss. His grip tightened at the back of her head and he leaned in, his thrilling masculine weight pressing against her as his lips plied hers. Coaxing, teasing, with a persuasiveness hard to resist.

She softened just a fraction. Then remembered she was supposed to be counting.

One . . . two . . .

His tongue slid across the seam of her lips.

Three . . . four . . .

He caught her bottom lip between his teeth, the faintest of bites, a teasing challenge to engage.

Goose bumps broke out over her skin.

She parted her lips.

His tongue swept inside, tangling with hers, and she nearly swooned. The scent of him coiled in her head, fogging her brain, filling her senses. Desperate for more, she touched her tongue to his, and the world narrowed to the wicked tangle of their mouths.

Desire pounded in her blood and pooled heavy between her legs. They weren't two beings but one, merged together, so close they shared a breath, a heartbeat.

Without thought she slid her hand up his chest and over his shoulder, solid muscle and cloth. Her fingers found the warm skin of his neck, above his cravat, and she pulled him to her, drowning in glorious sensation.

Morgan groaned, and the dark edge of hunger in the sound made her shiver. It should have frightened her, but the thought of him losing control because of *her* was so delicious, so forbidden, she could barely breathe.

Here be dragons.

She was sailing straight off the edge of the map, off the edge of the world.

She didn't care. Knowledge was power. *This* was power.

She could feel it. Drugging her, coursing through her veins, making her weak and strong at the same time. She knew how to kiss this man. It was as if she'd kissed him a thousand times before, a path so familiar she must have walked it in another life.

Morgan pulled back with a muffled curse and her eyes snapped open. Cool air danced across her wet lips and with a sudden shock she realized her left hand was still on his neck. She released him immediately and he did the same, letting his hands fall from where they cupped her head.

Her heart was pounding as if she'd run a race.

"Ten seconds!" Morgan panted.

Harriet blinked. Dear God, she'd completely forgotten to count! How mortifying, that he'd kept his wits while she'd lost all sense of time and place. Heat rushed to her face, but the tingling in her breasts and stomach barely abated.

Morgan's eyes were dark, his pupils jet black as he stared down at her. For a second he looked as shaken as she felt, but then his usual urbane mask slipped down over his features. His mouth curved into that slightly amused expression she knew so well.

"Consider that your first kiss paid."

It had been countless kisses, not just one. A conversation without words. A slow, wet slide toward delirium. But Harriet wasn't about to point that out. She took a deep breath, drew herself up, and tried to pretend that the map of her world hadn't just been redrawn. Expanded. With a whole new continent of sensation.

"I have to get back to the ball." She was proud of the decisiveness in her voice. "Good night."

Morgan took a step back, as if releasing her from his spell. "Two more kisses to go."

As if she could forget.

Harriet turned on her heel and forced herself to walk, not run, out of the arbor.

She made it back to the house without encountering anyone and it was only as she went to pick up a fortifying glass of ratafia that she realized she was still clutching Morgan's pocket watch in her hand. She opened her fist and stared down at it in wonder.

Her brain was churning. She wanted nothing more than to retreat to the quiet of her room so she could replay The Kiss in all its glory, but she forced herself to smile and mingle with the assorted guests instead.

She kept an eye out for Morgan, looking for the chance to return the timepiece, but didn't see him for the rest of the night. She could have given it to one of his brothers, of course—both Gryff and Rhys were in attendance—but then she would have had to explain why she had it, and her brain wasn't up to dodging such questions.

She would just have to wait until she saw him again.

Her heart pounded at the thought.

Chapter Ten

Morgan suppressed a wicked thrill of anticipation as his hackney carriage rocked to a stop in front of 18 Bury Street in Bloomsbury.

He'd visited Harriet's printshop only once before, years ago, when his curiosity had got the better of him and he'd sauntered inside on the flimsy pretext of wanting a map of Glamorganshire. Harriet hadn't been there—he'd made sure of that: He'd deliberately waited until he knew she'd be walking in Hyde Park with her cousin to do his snooping.

He'd been burning with curiosity to see where she spent her time when she wasn't visiting Newstead Park, the Montgomery residence adjacent to his own beloved Trellech Court in Wales.

It was much the same as he remembered. Two bulging bay windows flanked the door, and the dark green façade bore the gilt lettering: "H. Montgomery, Maps & Prints." Harriet and her father occupied apartments on the two floors above the shop, nothing large, but still neat and elegant.

The bell above the door jingled as he stepped inside and his stomach tightened as Harriet glanced up from behind the large wooden desk that served as a counter.

Her expression of surprise was delightful, almost as delightful as the look on her face when he'd kissed her last night. His cock twitched in memory. Her eyes had been dark with both shock and desire and it had taken everything he had not to pull her into his arms and keep on kissing her until they both forgot their names.

There'd been a slim chance that kissing her would have been an anticlimax. That his years of fantasizing about it would have created an impossibly unrealistic expectation.

They hadn't. If anything, he'd underestimated the effect she'd have on him.

Kissing her had been extraordinary. The taste of her, the smell of her skin, had turned his brain to mush and his cock to iron. And what he hadn't expected was the surge of possessiveness, the soul-deep feeling of *rightness*: the sense that after all his years of travels he'd finally found his way back home.

"Captain Davies!" Harriet's cheeks turned a delicious shade of pink. "I didn't expect you to come so soon."

He raised his brows. "You were expecting me?"

"Well, yes. I sent you a note."

"What note?"

She frowned. "I sent a note to your house an hour ago asking you to come."

"Ah. I haven't seen it. I went to breakfast with Carys and Tristan. Why did you want me? Eager for kiss number two?"

If possible, her cheeks turned even pinker. "Shhh!" she hissed fiercely, glancing over her shoulder toward the back of the shop. "Father's in the back room! And no, that's not why I wanted you at all. That Frenchman we discussed with Lord Melville was just here, in the shop."

Morgan's good mood evaporated.

"De Caen? Are you sure? What did he look like?"

Harriet shook her head at his disbelief. "Of course I'm sure. There can't be *that* many Frenchmen limping around London looking for maps. He used a silver-topped cane. He was about fifty years old, with dark hair, cut short. Ruddy complexion. Slightly bulging eyes."

"Hell, that's him all right. What did he want?"

"He asked for a map of the Caribbean. I showed him a few, including that one." She pointed to one of the framed maps that covered every square inch of the shop walls.

"That's an accurate, Montgomery version of the area drawn by my father, but your Frenchman rejected them all. He specifically asked for one made by Crusoe. Said he was buying on behalf of a wealthy collector obsessed with compiling a complete set of Crusoe's maps."

"What did you say?"

"I told him that Crusoe was an excellent mapmaker, but that we didn't have any of his in stock. De Caen was clearly irritated, but he left without incident."

Morgan frowned. The thought of a sadistic, unpredictable bastard like De Caen being within a hundred yards of Harriet made his blood run cold.

"You must tell me immediately if you see him again. Promise me. The man's determined, and capable of extreme violence."

Harriet nodded absently. "Very well."

God, he wanted to bundle her up in his coach and whisk her away to Trellech, far away from any hint of danger. Harriet, sadly, would see that as kidnapping, and to be fair, the weight of history was on her side. It wouldn't have been the first or even the tenth time a Davies had kidnapped a Montgomery—or vice versa. She'd never believe it was due to protective concern.

"I think this confirms our theory about the break-in,"

Harriet said, blissfully unaware of his mental detour. "De Caen can't have got the map he wanted from the Admiralty. I bet he's going around all the printsellers in town looking for a copy."

"Is there a chance one of them might have a Crusoe version to sell him?"

"Unlikely. Most of the ones we made for the Admiralty were planted on board French ships. They'll be dispersed all around the world by now."

"Did *you* keep a copy?"

Harriet's sly, secretive little smile would have made da Vinci's Mona Lisa look guileless, and Morgan quelled an unreasonable surge of lust. God, he loved clever women. This one in particular.

"Of course we did," she said. "We have copies of *all* Crusoe's maps."

"Where?"

In answer she bustled out from behind the desk and dragged a set of library steps until they were positioned below the map she'd indicated earlier. She was wearing a fetching pale blue day dress with a teasing little ruffle around the neckline, and Morgan enjoyed a glimpse of her slim ankles as she climbed up and lifted the map from the wall. His fingers twitched with the temptation to grab her by the hips and tumble her down into his arms.

"Here, take this; it's heavy."

He bounded forward to oblige, and placed the map she gave him on the leather-topped desk. Harriet came to stand by his side and they both looked down at it.

"I thought you said this was the Montgomery version?" Morgan said.

"It is. But this"—she turned the frame over to reveal a second map, almost identical to the first, attached to the reverse of the original—"is the Crusoe copy."

With a few deft twists she unpinned the second map, turned the frame back over, and placed the two versions side by side.

"Hidden in plain sight," Morgan marveled with a laugh. "It's like Janus, that two-faced Roman God." He gazed around the walls. "Are those *all* double-sided?"

"Many of them," she admitted. "It seemed a safer way to store Crusoe's maps than having them lying around in drawers. That's how the Admiralty stored theirs, don't forget."

Morgan glanced between the two pages. Apart from the different names engraved in the scrolling cartouches at the corner of each, they looked identical.

"Can you spot any differences?"

He bent closer. "Not really."

She shook her head and bent over too. Her shoulder brushed his and the scent of her perfume filled his nose. He reminded himself to concentrate.

"The differences are subtle, but they're there." She slid a slim finger toward a cluster of tiny dots in a vast expanse of ocean, and indicated the same area on the second map. "Look. This trail of islands just to the south of Martinique. On the real map there are only two, but for Crusoe's version I added three more, and moved them to the east, farther out to sea."

"You naughty girl." He gave her shoulder a friendly nudge, and enjoyed the way her blush spread down her neck and across her chest. He'd give anything to see how far it extended.

He cleared his throat. "I'll tell Melville that De Caen was here. Perhaps he can assign men to keep watch at the other mapmakers' in town and see if De Caen visits any of them. They might be able to catch him before he leaves the country."

Harriet straightened and he did the same, and her eyes widened as she realized they stood toe-to-toe. She was so small she barely came up to his chin; she had to tilt her head way back to look into his face.

He gazed down into her gray eyes. "It worries me that you've been in such close proximity with a man as dangerous as De Caen."

"Pfft. A Davies concerned for a Montgomery? That's a first."

"I'm merely looking out for my own interests," he drawled. "Can't have you dying before I've claimed my last two kisses, can we?"

Her lips parted in a surprised, "Oh!" and he fought the urge to bend down and kiss her.

As if she could read his mind, she darted another desperate glance toward the back room. "My father!"

Morgan swayed sideways to look through the open doorway. Sure enough, the elder Montgomery was sitting in a comfortable-looking armchair, a woolen rug tucked over his knees. His face was turned upward in the shaft of sunlight that filtered through the window, as if he was enjoying the warmth on his face.

Morgan glanced back down at Harriet. Her breathing had deepened at his proximity; he could see the frantic pulse beating against the thin skin at the side of her throat. To tease her even more, he glanced down at her lips. She moistened them in unconscious preparation for a kiss, but he simply raised his brows and sent her a wicked, taunting smile.

"Oh, no, Harriet. Kiss number two won't be on your mouth."

Chapter Eleven

Morgan turned back to the maps on the desk before Harriet could say anything. He located a bay on the island of Martinique.

"That's where De Caen kept us prisoner for six long weeks."

"You were lucky it wasn't longer."

"True," he said drily. "Bonaparte's exile to Elba secured our release. But I didn't feel lucky at the time. I felt hungry and miserable. Convinced I was going to die far from those who loved me. Far from those I loved."

Far from you, you infuriating woman, he added silently.

"At least you got to have an adventure. I've never been much farther than Wales." She traced her finger longingly over the paper, smoothing it over the lines. Morgan wished it were his skin.

"Last night you said something about me craving adventure," she said wistfully. "And it's true. I've always dreamed of seeing the world, of visiting the places I've drawn on maps. But as a woman that's nearly impossible. I'm stuck here, expected to be content with my lot, while the charts I've drawn enable men like *you* to go out and have amazing experiences."

"Married women have more freedom," Morgan said.

"I know several ladies who've taken a Grand Tour alongside their husbands. Perhaps you should consider chaining yourself to someone rich and adventurous?"

She gave an inelegant snort. "How can I marry? Father can't live alone, with his eyesight as it is, and I refuse to leave him to the care of servants. And what man would want their near-blind father-in-law living with them?" She cast another guilty glance backward. "Don't get me wrong, I *do not* mind caring for him. It's just frustrating, when there's a chance he might be able to regain some of his sight—and live a little more independently—and he refuses to even discuss it."

Morgen sent her a sympathetic look. "Can't he go and live with your uncle, over at Newstead Park?"

"He likes to visit, but he loves the bustle of London too much to ever move there permanently. Plus, the Aunts would drive him mad."

They both started when Henry Montgomery's voice echoed from the back room.

"Harriet, who's that with you? Is it the attorney's clerk, come about the case?"

"No, Father!" Harriet called back. "It's just a customer!"

Morgan sent her a mock scowl for relegating him to a mere client. "Embarrassed to be associated with a dastardly Davies?" he teased softly.

"Saving my father from unnecessary agitation," she amended. "He's already cross enough."

"Because of that court case he just mentioned?" Morgan hazarded. "What's all that about?"

"Oh, I don't want to bore you with our problems. You probably have a hundred things you have to get done today. Don't let me keep you."

Morgan laughed at her blatant attempt to get rid of

him. "The only thing I had penciled in my social calendar for today was '*annoy Harriet*,' so you might as well tell me. We Davieses have an innate nose for intrigue. Especially where Montgomerys are concerned. So—why would you need a lawyer?"

Harriet let out a resigned sigh. "Because someone—a fellow mapmaker here in London—has been copying our maps and passing them off as their own."

"That's stealing!" Morgan said, outraged on her behalf.

"Exactly."

"But how can you be sure that it's your maps he's copying? Surely all maps, if they show the same place, are identical?"

"Not at all. Every mapmaker worth their salt hides a series of safeguards in their own map to prevent copying." Harriet bustled to a large set of drawers placed against the wall, extracted a map, and smoothed it out on the table in front of him. He stared down at the city of London, with the river Thames winding, snakelike, through the middle. It looked almost anatomical, like a giant heart, with roads like arteries branching out in all directions.

"What safeguards?"

"The most widely used are trap streets or paper towns. They're fictitious roads, or even entire villages, put there with the express purpose of trapping a plagiarizer. How can they explain the inclusion of a place that doesn't exist if they haven't copied the original artist's work?"

She moved her finger to the center left of the map, over Mayfair. Morgan spied Hyde Park and his own house in Hanover Square.

"Sometimes the streets we add are completely nonexistent," Harriet continued, "but since that might hinder useful navigation, more often we do something less extreme, like add an extra bend to a street, or show a wide road as a narrow lane, without changing its location."

"That makes sense."

She found the neat rectangle of Grosvenor Square. "Here's Maddie's house. And *here's* proof that my maps are being copied." Her neat, oval fingernail indicated the Duke of Evesham's property. In the space behind the house and garden was an enclosed square, with a tiny emblem of a tree in the center.

Morgan squinted to read the tiny letters. "Paradise Court."

"Exactly. That walled area probably contains nothing more than a stable yard and mews, but I've drawn it as a fictional courtyard. Which means if Paradise Court shows up on someone else's map, they've copied it from this one."

"That's rather ingenious."

"Thank you."

Morgan sent her a sidelong smile. "Making things up seems to be quite a habit with you. Fake courtyards. Coral reefs in the wrong place."

She rolled her eyes at his dry teasing. "That was different. We were at war with France. Counterespionage is perfectly acceptable at times like that." She jabbed her finger down on the map. "*This* is to prevent plain stealing. That copyist is taking away my livelihood."

"Surely there are laws that protect you in cases like this?"

"There are. William Hogarth, the engraver, helped create them over seventy years ago." She sent him a faux-innocent look. "I'm sure you're aware of his series of prints entitled *The Rake's Progress*. They're a cautionary tale."

"I've seen them," Morgan agreed.

"Well, Hogarth's prints were so heavily plagiarized that he lobbied for legal protection from what he called 'piratical imitations.' He gathered together a group of artists and engravers and brought a petition before the House of Commons. The result was the Engraving Copyright Act, which grants the artist sole publishing rights of any original work for a period of fourteen years. After Hogarth died his widow, Jane, successfully petitioned to have the law changed so she could keep the sole rights to reprinting all of his artworks for *twenty* years."

"She sounds like a formidable woman."

"Indeed."

Morgan frowned. "So if you have the law on your side, what's the problem? Take this person to court, demand that he destroy the prints he's already made, make him hand over the printing plate so he can't make any more copies, and pay you damages for loss of earnings."

"Court cases cost both time and money. Father thinks we should engage an attorney to argue our case, but it will take months to go to court and even longer to settle the case. Lawyers are fiercely expensive: They're really the only ones who win. I don't think we should waste our money."

"You can't just let this person get away with it," Morgan said. "Do you know who it is?"

"I have a suspicion. There are only two or three other mapmakers in London who could make such good copies. I think it's a man named John Heron. He has a shop over in St. James's."

"Why do you think it's him?"

"All mapmakers have little stylistic traits. Our maps, for example, are known for their decorative cartouches." She pointed to the circular plaque in the corner of the map that bore her name. It was surrounded by a series of interlaced scrolls and vignettes of London landmarks, such as the Tower and Old London Bridge.

"Heron always writes the letters *F*, *K*, and *R* with a distinctive little swish at the bottom of the main stroke. It's there on the copies I've seen."

Morgan straightened. "Well then. Justice clearly needs to be served, and if you don't want to go through the courts, I say you should take matters into your own hands."

"What do you mean?"

"You should go to this Heron and demand the prints and printing plate yourself."

Harriet's face was the picture of scorn. "Oh, that's a fine idea. I'm sure he'll be quaking in his boots when one small woman and her half-blind father barge into his shop. I bet he confesses everything, *and* gives us an extra hundred pounds."

Morgan tried not to laugh at her delightful sarcasm. "I didn't say you should do it alone."

"You think I should hire some dangerous-looking thugs to accompany me, do you? I'll just pop over to Seven Dials or Limehouse and get myself robbed and killed—"

Morgan suppressed a snort. God, he loved her fire. Her eyes were flashing with irritation and her cheeks were becomingly flushed.

"I'll help you."

She didn't even try to hide her shock. "You? Why?"

He gave a careless shrug. "Because I'm bored, I suppose. This sounds like it might be entertaining."

"It sounds like it might be *dangerous*."

"Same thing."

She narrowed her eyes, deeply suspicious. "Davieses don't help Montgomerys. They hold them to ransom or push them in ditches."

"These are enlightened times," he said beatifically. "We're related by marriage now. You're basically family."

"Never!"

He chuckled at her fervent denial. "Oh, come on, let me help. What are you so afraid of?"

"Of being indebted to a Davies," she said without a pause.

"You're already indebted to me. You still owe me two kisses."

She scowled at the reminder.

"I promise I won't use violence. Not unless absolutely necessary. Usually the *threat* of unpleasantness is enough to persuade a man to comply."

Harriet bit her lip, clearly torn, and Morgan pressed his case. It was ridiculous how much he wanted to help her. She was usually so competent, so self-contained, but in this instance fate had provided him with the means to come to her aid, like some foolish knight in armor.

"I'm a man," he said, slightly more forcefully than he intended.

She blinked in surprise. "I'm aware of that."

"What I mean is, there are certain advantages to being a man, including brute physical strength. Plus, I have something you don't have."

Harriet's gaze immediately dropped to the front of his breeches even as her cheeks reddened even more. "And what's that?" she croaked.

He struggled not to laugh at the wicked path her mind had taken. The fact that she was thinking about what lay beneath his falls was *excellent* progress. Instead of celebrating, however, he pasted an innocent expression on his face.

"A brother with a title, of course. Gryff's the Earl of Powys. An aristocratic title is always extremely intimidating. Add in Rhys's natural ability to fight with every-one he meets, and we have a winning combination."

She shook her head. "You can't ask your brothers to come halfway across London just to confront a crooked mapmaker on my behalf."

"Why not? Rhys is bored out of his mind. He'll wel-come a diversion, especially if we tell him there's the chance of fisticuffs."

"But Gryff's far too busy. And Maddie will never for-give you if you rope him into something dangerous."

"Pfft. Gryff loves danger. In fact, the only problem you'll have is if Maddie hears what we're up to and de-cides she wants to come too. That woman is as attracted to intrigue as he is."

Harriet's brows lowered in confusion. She looked like she was about to argue, so Morgan did what he'd wanted to do all morning. He lifted his hand and cupped her face.

She froze in surprise.

"Let me help you, Harriet."

"But—"

"Where does this Heron fellow have his shop?"

"On Hart Street in Covent Garden."

"We'll pay him a visit first thing tomorrow. I'll take care of my brothers. You meet us outside at eleven o'clock. And bring this map with you, in case we need proof."

He dropped his hand from her face and stepped back, already regretting the loss of contact, and sent her an easy smile. "Who knows, maybe you'll be so pleased with the outcome you'll grant me an extra kiss?"

That snapped her out of her daze. She scowled up at him. "And maybe pigs will fly."

"Good day, Miss Montgomery. See you tomorrow."

Chapter Twelve

Harriet was no closer to deciphering Morgan's motives for helping her when she hailed a hackney carriage to take her to Hart Street than she had been the previous night. She'd lain awake long after she should have been asleep trying to ascribe some nefarious, twisted reason for his wanting to get involved.

It was too much to hope that he'd jumped at the chance to help because he wanted more time in her company. There were hundreds of women clamoring for his attention—sweetly docile, beautifully mannered, witty, and charming women who wouldn't dream of questioning his decisions or mocking him.

It *could* be because he relished the thought of a little excitement. London must be quite dull after years of warfare, Harriet supposed. Perhaps she ought to offer to take random shots at him with her pistol every now and again, just to keep him on his toes. She was a good enough shot that she could miss him deliberately.

If she wanted to.

Or perhaps he wanted justice? Despite being a Davies, he'd always had a strong sense of fair play. Even when he'd been tormenting her, there had been lines one simply did not cross. True, he was the rogue who'd thrown her favorite silver pencil into the stream at Trellech, but he was also the boy who'd punched Ifan Williams in the nose when he'd found him trying to drown a kitten in the well.

Maybe he just wanted to annoy her, and have her in his debt? That was certainly the most likely scenario. He'd even hinted at it with his parting comment yesterday.

Harriet bit back a snort. As if she'd show her gratitude with extra kisses. Just the thought of the two she still owed him was enough to turn her knees to jelly and her stomach to a swirling, writhing mass of nerves.

The cab let her off at the end of Hart Street and she walked toward Heron's shop with a deep sense of trepidation. She knew she was right about Heron being the copyist, but it was still a serious thing to openly accuse him of the crime.

The huge, shiny black Davies carriage clattered to a stop just ahead of her. The door swung wide—giving a glimpse of the crest painted on the side: a wyvern, a fanciful creature with the wings and head of a dragon and the tail of a snake—and all three Davies brothers spilled out onto the pavement.

Pedestrians stopped and stared.

Each man was impressive in his own right, but collectively they were enough to make any girl's pulse beat harder. Gryff was the fairest-haired of the three, with mid-brown locks, while both Rhys and Morgan sported darker brown, windswept curls. Comparisons to the wicked Lord Byron had regularly been made, but Harriet had never seen the similarity. None of the Davies boys were remotely pale or languishing. Gryff was tall and imposing. Rhys was charming and playful. And Morgan— she let out a silent sigh of appreciation—Morgan looked as though he'd been a pirate in another lifetime. He was one gold earring and an eye patch away from being a total ruffian.

All three of them had broad shoulders, outrageously long legs, and faces that made one seriously question the unequal allocation of good looks in the world. Why three such rogues should be so handsome was one of Mother Nature's greatest jokes.

Or perhaps it was the work of the devil. That was far more believable.

All three of them were dressed in deceptively simple jackets and breeches, but it did not take much of a practiced eye to discern the quality of their garments. Morgan's coat clung to his upper body with barely an inch of excess material anywhere, while his buff breeches and gleaming top boots fitted with a perfection only achieved by bespoke tailoring.

Harriet forced her feet to move, and was rewarded with a dazzling smile of greeting when Morgan spied her. "Miss Montgomery, good morning."

Her heart gave a pointless extra beat.

Gryff and Rhys both tipped their hats in greeting as Morgan took her arm and drew her into his side. His gaze flicked to the elaborate bonnet she'd chosen for the adventure. The straw concoction had a wide brim, several ribbons, and a fine net veil that could be pulled down to cover her face.

"That is a ridiculous hat," he said bluntly. "You look like a beekeeper."

Harriet smiled. "Oh, I know. But Heron might recognize me. The mapmaking world is surprisingly small. I thought a disguise might be in order, at least to begin with."

Morgan grunted, which she took to be begrudging acceptance of her brilliance.

"I hope you've come ready for a skirmish," he said.

"Always. Although it seems strange to be saving my powder for someone other than a Davies."

"Variety is the spice of life." Morgan grinned. "Did you bring your map?"

She patted the leather satchel she'd donned over her pelisse. "Aye aye, Captain."

He shook his head at her mockery but sent her a teasing look. "When we get in there, I'd like you to resist the habit of a lifetime and let *me* do the talking."

"Fair enough."

He dropped his jaw in feigned amazement. "Good God! Did you hit your head getting out of your carriage? Are you actually agreeing with me?" He reached out and placed his palm over her forehead as if checking for a fever.

She swatted him off. "For now," she said. She turned to Rhys and Gryff. "I apologize for putting you to such trouble. Please know that this was *not* my idea."

Rhys's eyes twinkled. "Oh, it's no trouble at all. The last time we had any fun was putting that escaped bear back into his cage back at Trellech, and that was weeks ago." He rolled his shoulders as if limbering up for a boxing match and sent her a wink. "This is my sixth-favorite jacket. Just in case things get physical."

"I'm sure it won't come to that." Gryff sent her a reassuring grin. "Maddie asked me to say she's sorry she can't be here. She told me to 'teach that stealing pig a lesson.'"

Morgan tugged on her arm. "Let's go."

Heron's shop had the same familiar smell of paper and ink as her own premises. Harriet squinted in the sudden change from light to dark, and when her eyes adjusted she saw a reed-thin man in a gaudy yellow waistcoat come bustling out from behind a set of shelves.

He gave an obsequious bow, clearly recognizing quality when he saw it. "Mornin', gents. And lady. What can I 'elp you with today?"

Gryff and Rhys feigned interest in the contents of a glazed cabinet off to the right, but Morgan drew Harriet forward to speak to the man.

"Are you Mister Heron?"

"I am, sir."

"Ah, then perhaps you can help me. I'm looking for a map by an engraver by the name of Crusoe. Do you have any?"

Harriet stiffened in surprise. What was Morgan up to?

Heron shook his head. "I'm afraid I don't, sir. And you know what's strange? You're the second person this week who's been in asking after a Crusoe map." He let out a disbelieving snort. "Don't get asked about one for years, and then two gents want one in the space of a few days."

Morgan sent him a sympathetic smile. "I don't suppose the man was French?"

"'E was, now you mention it. Why? Do you know 'im?"

"I do," Morgan said. "He's an employee of mine. I've asked him to help me find a complete set of Crusoe's maps. As a sailor myself I'm quite in awe of the precision of the man's charts. Brings back fond memories of sailing the ocean waves, you know?"

Harriet could only marvel at the seamless way he lied.

Heron nodded, despite Harriet's conviction that the closest *he'd* ever been to the ocean was to spit off the side a Thames wharf.

"Well, I'll tell you what I told 'im," Heron said. "Crusoe's maps are few and far between. They're Royal Navy issue, see. Not really wanted by your average man on the street. Your best bet is to apply to the Admiralty direct, see if they got any copies."

"Ah. That's a shame. Well, thank you, Mister Heron."

Morgan turned as if to leave, and Heron lurched forward, eager not to lose a sale.

"I've plenty of other maps you could try," he said a little desperately. "Perhaps the lady would like something? A map of Brighton, perhaps? Or Bath, if you're off to take the waters?"

Morgan turned back. Harriet, still clinging to his arm, followed suit. He looked down at her, his expression so fondly caring that it took her a second to realize his game.

"Would you like a map, my dear?" he murmured, in the perfect imitation of a besotted fool. "You know I'll buy you anything your heart desires."

Harriet returned his look through her veil with an equally saccharine smile. "Oh, darling, you're so *sweet*. And yes, as it happens, I *would* like something." She turned to Heron and summoned all her charm. "I don't suppose you have a recent map of London, do you? My cousin's coming down from Derbyshire soon, and I'd love to give her something as a gift."

Heron's shoulders relaxed. "Indeed I do, ma'am." He hurried over to a set of shelves and pulled down a rolled piece of paper.

He unfurled it on the glass-topped counter. "I can offer you a very reasonable price."

Morgan bent to look over her shoulder. His body was warm against her back and Harriet had to force herself to concentrate on the map in front of her and not the extraordinary feel of him surrounding her.

"Is it everything you wanted?" he murmured by her ear.

For a mad moment she imagined he was talking about having him so close, and bit back a groan. *Not quite everything. I want you closer still . . .*

Then reality reasserted itself. She located Paradise

Court, then checked the engraver's name at the bottom of the sheet: J. Heron, Covent Garden. Her blood started to heat. "Indeed it is."

She felt Morgan nod, then straighten.

"I'm afraid, Mister Heron, that your version won't do."

The mapmaker's face fell. "Why not?"

"Because this map is a piratical imitation!"

Chapter Thirteen

Harriet almost laughed at the overly dramatic way Morgan said *piratical imitation*. He would have been right at home in some terrible Drury Lane melodrama.

He swept his arm grandly at the map in front of her, like a prosecution lawyer confronting the accused with a bloodstained knife inscribed with their own initials.

"Harriet, would you care to explain to Mister Heron *why* this map is not to our taste?"

Harriet lifted her veil. She drew herself up to her maximum height of five feet, three inches and fixed Heron with a basilisk stare.

"Because you, sir, are not the original engraver. This is a copy from the version made by my father and myself last year."

Heron's eyebrows shot up as he finally recognized her, and his face grew red. "How dare you! What slander. You have no proof."

Morgan smiled in the same way Harriet imagined a crocodile would smile just before it ate you.

"Would you care to show him the proof, my darling?"

"I would." She pointed to Grosvenor Square and batted her eyelashes. "I assume you're aware of the concept of trap streets, Mister Heron? This courtyard, Paradise

Court, does not exist except on my version of the map. You'd know that, if you'd produced the map yourself. Instead, you've copied my deliberate amendment. How do you explain that?"

Heron slipped a finger into the collar of his shirt and tugged, as if it was suddenly too tight. Harriet fervently hoped he was imagining the squeeze of the hangman's noose.

"My son!" Heron blustered. "He's only fifteen, and a lazy lad. I've been trying to train him up as my apprentice. I tasked *him* with mapping that particular part of London. Told 'im to walk the streets himself, every inch, to make sure the map was accurate."

Morgan let out a disbelieving snort. "I bet he spent more time inside a nice warm coffeehouse than tramping around the streets. I bet he thought he could save himself a great deal of work by simply copying someone else's work and passing it off as his own. Where is the boy?"

Heron looked cornered. "Out. I don't know where."

His eyes darted left and right as if searching for an escape route and Harriet wondered if there really was a lazy son or whether the boy's existence was as fictitious as Paradise Court.

Morgan sent Heron a glower Harriet was certain he'd perfected to scare the living daylights out of subordinates on board ship.

"Plagiarism is a very serious offense. Miss Montgomery here can sue you, and win, according to the law brought about by—"

He glanced at Harriet in silent question.

"—William Hogarth," she supplied quickly, amused that Morgan knew she'd have the details on the tip of her tongue. "The Engraving Copyright Act of 1735, which confers exclusive rights, for a period of twenty years, to persons designing engravings and similar works. It says an engraver shall be entitled to profit from his—or her—designs, and gives them the sole right to print and reprint their original works without hindrance."

Morgan nodded. "If it goes to court you will lose, Mister Heron, no doubt about it." He gave another dramatic pause. "Lucky for you, Miss Montgomery is as kind as she is beautiful. She will not drag your name and professional reputation through the mud, if you promise to cease and desist. You will hand her the printing plate you have created, and swear never again to copy one of her maps."

"But!—" Heron sputtered.

"Have you met my brother, the Earl of Powys?" Morgan asked sweetly. "Gryff, do come over here a moment."

Gryff obligingly sauntered over and nodded to Heron.

"I hear your children's jigsaw maps are rather popular in the *ton*, Mister Heron," Gryff said easily. "My friend the Prince Regent would *hate* to learn you've been copying other people's work. He might withdraw his royal patronage if word gets about that you're a thief. Think what that would do for your sales."

A trickle of sweat slipped down Heron's temple. "Quite so. Wait here. I'll get you the plate."

He scuttled into the back room and returned a few moments later with the engraved metal map nailed to a wooden backing plank. Rhys took it from him with a smile.

"Now the paper copies," Morgan commanded.

With a scowl, Heron tugged open a drawer and pulled out at least ten pieces of paper. He slapped them gracelessly down onto the counter.

Harriet gathered them up with a glare.

"Pleasure doing business with you, Mister Heron," Morgan drawled. "And please remember that if I hear you've been copying other peoples' maps again—not just Miss Montgomery's, but anyone's—I won't simply ruin you. I'll let Rhys give you the beating you so richly deserve."

Rhys sent Heron a smile that was a hundred times more menacing than a frown. "I was the undefeated bare-knuckle boxing champion across six regiments," he said brightly. "Remember that, Mister Heron."

Heron's throat bobbed as he swallowed. "I will. Yes. Thank you."

Morgan tipped his hat and took Harriet's elbow once more. "Shall we, my sweet?"

Together they stepped out of the shop, with Gryff and Rhys close behind, and as soon as they were a safe distance along Hart Street Harriet gave her elation free rein.

"It worked! I can't believe it. Oh, thank you! You were all magnificent!"

Morgan smiled down at her, then turned to his brothers. "Just like old times, eh?"

"I liked your use of the phrase *piratical imitation*." Gryff chuckled. "It added a nice seafaring touch."

"We were always a good team." Rhys grinned. "Although you could have let me give him a little cuff around the ear, just to drive the point home. We let him off too easily. Remember that pickpocket we caught trying to steal your watch outside the theater?"

"We tied him to a lamppost with his own cravat to wait until the constable came," Morgan explained for Harriet's benefit.

"And pelted him with fruit," Rhys added. "Drury Lane has some very obliging orange sellers."

Gryff hefted the heavy printing plate in his arms.

"Enough reminiscing. This thing's heavier than a cannonball. Where's the carriage?"

The Davies carriage was waiting on the corner, and Gryff deposited the printing block inside with a groan of relief. He clambered in, followed by Rhys.

Morgan turned to Harriet and took the sheaf of fake maps from her arms. "Get in; we'll give you a ride back to Bury Street."

Harriet was about to protest, but Rhys simply reached out, grabbed her hand, and hauled her up into the carriage. "Come on, don't be missish. Whatever dreadful tales you've heard about Davies men, I promise we're only half as bad as they say."

Since escape was impossible, Harriet settled herself on the seat with a wry laugh. "Oh, yes, I was brought up on terrifying bedtime stories of wicked Davies monsters who eat unwary young women for breakfast."

The seat rocked as Morgan shouldered his way in and sat in the empty space next to her.

"Only if they ask very, very nicely," he growled.

Harriet's stomach did another little flip. She didn't entirely understand his meaning, but just the *way* he said it made her sure she should be blushing.

Chapter Fourteen

Harriet had never in her life imagined she'd share a carriage with all three Davies brothers. Not unless she'd been kidnapped and was about to be sold for ransom. But here she was, with both Gryff and Rhys swaying on the padded bench opposite her and Morgan's broad shoulder and solid thigh bumping against hers with heart-pounding regularity.

The three of them filled the space, but it was Morgan's proximity that sucked all the air from her lungs.

"Will you be attending Carys's costume ball on Friday, Miss Montgomery?" Gryff asked politely. "She's spent a small fortune on decorations and entertainments, I hear."

Rhys nudged him in the ribs. "Just be grateful she's bankrupting a Montgomery now, instead of us." He laughed and wiggled his eyebrows at Harriet. "Your poor Tristan must be ready to wring her neck by now."

Harriet laughed. The surprise wedding of her cool, constrained cousin Tristan to their flamboyant, wonderfully creative sister, Carys, had both shocked and titillated the *ton*.

Having known Tristan her entire life, she was beyond pleased that he seemed to have found his perfect match in flame-haired Carys. She'd seen the secret smile that curved his mouth when he watched his new wife from across the room. It was the look of a man deeply in love, and it had made her own heart twist in her chest.

If only a man would look at her with that same silent longing.

"I'm looking forward to it," she said briskly, replying to Gryff's original question. "Knowing Carys, it's going to be the talk of the town."

When they rattled to a stop in Bury Street Morgan hopped down and took her hand as she descended the steps. Her whole body tingled, even though she was wearing gloves. Rhys handed her down the roll of Heron's maps, and Morgan picked up the printing block from the carriage floor.

"Thank you again." Harriet smiled.

"You two don't need to wait," Morgan said. "I'll help Miss Montgomery put these away. Or burn them, if that's what you want to do," he said aside to her. "I'll get a hackney back to Hanover Square when we're done."

"As you wish." Gryff shrugged. "I'd better get back to Maddie and give her a full report."

"And I've got a fencing lesson with Signor Falconi in half an hour," Rhys added. "See you later."

The carriage rumbled away, and Harriet made her way into the shop with Morgan close behind. He placed the heavy printing plate on the desk with a thump.

"Harriet! You're back!"

Father's voice boomed from the rear of the shop. Harriet shot Morgan a fretful look, silently begging him not to introduce himself, but the infuriating man rounded the desk and strode purposefully into the back room to where her father was sitting in his customary place by the fire.

"Mister Montgomery? It's a pleasure to meet you, sir."

Father glanced up and squinted at him. "And who do I have the pleasure of addressing? Forgive me, but my eyesight's not what it once was."

"This is Captain Morgan Davies, Father. Of the Royal Navy." Harriet winced inwardly, awaiting the inevitable explosion.

"Davies, you say?" Father's bushy eyebrows lowered. "Daresay you're one of those dreadful Welsh Davieses, eh?"

Harriet closed her eyes and prayed for Morgan to deny all knowledge of Wales, but of course he did no such thing. He reached forward, grasped Father's hand, and shook it vigorously.

"I'm afraid so, sir," he said cheerfully. "A Davies of Trellech Court. But you could say I'm the black sheep of the family. I joined the navy, instead of the army like countless generations of Davieses before me."

Father harrumphed. "I expect you're still a scamp and a scoundrel. Still, m'brother William's working with that brother of yours to extract that seam of gold, is he not? Perhaps it's time to let bygones be bygones."

Harriet's jaw fell open in shock. She'd never heard her father express anything quite so benevolent about a Davies in her life.

"He is indeed, sir." Morgan sent her a laughing glance. "I think it's positive proof that collaboration between our two families might actually be possible."

Harriet scowled at the suggestive twist he put on the words. She knew *precisely* the kind of collaboration he had in mind, and it involved his lips and her skin in dangerously close proximity.

The very thought sent a hot flush over her body.

"Besides," Morgan continued, "the war has put a great deal of things into perspective. Petty rivalries like ours take on less significance when compared to more serious threats like Bonaparte."

"Quite so," Father agreed.

"I'd hardly call the Davies-Montgomery feud 'petty,'" Harriet muttered. "Natural disasters have wreaked less havoc. And we've kept it going for over five hundred years."

"Nobody ever said we weren't tenacious." Father chuckled. "But there haven't been any *fatalities* for decades." He turned his head toward Morgan again. "I heard about your capture of the *Brilliant*. It was mentioned in dispatches. Well done, sir. Any man brave enough to get out there and risk his life to defend his country can't be *all* bad."

Morgan laughed. "Maybe only fifty percent bad? Like most men?"

"I'd say you were eighty-twenty," Harriet said. "With the weight toward the wicked end of the scale."

He sent her a mocking glance. "Surely our adventure this morning has tipped the odds a little more in my favor?"

"What adventure?" Father demanded.

Harriet shook her head in silent reproach at Morgan. She'd been hoping to tell Father what had happened when they were alone.

"Captain Davies has been a hero yet again." She infused just enough enthusiasm into her voice to sound sarcastic. "He and his brothers confronted John Heron about copying our maps. They made him turn over all the prints he'd made and give up the plate. He promised never to copy someone else's maps again."

Father's brows shot toward his hairline and his mouth split into a wide grin.

"You did, sir? By God, I wish I'd been there to see it! I tell you, if I'd been ten years younger and able to see more than a few blurry shapes I'd have visited him myself and knocked the stuffing out of him, the cheeky blighter."

"My brother Rhys threatened to do the same if Heron ever repeated the crime."

Father slapped his palms down on the arms of his chair in jubilation. "Well, thank you, Davies. I never thought I'd have cause to say it in my lifetime, but I'm in your debt."

Morgan bowed, even though it was doubtful Father could see more than a flicker of movement. "My pleasure." He turned his gaze toward Harriet and his eyes took on a wicked twinkle that put her immediately on guard. "Oh, I nearly forgot! I have something for *your* pleasure too, Miss Montgomery."

That sounded ominous.

He slid his hand into the inner pocket of his jacket, withdrew a small board-bound book, and handed it to her.

"What is it, Harriet?" Father queried.

"A book. Of prints, by the look of it."

"It's a bound set of engravings by Thomas Rowlandson," Morgan said with a smile. "I'm sure you're familiar with his satirical works."

Father nodded enthusiastically. "I am indeed. Such a vibrant, amusing artist! His scenes are full of humor and vitality. He captures the most fleeting of moments with just a few lines. What do those drawings show?"

Harriet inspected the cover. "It's titled *Pretty Little Games for Young Ladies and Gentlemen. With Pictures of Good Old English Sports and Pastimes.*"

That sounded innocent enough, but she didn't trust the curl of Morgan's lips. He was up to something.

"It's actually a rather rare series of etchings Rowlandson produced for an anonymous royal patron a few years ago," Morgan said. "He made a few extra copies for some of his artist friends, and I managed to get hold of one. I thought you might enjoy it, Miss Montgomery."

Harriet opened the book at a random page and choked back a gasp of shock. The hand-colored drawing showed a woman, completely nude, surrounded by the discarded tools of a stonemason: a sculptor's mallet and a hewn block of stone. It was titled *Pygmalion*. The colorist had been overly generous in the use of paint; her cheeks and nipples were a rosy, gaudy pink.

She flicked the page over. A jumble of men and women were all tumbling down a curving staircase. Since none of the ladies were wearing underwear, there were naked limbs, exposed breasts, and bare bottoms everywhere she looked.

Her cheeks flamed.

"Are they amusing scenes?" Father chuckled. "How I wish I could see them again."

"Yes, they are quite funny!" Harriet croaked.

Morgan's eyes were brimming with amusement. "There are a few others in there, drawn by Continental artists."

He reclaimed the book, turned a page, and held it out in front of her.

Heat flushed from her head to her toes. The print showed a woman and a priest on a bed doing decidedly unholy things. The priest had his fingers between the woman's legs, while she had her hand wrapped around the fleshy rod that sprang from his clerical robes.

Cock, she reminded herself sternly. *It's called a cock. Stop being so missish.*

She could barely catch a breath.

Morgan turned the page. This print was entitled *Train de Plaisir*. Two ladies and one gentleman were entwined in a carriage. The first lady was kissing the man, while the second lady pleasured him with her mouth.

Harriet's corset felt increasingly tight. Drowning in embarrassment, she shot Morgan a furious glare for showing her such shocking things in front of her father.

Utterly unrepentant, he pressed the book into her hands. "I'll leave you to ponder the artistry, Miss Montgomery."

Oh, the beast! Her cheeks felt hotter than the fiery pits of hell—surely his ultimate destination for pulling such an outrageous trick on her.

Morgan stepped closer to her father again. "Before I go, sir, I have a question for you."

"Go on."

"One of my father's old school friends, John Saunders, was one of the navy's top surgeons. He spent years in Egypt studying the effects and treatment for sand blindness in our troops during the Egyptian campaign. When he left the navy, he set up his own practice on Harley Street, in Marylebone, and for the past few years he's specialized in eye surgery, most especially on cataracts like yours. I wonder . . . would you might like to meet him?"

Harriet's body was still tingling from the effects of the erotic prints, but she held her breath, certain her father would refuse his offer. She hardly knew what to think of Morgan; the dreadful man humiliated her in one moment, then tore at her heart with a generous and utterly unexpected offer the next.

Father's brows lowered as he steepled his hands together, his elbows resting on the arms of his chair. "Yes, all right. Why not?"

The floor tilted oddly beneath her feet. He'd *agreed*? She'd spent the last two years alternately nagging and pleading with him to get an opinion from a qualified doctor. And now Morgan ambled in here—one of the devilish Davieses no less!—and Father agreed to his suggestion as docilely as a lamb?

Harriet didn't know whether to laugh or cry.

Perhaps Father was only agreeing so as not to look cowardly in front of a Davies. *That* she could quite understand. She'd done the same thing herself on countless occasions.

Still, it was impossible not to feel grateful to Morgan for bringing about such a miracle.

"Excellent!" Morgan said brightly. "I'll set up an introduction between you as soon as I can." He sent Harriet a jaunty little salute—a mocking parody of a real naval show of respect—and started for the door. He nodded toward the book she'd unconsciously clutched against her breast.

"Enjoy your book of prints, Miss Montgomery. I hope you think of me whenever you look at them."

That put the heat back in her cheeks. Cursing his shameless flirting, she ushered him back out into the shop.

"Thank you for your help today, Captain Davies," she said severely, loudly enough for Father to hear. "I am truly appreciative of all you've done."

Morgan swept her an elegant bow. "I'll see you at Carys's costume ball." He leaned closer and lowered his voice. "Make sure you wear something low-cut. Those engravings have given me all sorts of ideas about where to put kiss number two."

Harriet sucked in a breath, but he merely gave her a teasing flick under the chin with his fingers and sauntered out of the shop.

She watched him go with mingled relief and regret.

Chapter Fifteen

It had been impossible not to take another look at that terrible book that night when she was alone in bed.

Each drawing was worse than the next, and they made Harriet's stomach feel all hot and squirmy. And yet she was luridly fascinated by the sheer variety of possibilities depicted.

Living so close to the less genteel parts of town, she was far from a complete innocent. She'd glimpsed harlots beckoning men into darkened alleyways, seen couples fumbling and kissing in doorways. She'd seen animals copulating in the fields. She had a vague idea of the basic mechanics of lovemaking, but this—this tiny book—had expanded her universe exponentially.

Almost without volition she stroked her finger over the exposed bosom of a woman and felt her own breasts tingle in response. What would it feel like for Morgan to touch her there? And the image that showed a man with his head between a woman's legs—what was all *that* about?

She flipped the book closed with a guilty snap.

Morgan Davies was a wicked man.

There was no point in denying that she was physically attracted to him: She'd been pining after him ever since she was fourteen. But now her longing had taken on a far less abstract—and far more *physical*—dimension.

He seemed to be doing his level best to produce lustful feelings in her, too, but his endgame was still infuriatingly unclear. He'd told the Aunts that he was going to start looking for a wife: Shouldn't he be concentrating on *that*, and not driving her to distraction by dragging out their kissing bet for weeks on end?

It didn't help that he was proving himself far more than just a handsome nuisance. Not only had he solved her problem with Heron, but he'd made incredible steps toward helping her father too.

Harriet fell back on her pillows and let out a long sigh. *Oh, the man was a menace.*

Friday, and the costume ball, came much too soon.

Since Carys was infamous in the *ton* for her spectacular wardrobe, Harriet knew that outfits for the evening would be even more outrageous than the usual society affair. It was the only reason she'd plucked up the courage to wear something more daring than normal.

Wear something low-cut.

Morgan's wicked command echoed in her ears. *Ha!* She wasn't one of his sailors, bound to follow his orders.

She'd managed to scrounge a small navy-issue jacket from her neighbor, Jem Cooper, who'd spent his teenage years as a "powder monkey"—ferrying gunpowder and cartridges from the powder magazine in a ship's hold to the artillery pieces in the decks above. She'd teamed that with a pair of baggy striped trousers, a jaunty red knitted cap, and a linen shirt that buttoned all the way up to her throat.

Her father, much to her surprise, had elected to join her. He'd cleverly decided to go as "a curmudgeonly old mapmaker," thereby eliminating the need for a costume altogether. Harriet helped him tie his cravat and don his jacket, then took his arm and assisted him up into the carriage waiting to take them to Carys and Tristan's London home.

The queue of vehicles stretched right along the street when they arrived, and it took at least fifteen minutes for them to reach Carys and Tristan in the receiving line at the top of the steps.

Never one to disappoint, Carys was dressed as a Valkyrie, in a flowing white dress and a shining metal breastplate. Her glorious Titian hair was upswept in a wild, elaborate series of knots, and a curved Viking drinking horn hung from her belt.

Tristan, presumably to complement his wife, was dressed as Odin, complete with an eye patch over one eye, as befitted the god who'd sacrificed an eye in exchange for knowledge of the universe.

"Harriet!" Carys exclaimed, transferring the spear she held to her left hand so they could hug. "You've come as a sailor? How wonderfully scandalous!" She sent Tristan a cheeky glance. "I've dressed as a boy myself, on a few notable occasions, haven't I, Tristan?"

This, clearly, was some private joke; Tristan's lips twitched in amusement. "You have indeed, my love."

Carys turned back to Harriet with a laugh. "Just be careful, or Morgan will mistake you for one of his cabin boys and start ordering you around."

"I'll do my best to ignore him," Harriet said, not entirely truthfully.

Tristan drew her father forward. "Good evening, Uncle Henry. I think Constance and Prudence are in the ballroom. Would you like me to take you to them?"

"Dear God, no!" Father said, aghast. "I'd have to be

deaf as well as blind to endure the constant gossiping of those two harpies. Take me to the cardroom, Tris, there's a good lad. I might not be able to play, but at least I'll be able to converse with the gentlemen about something other than who's marrying who."

Tristan, laughing, led him away, and Harriet made her way into the crowded ballroom.

Carys had taken a nautical theme for her decorating. The room had been transformed into an underwater paradise. Huge garlands of green and white flowers festooned the walls and tables, studded here and there with coral and seashells. Gauzy fabric in shimmering silver, gold, and blue floated gently in the breeze coming from the open doors, giving the impression of fronds of seaweed waving in the ocean currents.

The orchestra, on a raised dais at one end of the room, was surrounded by what looked to be the wreckage of an actual ship, draped with dried seaweed and encrusted with barnacles. The violinist was seated inside a giant shell. Harriet could only assume that Carys had borrowed the scenery from one of the Drury Lane theaters. *The Tempest*, perhaps?

She spied Aunts Prudence and Constance at the side of the room and made her way over to them.

"Harriet, my love!" Prudence set her knitting on her lap. She seemed to be making an inordinately long scarf. "You look intriguing. Who are you?"

"The first woman to circumnavigate the globe: a Frenchwoman named Jeanne Baret."

"My goodness. How did she manage that?" Aunt Constance asked.

"Her lover, a botanist named Commerson, was hired for a round-the-world expedition. Jeanne had been his assistant for years, but since the French Navy forbade women on their ships, she disguised herself as a man and went aboard as his valet and secretary. The crew didn't discover 'Jean' was a woman for *three whole years*."

"How extraordinary!" Constance said approvingly.

"Circumnavigating the globe sounds *exhausting*," Prudence sniffed. "I get fatigued just thinking about circumnavigating the Serpentine."

Harriet laughed. "Yes, well, I'm rather envious of all her adventuring. But I expect you're right. Perhaps *halfway* around the globe would be enough."

"Don't you just adore Carys's outfit?" Constance sighed. "Tristan said she wanted to bring her ravens, Huginn and Muninn, up from Wales to sit on her shoulders, but he managed to talk her out of it. Said they'd be too disruptive, and steal things from the guests."

"He's probably right,' Harriet said. "But you can't deny that Tristan's life is far more exciting with Carys as his wife. In a good way," she hastened to add.

Constance chuckled. "That's precisely how it *should* be. Davieses have been livening up the existence of Montgomerys for hundreds of years. And vice versa."

"In a *good* way," Prudence echoed drily. "Most of the time, at least."

"Speaking of enlivening, is that Morgan Davies I see over there dressed as a pirate?"

Harriet forced herself not to spin around and look. She grabbed a glass of champagne from a passing footman's tray instead and took a fortifying swig. "He was bound to come as something nautical. Being in the navy, and all that."

"Shame he didn't come as Neptune. Or a merman. That man has a chest that deserves to be seen. It's a crime to hide it away under layers of fabric."

"Aunt Prudence!" Harriet choked on her champagne.

"Oh, pfft." Constance waved her fan. "When you get to be as old as Pru and I, you get to say whatever you like."

"I'm not sure that's an *actual* rule—"

"Course it is. And if it isn't, it should be."

Harriet had no way to counter such logic. Bowing to the inevitable, she turned and found Morgan in the crowd, predictably surrounded by a gaggle of women. Unlike Tristan, he wasn't wearing an eye patch, but a jaunty red kerchief was tied around his throat above an open-necked shirt that seemed to have far too many buttons undone for decency.

She tried not to stare at the illicit snatches of smooth, tanned skin she glimpsed whenever he moved. A pair of black buckskin breeches hugged the contours of his legs and he'd tied a black, fringed scarf around his hips in lieu of a belt.

Her breathing hitched just a little.

Morgan glanced up and caught her eye over the heads of the women around him. With a charming smile he extricated himself from their clutches and weaved unerringly through the crowd to stand before her. He bowed with an extravagant flourish.

"Miss Montgomery."

Since she, too, was wearing trousers, she gave him an extravagant bow back.

"Captain Davies."

"I've just seen your father, in the cardroom. I introduced him to my surgeon friend John Saunders."

"Oh, thank you."

"And since Montgomerys need more-than-average persuading," he continued, "I *also* introduced him to a Mister Edward Bronte, on whom John successfully performed cataract surgery last year. It's one thing to speak to a doctor about an operation, quite another to meet a man who's actually had it done. Edward can answer any questions or concerns your father might have."

"Thank you," Harriet said again, truly meaning it.

Aunt Prudence snorted elegantly from her seat at Harriet's side. "Good Lord. If you can convince Henry Montgomery to change his mind about anything, Captain Davies, then you deserve another shiny medal from the Admiralty. The man's as stubborn as a mule."

"A trait I suspect runs in the family," Morgan drawled, so politely that it took Harriet a moment to realize she'd just been insulted.

"I'm not stubborn. I'm principled. There's a difference."

"Whereas I'm thoroughly *un*principled." Morgan sent Aunt Constance a smile that had the older woman fanning herself vigorously. "I confess, diverting her father's attention was all part of my wicked plan to steal Miss Montgomery away."

Aunt Prudence chuckled. "You're a handsome rogue, I'll give you that. Off you go, then. You young things get out there and dance." She made a shooing motion with her knitting needles toward the center of the room where several couples were forming for the next set.

Morgan put out his hand. "Shall we?"

Harriet couldn't think of a way to refuse. She surrendered her empty champagne glass and took his hand.

Chapter Sixteen

Neither of them was wearing gloves. The moment Harriet placed her fingers in his, a jolt of energy flashed between them. He sent her a private smile that made her stomach roll over like a breaker on the shore.

Instead of joining the dancers, though, he led her around the edge of the dance floor and out into the main hallway. Carys and Tristan were still welcoming guests, but Morgan ignored the commotion and drew her away from the crowd.

"What are you doing?" Harriet hissed in alarm.

"Isn't it obvious? I'm abducting you. Like any self-respecting pirate."

His grip was firm and impossible to escape. He tugged her round the corner and into one of the mansion's long corridors. A footman carrying an armful of cloaks, hats, and canes turned into a doorway on the left, but Morgan kept going until he finally ushered her through the very last door on the right.

He closed it behind them with an ominous-sounding click. The noise of the party muted, as if they were suddenly underwater.

The room was clearly Tristan's library-study. Shelves

of books lined the walls, and various chairs and tables filled the space.

Desperate to put some space between them, Harriet tugged her hand free and strode into the center of the room where a wide leather-topped desk held court. A large terrestrial globe stood by the fire and she hurried over to it, feigning interest in the seas and continents caught up in the elegant net of latitude and longitude.

Her heart was pounding quite alarmingly in her chest. They were indisputably alone, and she had no idea what wickedness Morgan had planned, but she couldn't deny she was looking forward to whatever it was. She could be sailing toward triumph or disaster, but being with him was the best kind of adventure.

He leaned back against the door. "It's time for kiss number two, Harriet. I bet you've been wondering where it's going to be."

"I hadn't given it much thought."

"Reall-l-ly?" He drew the word out just long enough to underscore his skepticism.

"Yes, really. I've been busy."

"Poring over those naughty prints I gave you, I hope?"

Heat scalded her cheeks and he chuckled as he pushed himself off the door and stalked toward her.

"But before we get to that, I'd like to tell you about a maritime tradition. It's rather apt, considering Carys's choice of décor for the ballroom. And your own choice of costume."

"I'm the first woman to circumnavigate the world."

"Of course you are. And as such," he continued silkily, "you would certainly have crossed the equator. Which means you should have taken part in a 'crossing the line' ceremony."

Harriet wrinkled her nose. "What's that?"

"An initiation all 'griffins'—that's sailors who've never crossed the equator before—must complete to be inducted into the solemn mysteries of the deep. And to gain the respect of their peers."

"I don't—"

His expression was pure challenge. "Come, now. You're always saying how much you want a taste of adventure."

Harriet swallowed the nervous lump that formed in her throat as he stepped closer.

"What precisely does this ceremony entail?"

He reached down and untied the black silk scarf that wound around his waist in lieu of a belt. The suggestive, slightly menacing way he slid the silk through his hands was both a threat and a promise. Her heart gave another excited jolt.

"Well, first of all the griffins are put in the lower deck and the hatches battened down. One by one, they're stripped, blindfolded, and led up to the deck to face the Ruler of the Deep, King Neptune himself."

She reared back in alarm. "You're not stripping *me*!"

"Of course not. But you need to be blindfolded if you want to prove yourself worthy of sailing across Neptune's realm."

Her instinctive retreat was stopped by the giant globe behind her. This was utterly ridiculous. She didn't want or need his respect. And yet a wicked, excited kind of fever was taking hold of her. She didn't want to stop.

Morgan reached out and tugged the woolen cap from her head, releasing the tendrils of hair she'd tucked underneath. He stepped closer, and her entire body tensed as if preparing to flee. Or to fight.

She did neither.

He loomed over her, deliciously close. "Are you going to cry off?"

She narrowed her eyes at his taunting. She should say yes. Make him leave. Stop this madness.

But the words froze on her tongue. She'd never been able to tell this man no.

"You can't blame me for feeling a certain amount of . . . trepidation," she breathed.

He shook his head, as if disappointed in her cowardice. "A ship in the harbor is safe, but ships aren't built to stay in port. They're built to explore. They're strong enough to face the fiercest of storms. Be *brave*, Montgomery. Set sail."

He was the last person in London she should trust. And yet she did.

"Oh, fine," she huffed. "Go ahead. Do your worst."

He chuckled. "Oh, I intend to do my very *best*."

A nervous thrill of anticipation twisted low in her belly.

He raised the scarf and wrapped it over her eyes, abruptly cutting off her vision. His arms brushed her ears as he reached around and tied a tight knot at the back of her head. Darkness consumed her.

This must be what it's like for Father.

All of her other senses came alive. She became aware of the pounding of her own heart, the soft crackle and heat of the fire against her legs. A disturbance in the air told her that Morgan was standing right in front of her. He was looking at her: Even without sight she could feel his gaze burning her skin.

She really was crossing the line, in more ways than one. This was stepping beyond the personal boundaries she'd always set with him. They were heading into uncharted territory.

She cleared her throat and tried to maintain a pragmatic tone. "So, what happens to the griffins next?"

"Oh, all manner of foolish things. Sometimes they're made to do ridiculous tasks, like walk the plank into a bath full of water, or they're 'baptized' by being thrown overboard and rescued."

His voice was hypnotic, deep and gravelly. "But most of the time we just paint their faces with tar, then 'shave' them with a rusty iron ring."

Harriet gave a little start as the pad of his thumb brushed across her cheek, and then her lips, as if anointing her own face. His fingers slid up to cup her jaw, and his thumb rolled down her lower lip.

Her whole body tightened.

His thumbnail clicked against her teeth, and she had the oddest urge to part her lips and suck it into her mouth, but before she could make sense of that, his warm breath sloughed over her cheek.

And then the tip of his tongue traced the same path his thumb had taken, along her lips.

Harriet jolted in shock, but he withdrew, leaving her lips moist and tingling.

"Was that—kiss number two?"

His low chuckle did sinful things to her insides. She clenched her thighs together to try to ease the heavy ache that had started there.

"You wish. That wasn't a kiss; that was a lick. You taste like champagne."

His hand was still cupping her cheek. Slowly, so slowly she almost screamed, he slid it down the side of her neck until he reached the buttons of her shirt. He clucked his tongue.

"I thought I told you to wear something low-cut."

Her stomach somersaulted at the teasing gravel in

his voice. That same voice had filled her most forbidden nighttime fantasies. Now it shimmered across her nerve endings like rough silk.

"This shirt seriously hampers my plans." He toyed with the first button. "May I?"

Harriet struggled to find her voice. "Yes."

He popped open the first button. And the next. The sound was unnaturally loud in the quiet room.

She was wearing stays beneath the shirt. Harriet stood immobile as he flicked more buttons open, his knuckles brushing the warm skin he exposed. She felt a rush of cool air against her throat and upper chest as he tugged the fabric from her trousers, then undid the final buttons, and spread the fabric wide.

She waited, breathless, ears straining for his verdict. Her stays were new, a gorgeous, lace-edged set the pale pink of a seashell. She'd bought them with the fantasy of his reaction in mind, but never imagined she'd actually be in a situation where he'd *see* them.

The corsetry pushed her breasts up and slightly together, making two pleasing mounds that suddenly felt far too exposed.

With every breath she inhaled the dark, masculine scent of him. She parted her lips, desperate to drink him in, to revel in his heady, intoxicating scent.

Morgan gave a slight, sharp exhale, and her skin tingled as his finger touched her collarbone and traced a path down, along the edge of the corset, skating in a teasing scoop over the top of her breasts. Goose bumps pebbled her skin.

"You're beautiful, Harry."

His voice was deeper than before. Rougher. Darker. She shivered as his fingers continued their petal-soft exploration.

He was *mapping* her body, discovering every dip and

curve. His thumb slid into the hollow at the base of her throat and she cursed the betraying pounding of her pulse. His fingers skimmed the hillocks of her breasts, then dipped teasingly into the valley between, and her stomach twisted in hot agitation.

His breath tickled the sensitive shell of her ear as his hand slid down to cover her breast, over the stays.

"For kiss number two, I choose here."

Harriet almost groaned in delight.

"Yes?" he rasped. "Say yes or I'll stop."

She summoned every ounce of her courage. "Yes."

He pushed down the fabric, exposing her whole breast to the cool air, and she sucked in a shocked breath as his big hand cupped her, a perfect fit. Her nipple puckered and pressed into his palm.

A rumble of pleasure escaped him.

Dear God, what a sensation.

She felt a disturbance in the air, and his lips brushed her skin an inch above her nipple. With a gasp, she lifted her hands from her sides and grabbed his head, threading her fingers through the cool waves of his hair.

He was kissing her: not one kiss but many, his lips fluttering over her skin like a butterfly that couldn't decide where to land. The faint scrape of his evening beard turned her knees to water, and her stomach clenched as she felt the rasp of his tongue over her aching nipple.

With a sound that seemed part rapture, part pain, he drew her into his mouth, sucking on her, hot and wet, a tug that caused a corresponding tug deep in her belly. His left hand covered her other breast, squeezing it lightly, and she tightened her grip on his hair, unsure whether to hold him close or push him away.

It was torment, but of the wickedest, most incredible kind. Without sight, she was aware of nothing but the delicious friction of his skin, the heat of his mouth, the strength of his body.

"Morgan!"

"Yes-s-s-s." He groaned it against her, as much a vibration as a sound, but the word seemed to recall him to what he was doing. He leaned back, putting space between them, dislodging her hands from his hair.

The cool waft of air against her skin jolted her from the drugging sensual haze he'd created. Dear God, what must she look like? Blindfolded. Bare-breasted in the firelight. Like some ancient pagan reveler.

Heat scalded her cheeks. She tugged her stays back up to cover her breasts, then reached up and pushed the scarf up over her head, blinking at the relative brightness of the library again.

Morgan stood in front of her, his expression impossible to define. His breathing seemed as labored as hers, his eyes dark pools.

Harriet's entire body was alive, tingling with desire, and when she tried to button her shirt, her hands were shaking so badly she fumbled them.

He brushed her hands aside. "Let me do it."

She looked up into his face with a sinking feeling. Oh, she was in so much trouble. Not because she'd let him do this wicked thing. But because she wanted him to do it again.

"This is a wicked game."

She hadn't meant to say that *out loud*.

Morgan's head was bent as he concentrated on her buttons, but she saw his lips twitch.

"A very wicked game," he agreed. He fastened the last of her buttons neatly under her chin and stepped back, his face assuming its standard, amused expression. "But there's no one I'd rather be playing it with than you."

Chapter Seventeen

Harriet gazed at him, her thoughts in a whirl. Should she scold him for taking such liberties? Or be ashamed of herself because she'd encouraged them?

This kind of education was precisely what she'd hoped for when she'd engineered their bet. Admittedly, she'd only thought to enjoy three wonderfully passionate kisses, but that was because her imagination hadn't been nearly as broad as Morgan's. He'd taken things to a whole new level.

She cleared her throat, determined to take control of the situation. "You only have one kiss left." Her voice was a croak, as if she was parched.

His eyes bore into hers. "Can you guess where it's going to be?"

Her stomach somersaulted as he let his gaze drop down her body and settled at the juncture of her thighs.

"It's going to be there. Between your legs."

Blood rushed in her ears as her heart began to pound in earnest. God, he wasn't even touching her, but she could feel her pulse there, low down, where he mentioned. A dark ache.

"Did you see the drawing of the man doing that to the woman?"

Harriet nodded. Words were beyond her.

"That's what I'll do to you. And you're going to love it."

Her wicked imagination could almost feel his lips: she wanted to rub against him, hot and shameful—

Sanity made a welcome reappearance. *What was she doing?* Three kisses on the mouth would have been acceptable: a welcome way to rid her of her inexperience. Plenty of unmarried girls stole illicit kisses before they wed. Some even went so far as to indulge in the kind of ribald fondling she and Morgan had just done. Such things could be dismissed as harmless fun, no real impediment to a woman's virginity or marriage prospects. Or, as in her case, a memory to cherish in her long remaining years as a spinster.

But what he was suggesting now went far beyond the realms of decency. He might not *technically* be relieving her of her virginity by kissing her there, but he would certainly take her innocence.

Harriet bit her lip.

Why was he insisting on raising the stakes so high? On deepening this game they played?

Was it revenge? She'd teased him for so long there would doubtless be satisfaction in finally having her at his mercy.

Was he only playing with her? Was this a form of humiliation, of subjugation—an adult version of making her kneel and swear fealty, as he'd done in the woods all those years ago?

Perhaps he meant to take her to the very edge of ecstasy and then stop.

There was little doubt that he had mastery over her body. She could barely think when she was near him: She'd been dangerously close to begging him to continue tonight. What on earth would she do if he kissed her *there*?

Every naughty, forbidden thought whispered at her to let him do the things he promised. To let him give her pleasure. But what would happen then? Their wager would be completed and Morgan would leave her without a backward glance.

He might be receiving some physical enjoyment from their interactions, but he'd probably feel the same enjoyment with *any* woman. His emotions—unlike hers—weren't involved at all. He'd go and marry some foolish debutante and continue sailing around the world, while she would remain unwillingly single, haunted by the memory of these stolen moments.

She put her hands on her hips.

"Why are you doing this to me?"

His brows lowered. "Doing what?"

"Teasing me like this. Is it revenge? Are you trying to make me forfeit?"

He mirrored her stance. "Of course not. I'm *trying* to show you pleasure." He dipped his chin and returned her frown. "And succeeding too. Don't tell me you aren't having any fun, because I heard those little sounds you were making just now and believe me, they didn't mean '*Morgan, stop!*'" He said the last words in a ridiculous falsetto, as if he were her.

Her cheeks flamed. That was precisely the problem. She hadn't been saying no. If she let him claim kiss number three, she might lose her senses entirely and beg him to keep on kissing her. Beg him to make love to her completely. Her desperate yearning would be revealed, and she couldn't, *wouldn't*, give him the satisfaction of knowing how much she wanted him when those feelings clearly weren't reciprocated. She still had her pride.

And so did he. The thought came to her on a flash of inspiration. He was as proud, as arrogant, as ever. And that was her way out of this predicament.

Having Morgan fulfill kiss number three was something she wanted beyond anything. But on her terms, not his. She wasn't one of those biddable, simpering debutantes. She was his equal, in cunning and wit.

She shook her head and sent him a pitying look guaranteed to drive him completely insane.

"Poor Morgan. Do women only do these things with you because they lost a bet? How lowering."

His eyes narrowed and her heart started to pound. *Oh, she loved sparring with him like this.*

"No," he growled. "They do *these things* with me because they feel like they'll die if they don't."

"That's a little dramatic, isn't it?"

"Let me give you kiss number three and we'll see what you have to say about it then," he drawled. "I guarantee you'll be screaming for more."

Dear God. What arrogance!

Harriet was about to laugh when he raked a hand through his hair in a frustrated gesture and dipped his chin.

"*Bloody hell. You're* not only doing this because of the bet, are you?"

His voice was quiet, more unsure than she'd ever heard before, and her conscience gave her an uncomfortable stab in the gut. Making him think he'd coerced her into doing something she didn't want to do was a low blow. She'd been enjoying their byplay just as much as he had. More, probably. But how could she admit that without revealing how much she wanted him and humiliating herself?

"I have been enjoying the game," she said carefully. "But you have to admit that you've twisted the rules. You knew I was expecting to give you three kisses on the mouth, not grant you free rein to my body. I didn't know what I was getting into."

A muscle ticked in his jaw, but he didn't deny it.

"So what if . . . we make a new bet? Now I know exactly what's at stake."

He raised his brows for her to continue.

"If you win," she said quickly, "I'll willingly grant you kiss number three. Wherever you like."

"And if you win?"

"Then I get to choose your forfeit."

Harriet held her breath, praying that he'd agree.

"Fine," he grumbled at last.

Her heart soared.

"What do you suggest?" he asked. "A coin toss? Game of cards?"

She shook her head. Both of those were too reliant on luck. She needed something she could definitely win. "A footrace."

He gave a bark of surprised laughter. "A *footrace*? You're joking."

"Not at all. Over a distance of a hundred yards."

Morgan's lips had resumed their customary curl. He shook his head, good humor fully restored. "You're just delaying the inevitable. Look at us. Even if you wear those breeches instead of skirts, I'll still win. I'm faster than you. It's simple biology."

Harriet held up a hand. "I have two stipulations. One, I get to choose the course. And two, you give me a twenty-foot head start. To compensate for all that unequal biology."

"Done. Even so, there's no way you'll win."

She tried and failed to keep the delighted grin off her

face. Morgan might think he had the upper hand, but she had an ace up her sleeve.

"Shall we shake hands on it?" she suggested.

"Fine." He took her outstretched hand and gave it a threateningly hard squeeze. "May the best man win."

"Or woman." She smiled at him. "And thank you, I intend to."

Chapter Eighteen

Morgan was in a daze as he and Harriet made their way back to the ballroom, making sure not to be seen together. Harriet peeled off in the direction of the ladies' cloakroom, and he slipped easily into the crowd of newcomers filing into the hall.

Her counter-bet had come as a surprise. He'd hoped she was enjoying their game as much as he was, but perhaps he *had* been pushing her too hard. She was a virgin, after all, and presumably still thought she should be saving that virginity for her future husband.

The idea that *he* could be that husband clearly hadn't yet occurred to her.

He still had work to do.

Her suggestion that she was only enduring his kisses because of the bet had stung, but he didn't believe it for one minute. Harriet was no weak-willed debutante. If she truly hadn't wanted him to kiss her that first time in the garden she would have kneed him in the groin or bitten his lip. She'd never been one to hide her displeasure. If she'd had a branch handy, she would have hit him with it. He traced the scar beneath his chin in fond memory.

And if she hadn't wanted to continue the game tonight, she would have refused to have let him blindfold her. He would have stopped the moment she asked.

Surely she knew that?

Morgan frowned. She *did* know that. Despite the fact that he was a Davies, she'd always trusted him when it came to important things like this.

He skirted a group of dancers and smiled vaguely at an acquaintance while his mind continued to turn.

She'd definitely enjoyed him kissing her breasts. Her fingers had clutched at his head and she'd arched her back, silently offering herself to his mouth. He hadn't mistaken the little gasps of pleasure she'd made.

Perhaps it was *herself* she didn't trust? Had the intensity of her own reaction shocked her? It had shocked *him*, and he wasn't even a virgin.

Morgan's lips curved upward as a new explanation presented itself. Perhaps her desire to avoid kiss number three was less about the fact that she didn't want him to kiss her, and more about her wanting him to kiss her *too much*.

If that was the case, then winning this race was critical. If Harriet won, there would be no more kisses. No more chances for him to demonstrate just how amazing making love together could be.

He longed to pleasure her with his mouth, to show her *everything* they could do, but he wouldn't take her virginity. He didn't want her to feel like she had to marry him because he'd "ruined her." She had to marry him because she loved him. As much as he loved her.

Proving their physical compatibility was only one part of convincing her to marry him, of course. Any good military strategist knew the importance of engaging an opponent on more than one front, and Harriet's *brain* needed to be involved in the decision too.

Since she yearned for adventure, he'd been trying to think of ways to provide it. Ways that—naturally—included himself. Confronting Heron had been ideal: a low-risk way to show her how well they could work together even when they *weren't* in bed. They could be a team. Supporting and complementing each other.

Just as if they were married.

Chapter Nineteen

The following morning Morgan received a note from Harriet, along with one of her own maps of London, carefully folded. A circle had been penciled around a particular area in Holborn, and he squinted to read the name of the place she'd chosen for the race.

The note merely said: *Eleven o'clock. Bleeding Heart Yard.*

He chuckled. London certainly had some interesting place-names. Had Harriet chosen that one deliberately as the starting line? Was it a threat? Or a promise? If any woman could make his heart bleed, it would be her.

He'd seen her sneaky little smile when they'd shaken hands last night. For some reason she genuinely thought she could win this race and the fact that she'd clearly hatched some devious plan delighted him as much as it worried him.

Any other time he might have considered letting her win. He might have stayed behind her just to enjoy the sight of her delightful bottom jiggling around ahead of him.

But in this instance, he couldn't afford to lose. Honor and chivalry be damned.

He wondered if she'd be wearing breeches again. She'd looked delicious dressed as a sailor.

His cock stiffened at the thought. God, no wonder the navy didn't allow women on board. Nobody would get any work done at all.

She was already waiting for him when his coach arrived at the location, but to his surprise she wasn't alone. Gryff stood with her, along with Maddie.

"What are they doing here?" he demanded as soon as he stepped down onto the cobbles.

"And good morning to you too!" Gryff chuckled.

"We're here to support Harriet." Maddie smiled. "And to act as race officials."

"Speak for yourself," Gryff said. "I'm here to see Morgan get beaten by a girl. Again. It's always fun to watch you two each try to best the other."

Morgan glared at him.

Harriet, disappointingly, wasn't even wearing trousers. In fact, it seemed her only concession to sporting attire was to wear a shorter-than-average skirt and petticoats that gave an excellent view of her ankles. Her luxurious hair had been tamed into one long braid that rested over her shoulder and snaked down over her chest. The tail of it curled suggestively right where he imagined her nipple would be beneath her corset.

Morgan dragged his gaze back upward and met Harriet's mocking gaze.

"If I could have your undivided attention for a moment, Captain Davies?"

Her tone was drier than the sands of Egypt.

Oh, she was a cheeky wench. She needed a good spanking.

"Yes?"

"We need to discuss the course."

"Very well. We agreed a hundred yards. Where do we go?"

"We start here. Turn right at the corner, run along Knight Street for fifty yards, then turn left into Squeeze Gut Alley. The race will finish at the far end of the lane."

Morgan narrowed his eyes at the name of their destination. "Squeeze Gut Alley?"

"Yes." Harriet's eyes held a wicked twinkle that made him want to grab her and kiss her. "It's very well-named. You'll see."

Gryff clapped his hands. "Maddie, you stay here and act as starter. I'll go and wait at the end of the course to judge who comes in first." He trotted off around the corner.

Morgan made a shooing gesture with his hands at Harriet. "Off you go then. You get a twenty-yard head start."

"I doubt I'll need it," she taunted. "But thank you."

She carefully took twenty large steps toward the entrance to the cobbled yard, counting aloud as she did so. "Here?"

"That'll do!" he shouted back.

Morgan's heart began to pound at the thrill of the chase. Despite Harriet's head start she would still be hampered by her skirts. He had a longer stride. The street beyond was relatively quiet; he shouldn't be slowed by carts or stray dogs.

"Ready?" Madeline called.

Both he and Harriet nodded.

"In that case . . . *go!*"

Morgan pushed off, pumping his arms as he set off in pursuit. Harriet turned the corner in a flurry of skirts, and when he followed only seconds later he was pleased to see he was already gaining on her.

The road ahead was clear. His boots slipped a little on the damp cobbles, but he'd had years of sliding around on ships' decks, and righted himself with ease.

Harriet glanced over her shoulder and gave a squeal of dismay.

He laughed, already scenting victory.

A pigeon flew up in a puff of feathers as he pounded past a shop window, but he was only ten yards behind her now. The open mouth of the alleyway loomed to her left and Morgan grinned. It was wide enough for a horse and cart. He would definitely be able to catch her before the end.

She veered sharply into the alley, her braid flying behind her like a loose rope in a gale, and he followed, but his heart sank as he rounded the corner and saw what lay ahead.

The sneaky little weasel!

Past Harriet, at the very end of the lane, a tiny sliver of daylight indicated the exit. A dark shape—doubtless Gryff—hovered just beyond.

Damn!

The lane grew steadily narrower, the buildings on either side getting closer and closer together until a gap of less than a few feet remained.

Morgan bellowed his displeasure. *"No!"*

Harriet, the devil woman, *laughed*. The joyous sound echoed off the looming walls.

He put on a spurt, leaping over crates of refuse and closing the distance between them even more. The walls closed in as the light became more sparse. He was almost near enough to grab her braid, but she darted back and forth like a rabbit, deliberately hindering his ability to get past.

His shoulder scraped the wall, and then the other one hit, and he realized with mingled outrage and disbelief that he couldn't pass her. Not without tackling her to the ground and leaping over her.

Even as the thought materialized, he was forced to slow as both of his shoulders made contact with the crumbling bricks. Harriet, with her smaller frame, surged ahead, victory clearly within her grasp. He was about to turn sideways in a last desperate attempt to grab her when she skidded to a stop and whirled around to face him.

Morgan stilled in surprise.

Her shoulders and skirts touched the walls now too, filling the space, blocking out even more of the light. The gap could only be two feet wide at most. He lunged forward, but he was well and truly wedged.

She took a step back toward him until they stood face-to-face.

"Now I see why it's called Squeeze Gut Alley!" he panted, trying to sound offhand when bitter disappointment was squeezing his own guts. "Well played, Montgomery."

Harriet's cheeks were flushed and her eyes glittered with triumph. "Do you admit defeat, Davies?"

He tried to free his shoulder and heard fabric rip. He'd have to get a new jacket. "I suppose I do."

She gave a little crow of delight. "Ha! And don't you dare say I cheated either. All's fair in love and war. I merely used my superior knowledge of the local terrain to gain victory. Like any good general."

"Wellington would be proud," he grunted.

He was wedged tight, restrained by the coarse bricks as efficiently as if two men held him. He could have turned sideways and freed himself, but instead he strained forward so they were nose to nose. In the semidarkness it was as if they were the only two people in the world, despite the fact that a busy thoroughfare clearly existed not six feet farther on.

Harriet stared up at him. Her pupils were huge, her

chest rising and falling with exertion. She looked like she'd just tumbled out of bed after the best sex of her life, and Morgan's body hardened instinctively at the thought.

"You win," he growled. "Which means I don't get kiss number three. And you get to choose my forfeit. What's it going to be?"

She lifted her hands and pressed them, palms out, against the rough walls just by his ears. She leaned closer. Her mouth was tantalizingly close to his own.

"I want . . ."

"You want—?" he prompted impatiently. "Me to run naked around St. James's Square? A hundred pounds? What? Out with it."

She licked her lips and looked him dead in the eye. "I want kiss number three."

Chapter Twenty

Harriet's heart was pounding so hard she thought it might explode. Had she really just admitted that she wanted kiss number three? Elation and terror fought for supremacy in her chest.

"You what?" Morgan asked.

She glanced over her shoulder to make sure Gryff was out of earshot.

"You heard me. I want kiss number three."

Morgan's eyes narrowed into suspicious slits, and she had to stop herself from laughing. He looked like a pirate who'd just lost a ship full of gold bullion.

"*Where* do you want it?"

She opened her eyes wide. Really, it was so much fun teasing him. "You mean geographically?"

He bared his teeth.

"Oh, you mean *physically*."

She let her gaze linger meaningfully on his lips, then gazed back into his eyes, and her humor fled as the enormity of what she was about to do struck her. She should say *on my cheek* and have done with it.

But she'd come to a shocking realization: She wanted Morgan to kiss her everywhere. Even if it was only for one night, she would have his complete and undivided attention. She would have his expertise.

She just needed to be brave and grab what she wanted with both hands. She was tired of being ignorant of the pleasures between men and women. It was one thing to see them in two-dimensional drawings—like in that naughty book he'd bought her—and quite another to actually experience them in real life. A flat map was no substitute for hiking up a real mountain.

She wanted that discovery, the danger of the adventure.

Plenty of navigators never returned home, of course. They simply sailed off the edge of the world, never to return. But maybe they hadn't been lost. Maybe whatever they'd found in those mysterious places was so extraordinary, so compelling, they simply hadn't wanted to return to "civilization."

It was time to find out what the dragons were really like. Or if they existed at all.

"Where do you want it, Harriet?" Morgan repeated.

His low question snapped her from her reverie and she took a deep breath, as if she were a diver about to leap off a cliff into the ocean below.

"Where you said." She dragged her hand down the wall and hovered it in front of her skirts, at the juncture of her thighs. "Here."

He sucked in a breath. "Why?" His voice was scarcely more than a whisper, a gravelly demand. "*Why* do you want it, Harry?"

"Because I want the adventure."

He shook his head. "Not a good enough reason."

Her mouth fell open in shock. She'd thought he'd jump at the chance. Panicked that the opportunity might be slipping away, she blurted out the truth.

"Because I want *you*."

His eyes darkened. His big body loomed over her, crowding the tiny space, like a wild animal straining at the end of a leash.

"Yes!" he breathed. "That's the right answer."

Dear God! Now what should she do?

She swallowed and tried to sound as if she made assignations of this magnitude all the time. "Well. Good. Ah . . . excellent. Where do you suppose we should—? When should we—?"

He grinned at her embarrassment, but before he could answer, Gryff's impatient tones echoed toward them.

"Are you two stuck?"

Harriet thought she heard Morgan mutter, "Only with each other," but she couldn't be sure.

She turned sideways and called out, "Oh, no! At least *I'm* not. Captain Davies might be."

"Need me to give you a shove?" Madeline's amused tones came from directly behind Morgan—she'd followed him along the alleyway. "I'd be more than happy to give you a kick in the—"

Morgan shook his head. "I'm fine, thank you." With a hideous scrape of fabric, he turned and sidestepped after Harriet toward the narrow egress.

Harriet emerged on the brightly lit street next to Gryff. Morgan, then Madeline, followed, but Harriet could scarcely bring herself to look Morgan in the eye.

"I think it's fair to declare Miss Montgomery the winner," Gryff said with a taunting smile at Morgan as the four of them began walking back to the carriages.

Morgan sent Harriet his own secret smile. "Oh, I think we're both winners."

Maddie frowned, clearly about to ask what he meant, and Harriet's cheeks heated even more. Luckily, Gryff interrupted before his wife could follow up.

"So, what were you playing for? What's the winner's prize?"

"The lifelong satisfaction of having beaten a Davies," Harriet temporized quickly. "It's worth more than gold."

Madeline glanced up at her husband with a sly smile. "Oh, I quite agree. No money in the *world* can beat that."

They reached Bleeding Heart Yard, and Gryff helped Maddie back into their carriage. He turned to assist Harriet, but Morgan cleared his throat.

"I can take Miss Montgomery if you like. I'm going past Bloomsbury."

Gryff glanced at Harriet in question. "Are you sure you want to share a carriage with this reprobate?"

She met Morgan's eyes. "Oh, yes. That would be fine."

Maddie poked her head out of the carriage and shot Morgan a threatening glare. "Morgan, I know what you're like. Promise me you'll be nice to Harriet while you're alone. You used to be horrid when we were younger."

"She gave as good as she got." Gryff chuckled. "Don't you remember that time she whacked him with a sword?"

"It was a stick," Morgan countered evenly. "*I* was the one with the sword."

"And she still bested you," Gryff snorted.

"She did indeed." Morgan slid another hot glance over at Harriet as he touched his chin, then looked back to Maddie. "And *of course* I promise to be nice. Miss Montgomery will have nothing to complain about from me."

Harriet's heart pounded at the double meaning of his words.

Maddie looked as if she wanted to say more, but Harriet stepped up into Morgan's carriage and sent her cousin a cheery wave through the open doorway. Morgan settled himself on the seat opposite her.

"See you at Lady Scarborough's on Sunday?" Maddie called out.

"Yes." Harriet could barely choke out the word.

Gryff sent Morgan a hard stare. "Take care, Brother."

Morgan nodded. "I will."

The other coach rattled off, and Harriet grabbed the leather strap above the window in preparation for their own departure, but Morgan didn't call out an address to the driver. She glanced over at him and was disconcerted to find him watching her with his usual amused, slightly mocking look on his face.

"Where shall I direct him, Harriet? To Bloomsbury? Or back to my house?"

Her eyes grew wide as his meaning sank in.

"Good Lord, you can't mean to do it *today*? Now? In the daytime?"

He chuckled at her obvious shock.

"Yes, that's exactly what I mean." He brushed some brick dust from the sleeve of his jacket. "This may offend your maidenly sensibilities, Montgomery, but people—many, many people, in fact—engage in all manner of scandalous behavior before the sun goes down."

Harriet was lost for words. Whenever she'd been brave enough to imagine it—*them*—her brain had always pictured soft, flattering lighting and plenty of concealing shadows to preserve her modesty.

"But . . . won't Rhys be at your house?" she stammered.

"Not until Friday. He's gone to visit an army friend down in Kent."

"We can't. I mean . . . I'm sure we *can*, technically, but I hadn't expected it to be so—"

"Imminent?" he finished with a wicked smile. "So urgent?"

"I think I need time to prepare."

He snorted. "This isn't a pitched battle. You don't need to prepare anything."

"I got all sweaty from the running." A lady *never* mentioned perspiration, but she was past the point of desperation now.

"You'll get even sweatier with me."

She swallowed audibly and Morgan laughed.

"Just come to my house, follow me upstairs to my bedroom, and let me do unspeakable things to you."

She sent him a scolding look. "You make it sound so easy."

"It *is* easy. Seriously, the longer you put it off, the more nervous you'll get."

"I'm not nervous."

"No? Then why is your knee jiggling about like that?"

Harriet slapped her hand over her thigh to still the instinctive tremor. "I'm unused to running."

"If you've changed your mind—" he drawled. "I quite understand. The life of an adventuress isn't for everyone."

Oh, he knew just how to taunt her, the beast.

She lifted her chin. "I haven't changed my mind. Tell him 'Hanover Square.'"

He eyed her a moment longer. "You're sure? Won't your father be expecting you home?"

"He's gone to visit that Mister Bronte you introduced him to the other night. He won't be back until teatime."

Morgan looked entirely too pleased with himself. "That leaves more than enough time for debauchery." He lifted his fist and hammered on the ceiling of the carriage to get the driver's attention. "Hanover Square."

Chapter Twenty-One

Harriet couldn't decide if this was the best decision she'd ever made in her life or the worst. She'd thought turning the tables on Morgan would be so clever, that she'd be the one controlling her own seduction. Demanding it, even. But she didn't feel in control at all. Her pulse pounded in her throat as the carriage bowled along, and she stared out of the window to avoid looking at him.

She could do this. She wanted this. She'd wanted this for *years*.

Morgan was right. Women all over London were probably making love right now.

In a few short minutes she'd be one of them.

She gulped. This was going to be her first great adventure—and all without leaving London.

The coach clattered to a stop in Hanover Square far sooner than she would have liked. She briefly considered telling him she'd changed her mind, then saw the knowing glint in Morgan's eye and just knew he was waiting for her to cry off.

Never.

"We can't just go in through your front door!" she hissed. "What if someone sees me? I'll be ruined."

"True." Morgan directed the driver around the back of

the house, and they pulled into a cobbled mews yard. He helped her down. A tall iron gate led to a neat rectangular garden, and then they were ascending a short flight of steps and passing through a shiny black door.

Harriet glanced around with undisguised interest. The tiled hallway was large, with a handsome console table and pier mirror on one side and a large Chinese porcelain pot that the brothers were using as an umbrella stand on the other. A set of stairs led down, presumably to the kitchens, while another set curved upward overhead. A silver card tray sat on the table, filled with an abundance of letters and invitations.

"Well?" Morgan asked drily. "What do you think of my evil lair?"

"I've never been inside a bachelor's lodgings before. It's . . . tidy."

He smiled at her surprise. "What were you expecting? Half-dressed harlots swinging from the chandeliers and half-eaten dinners on every surface? Muddy boots all over the floor?"

"Something like that," she admitted wryly.

He glanced around the perfectly clean hallway. "Sorry to disappoint. I keep Trellech as my den of iniquity. Rhys and I have a valet and a cook when we're here, but I've given them both the day off."

She raised her brows. "Rather presumptuous, wasn't it? Were you so confident you'd win?"

He shrugged. "I've always been lucky. And here we are."

Here they were indeed.

She clenched her fingers in her skirts. "So, what do we do now?"

He took her hand and threaded his fingers through

hers. Her pulse rate doubled. His fingers were warm and slightly rough, so much larger than hers.

"Now we throw off the bowlines. Catch the wind in our sails." He sent her an irresistible smile and tugged her toward the staircase.

Harriet let herself be drawn along the corridor and up the stairs. She could scarcely believe that this was happening, that she was actually here, in Morgan's house—in his bedroom—as he led her into a surprisingly large room decorated in navy and gold.

Her steps faltered.

A large wooden-framed bed stood against one wall, the headboard crested with a carved shell and a confusion of rococo scrolls, like a cartouche on one of her maps. The bedspread was a rich royal blue piled high with an assortment of pillows.

She barely glanced at the rest of the room: She was vaguely aware of the dark shapes of a wardrobe and dressing chest, a couple of armchairs. The bed dominated her attention.

Morgan released her hand. Without prompting, he strode to the windows and drew the curtains closed, shutting out the daylight, enclosing them in a cocoon of shadows.

Still without speaking he crossed to the fireplace, took a tinderbox from the mantel, and crouched to light the fire that had been laid. Only when bright flames danced merrily in the grate did he rise and turn to her again.

Harriet was practically shaking with nerves. It was one thing to fantasize about being a wicked adventuress, quite another when faced with the opportunity in real life. Her breathing quickened as he stopped an arm's length away from her. Holding her gaze, he tugged at the cuffs of his ruined jacket and shrugged out of it, tossing it carelessly on the back of one of the armchairs that flanked the fire.

Harriet stared at him, a queer, intense squeezing sensation in the region of her heart. In the fire glow he looked perfectly wicked, a pirate prince in his shirtsleeves. A brigand who promised nothing but adventure and heartbreak.

Irresistible.

Well, if she was going to get her heart broken, it might as well be with the only man she'd ever really wanted. The only man she'd ever imagined giving herself to.

Summoning her nerve, she unbuttoned her own fitted jacket and placed it on the opposing chair, a mirror image of his own, and his eyes brightened at the hint of a new game. As if to test her, he put his hand up to his throat, untied his cravat, and laid it over the jacket.

She tugged the thin lace fichu from her neckline and put it on hers.

Tit for tat, a silent game of one-upmanship.

His lips twitched in appreciation. He flicked open the first button of his shirt and sent her a raised-eyebrow challenge.

She undid the first button of her own shirt, glad that the design fastened at the front and not at the back, and bit her lip to quell her own spurt of laughter. It had been like this between them forever. Why should lovemaking be any different?

His shirt didn't button all the way down. He undid the remaining three buttons, revealing a wedge of smooth, tanned skin at his throat, but when Harriet was about to do the same, he closed the distance between them and caught her hands.

"Allow me."

She held her breath as he undid her buttons all the way

to her waist, revealing her thin chemise and stays, and slid it down her arms. She shivered, despite the warmth from the fire, as his hot gaze roved over the top swell of her breasts, the smooth curves of her shoulders. He reached out and stroked her neck, the jut of her collarbone, and her stomach contracted in sweet confusion.

"As someone who's done this before, might I make a suggestion?" he murmured.

"By all means."

Their exaggerated politeness only reinforced the crackling tension arcing between them.

"Allowing me just *one* kiss is extremely restrictive. I guarantee you'll have a more enjoyable time if you grant me a series of kisses."

Harriet tried to ignore the heat rising in her cheeks and the way his fingers stroked oh-so-softly over her skin. "Very well. I suppose I should bow to your experience in this matter. Carry on."

His lips quirked. "Your wish is my command."

She stayed perfectly still as he caught the end of her braid. He unwound the strip of ribbon that secured it, then teased the woven strands loose, unthreading them from one another with infinite patience. When he was done, he fanned her hair, bringing it forward to tumble in dark waves down over her shoulders.

"You always used to wear your hair down when you were in Wales," he said softly.

She nodded, struck dumb with nerves.

He slid his fingers down her arm and caught her hand, then gently turned her so her back was to him. His soft exhale lifted the hairs on her exposed nape and she could feel the heat of his body all along her back, even though they weren't touching.

And then his lips pressed against her shoulder and his

arms slid around her waist, his fingers spreading across her stomach, and even through the fabric of her stays and chemise, it *burned*.

A heavy pounding started in her blood.

To her surprise, he sank to his knees behind her. His hands slid to her hips and she sucked in a breath as he rested his forehead in the curve at the base of her spine.

"Turn around."

His gravelly command made her knees turn to water. She obeyed, staring down at him as he remained on his knees, his hands resting at her waist. The sight of him there, like a supplicant, as if he truly meant to worship her, did funny things to her insides.

Without thought, she put her palm on his jaw, loving the rough texture of his cheek. She'd asked for an adventure; she couldn't wait to discover what lay in store.

Chapter Twenty-Two

Harriet let Morgan guide her backward until she sat on the edge of the bed. Still kneeling, he removed her shoes with brisk efficiency, then slid his hands beneath her skirts and lightly encircled her ankles.

Her breathing hitched, but she was determined to remain in control of herself.

He moved higher, his palms gliding up her calves, over her stockings, and she sucked in a breath as he reached the sensitive hollow at the back of her knee. His clever fingers found the ribbons that secured her stockings, and she bit her lip as he toyed with them.

Oh, he was wicked. She could barely breathe for the anticipation. And he knew it.

In an effort to relax, she leaned back, supporting herself on her hands; the soft mattress dipped beneath her weight.

He found the bare skin above her garters. She wasn't wearing any undergarments; she hadn't wanted the additional fabric to hinder her sprint, and the waft of cool air against her most feminine flesh made her shiver. She felt wicked, wanton, like those scandalous women in the Rowlandson cartoon tumbling down the staircase.

Embarrassed, she tried to press her knees together, but Morgan's big body was in the way.

"Relax," he murmured.

"Easy for you to say. I've never done this before."

He glanced up from between her knees, and his knowing smile made her heart pound. "You'll like it, I promise."

Harriet could only watch in a daze as he pushed her skirts over her knees and slid his palms up her thighs. And then he bent his head and pressed a kiss to the inside of her leg, just above her garter.

She arched off the bed, caught between terror and bliss.

He tightened his fingers on her thighs, a subtle reminder to stay still, and pressed another kiss higher up. And then another—a series, just as he'd promised—and her whole body tightened and shivered.

Closer. Closer. His fingertip brushed the ticklish crease where her leg met her torso, and she yelped as he followed it up with another kiss on the inside of her thigh.

A restless ache gnawed at her belly. She glanced down to find him staring up at her, and her heart somersaulted again.

Dear Lord, he was handsome. Dark and wicked, with one lock of hair falling over his forehead and that beloved scar just visible beneath his chin. Only in her wildest dreams had she imagined him like this.

His index finger traced a devilish figure-eight pattern at the very top of her leg as he held her gaze in challenge. She stared right back at him, refusing to be the one to break eye contact.

She imagined herself a queen. An empress with the power to command. A woman for whom men would willingly lay down their lives to fulfill her every desire.

His lips twitched, as if he could read her thoughts. Very deliberately he let his fingers trace inward, skimming her damp folds, then parting them, sliding in the slippery wetness her body had produced. Her cheeks blazed, but she couldn't look away. She arched against him, desperate for him to ease the ache he'd started—

He withdrew his hand.

"Not like that," he chided. "I promised you a kiss." He glanced between her legs and whatever he saw there, within the frothy tumble of her skirts, made him bite his lip. His throat bobbed as he swallowed. "I've dreamed of tasting you for *fucking years*."

Her mouth dropped open in surprise, but there was no time to process his unexpected admission. One of his hands slid to her hip while the other slipped beneath her bottom. She fell back onto her elbows, and then his mouth was between her legs, hot and wet, and she could only gasp in astonishment.

He kissed her with lips and tongue, alternately licking and teasing. Feasting, then savoring, as if he couldn't decide whether to take his time, or devour her in one fell swoop.

Dear God, what a sensation! His lips found the sensitive bundle of nerves within her curls; he flicked it with his tongue and then tapped lightly with his fingers and Harriet nearly shot off the bed.

"Morgan!"

He groaned against her, a sound of pleasure and agony, like a dreamer, and the vibration made her even more feverish. Utterly unable to keep still, she grabbed his hair, holding him in place, silently begging him to continue this wicked torment. In that moment she didn't know whether she loved him or hated him. Perhaps it was both.

"Don't stop!"

Kisses. More kisses: wicked and wonderful. Darkness and pleasure swirled behind her eyelids. Her entire being seemed centered at the junction of her thighs, her stomach muscles tensing as his touch wound her higher and higher even as she was sinking, falling. *Dying*.

She was about to beg for mercy when his tongue slipped *into* her, stabbing deep, and her body clenched around him like a fist.

She was beyond embarrassment now. Past shame. And he seemed to know exactly what she needed. He quickened his pace, tongue and fingers working in wicked harmony, and she gasped his name, clutching at his head, striving for that pinnacle of joy.

She splintered apart. Waves of pleasure rolled over her, as powerful as breakers in a storm, pitching her to the depths of smothering, drowning ecstasy.

When she finally regained her senses, Harriet found herself staring up at the ceiling, her chest heaving, her limbs still shaking with tiny tremors. Her entire being seemed to glow with satisfaction. She glanced down her body, past the voluminous puff of her skirts, and found Morgan still crouched between her thighs. Heat flashed over her skin, and for an endless moment they just stared at each other, as if neither of them could quite believe what they'd done.

And then he sent her a cocky, knowing smile, and the spell was broken.

"Welcome back."

He stood, wiping his glistening mouth on his shirtsleeve, then fluffed her skirts down over her knees. For a heart-stopping moment he stood looking down at her, and she wondered what would happen if she simply opened her arms and beckoned him down.

Would he cover her with his body? Would he kiss her? Touch her? Strip them both of their remaining clothes and make love to her fully, as she was so desperate for him to do?

Unable to stop herself, she dropped her gaze to the front of his breeches to see if he'd been remotely affected by what they'd just done, and her eyes widened at the obvious bulge outlined by the snug fabric.

His eyebrows lifted as he saw the direction of her gaze. "See something you like, Montgomery?"

Without a hint of embarrassment, he molded his hand over the bulge and shifted it to what was presumably a more comfortable position. "Because if you want to add kisses four, five, and six, I have plenty of suggestions."

She hadn't thought it possible to get any hotter. Feeling at a distinct disadvantage flat on her back, she struggled to sit up, but the mattress was so soft it thwarted her every move. With a snort of amusement, he reached out a hand, caught her own, and hauled her up.

The ease with which he did it reminded her just how strong he was; and how careful he'd just been with her. Her heart compressed a little more.

Oh, God, she was in trouble.

Chapter Twenty-Three

Morgan fought to clear his swimming head. He felt drunk, utterly intoxicated. Harriet's scent, her taste—dark and sweet—lingered in his mouth, his nose. His only thought had been to pleasure her. Every pulse of his blood had been filled with the same desperate refrain: *Love* this. *Need* this. Need *me*.

He'd tried every trick he'd ever learned, following the cues of her body, the way she grasped him tighter, or arched, or the way her breath caught on a groan. The sound of her climax had made his heart almost burst with satisfaction.

He'd envisioned her like this in his darkest moments, her skirts rucked to her waist in a frothy foam of petticoats, long hair fanned out around her head, wallowing in the silken ripples of his bedspread. Now the image was seared into his brain like a brand.

God, he was so close to losing control. She was laid out before him like a feast, and he was as starving as he'd been in his prison cell.

He sucked in an unsteady breath. Her thighs had been so soft, like cream silk. He wanted to see her naked. His cock was stiff and throbbing in his breeches, and when her curious gaze rested there, he thought he might explode.

She had no idea what she was doing to him, thank God. If she did, he was bloody sure she'd keep on doing it, just to drive him mad.

He was probably there already.

Lust held him on the knife-edge of reason. Every muscle roared at him to sate himself. It would be so easy. Tumble her back down onto the bed, kiss that gorgeous mouth of hers, bare every inch of her skin, and his, and push himself into her. He wanted it so badly he was shaking with it.

Do it!

He ignored the insistent whisper. *Enough.* This would have to be enough. He had no more kisses left.

He frowned. Had he actually pushed his finger inside her, or just his tongue? The past minutes were a bit hazy. It was probably a moot point anyway. Even if he hadn't ruined her in strictly technical terms, she'd ruined him. For every other woman, ever.

She'd won, and she didn't even know it.

She was watching him from her seat on his bed. Her gray eyes were dark and dreamy, her hair in delightful disarray around her face. Her lips were pink—and still unkissed. A shaft of outrage pierced him. *What a fucking waste!* Those lips were made to be kissed. Daily. Hourly.

He started to lean forward to remedy the oversight, then remembered he was out of kisses and forced a light, teasing smile onto his face instead.

"So. Kiss number three. Did it meet expectations?"

God, his voice was low. He sounded like he'd been bellowing orders over a force nine gale. He cleared his throat.

Harriet let out a shaky laugh. "It surpassed them. But then, you knew it would." Her face fell a little. "You're very skilled. I suppose that comes from practice."

His euphoric mood plummeted. Yes, he'd done that to other women on occasion, but every one paled into insignificance compared with her. Harriet wasn't just one of many: She was the *last* of many. The only woman he wanted to make love to ever again.

"No!" he growled, more harshly than he'd intended. "It comes from *desire*."

Her eyes widened at his fervency and he cursed himself for not keeping things light. He didn't want to frighten her with the force of his feelings; she was probably already embarrassed enough by what they'd just done.

She stood, suddenly awkward, and bent down to fasten her shoes. "So. Your forfeit is paid," she mumbled at the carpet. "Thank you. It was most . . ."

"Extraordinary?" he suggested. "Unforgettable?"

"Educational."

Morgan frowned at the top of her bent head. *Educational?! Bloody woman!* He'd show her educational—

No. He bit his lip to stop the words from tumbling out. She needed time to process everything.

And he needed a swim in an ice-cold lake.

She crossed to her discarded clothes on the back of the chair and struggled to refasten her shirt over her stays. "I should go."

He clasped his hands behind his back to stop himself from taking her in his arms and kissing her senseless. Her color was still high and she was looking everywhere but at him; she was clearly mortified.

"Of course," he said. He grabbed his own clothes and crossed to the door. "I'll tell Mason to ready the coach."

As he headed down the stairs, he realized how dismissive that had sounded, as if he couldn't wait to get her out of the house. She wasn't some harlot to escort off the premises now their liaison was at an end. *Idiot!* He might as well have warned her not to steal the silver on the way out.

His own hands were unsteady as he pulled on his jacket and retied his cravat using the mirror by the door. When he returned from the stables—ignoring his coachman's cheeky comments about the brevity of the lady's visit and how Morgan must be losing his touch—Harriet was waiting in the hall.

She followed him to the coach without a word, but when he climbed in after her, she finally looked him in the face again.

"Oh! I thought you would be sending me home alone."

He feigned scandalized horror. "Unchaperoned? My dear Miss Montgomery, I wouldn't dream of it."

"I dread to think what you *do* dream of," she countered, then bit her lip as if shocked by her own unguarded words.

Relief surged through him at the reappearance of her customary sarcasm. "Oh, all manner of wicked things, you can be sure."

She flushed and frowned at the same time and he laughed, glad they'd found their way back to their usual footing.

"You'd be surprised at how many of those dreams concern you, Harry," he teased.

"Don't call me that. You make me sound like a man."

He let his eyes linger on her face for a long moment. "Believe me, I could never, ever make that mistake."

It took less than ten minutes to reach Bury Street, but instead of allowing her to escape, he followed her into the shop.

There was no sign of her father. The sign in the window read Closed, but she turned it over to read Open and hastened into the back room, then disappeared through an adjoining door, presumably to check the upper part of the house.

"Father's not back yet, but you don't have to stay," she said when she returned. "I'll be perfectly fine on my own."

She was clearly keen to be rid of him, but Morgan was in no mood to comply. He wanted more of her company, and he was ruthless enough to use any excuse to keep her nearby. Now that their kissing game was done, he'd have to be more creative about finding reasons to see her.

"I don't like the thought of you here alone. What if someone decides to rob you?"

"I keep a loaded pistol under the counter," she said evenly. "And I know how to use it." She sent him a meaningful glare, as if she were considering using it on him.

He repressed a smile. "Good."

She folded her arms, but he didn't leave. Instead, he wandered over to inspect the papers and paint box that were strewn on a leather-topped desk against one wall. Harriet let out a little huff of irritation. "That's my work station. Do you mind?"

He pulled one of the pages forward. "Not at all. What's this?"

"It's something I've been working on for Lady Melville."

She tried to take it from him and failed.

"*A Map of the Heart*," he read.

She sighed in defeat and let him look.

"Indeed. It's an amusing map showing all the different parts of love. Lady Melville already owns several examples of this type of thing—there's one called *The Empire of Love* by a German mapmaker named Breitkopf, and a French version called *The Map of Tenderness* by Madeleine de Scudéry—but she asked me to produce one in

English to entertain her friends. I've been having a great deal of fun with it."

Morgan looked closer. The map appeared to be ordinary enough, with a series of lakes and rivers, hills and valleys. Various sections had been painted with different colors to denote their borders, as the counties of England were often shown on a regular map, but his lips twitched as he started to read the place-names.

There was the Land of Youth, filled with such places as the Forest of First Love, Kiss Field, and Charm Castle. Was it his imagination, or did some of those look like the places he and Harriet had played as children in Wales? Charm Castle looked a lot like the ruined folly near Trellech where he'd tried to get her to swear fealty. And almost kissed her.

Next to the Land of Youth, however, was the rather more sobering Mountains of Loathing.

"'Vale of Tears'?" he read, highly amused. "'Swamp of Profanity.' 'Desert of Melancholy'? Someone was having a bad day."

She shrugged. "My aim is to show *all* the emotions, not just the happy ones. The peaks and troughs of amorous pursuit, if you will."

He snorted and carried on reading. "Ah, 'the Land of Lust.' What have you put in here? 'Intoxication County' . . . 'Lake of Lechery' . . . 'Flirtation Field' . . . All a bit cynical, isn't it?"

"I've drawn the Land of Happy Love too." She slid her finger to the section next to his. "See, there's Tenderness Tavern, Satisfaction Valley. I even put a Well of Granted Wishes in honor of Maddie and Gryff. And a Fountain of Joy."

"But what's this here? Bachelor Country." He tilted his head to see better. "Of course; Stupidity Town, Rejection

Place, the Cave of Contempt." He struggled to contain his laughter.

"The Aunts have been particularly helpful in naming places."

"What's Exasperation Heath? And who lives in the *Hamlet of Death*?"

"There are nice parts too. Look, there's a City of Dreams. And the Bridge of Hope."

"All by the Sea of Doubt," he pointed out.

"I drew a Marriage Harbor."

"Right next to Spinstertown. And I can't help noticing that the River of Inclination leads to the Lake of Indifference. Is that a warning?"

"Pure coincidence."

Morgan shook his head. He loved her humor. But for all its levity, this map was symbolic of their own situation. He'd taken her to the Peak of Desire this afternoon, but could she be convinced to pay a visit to the Dale of Permanent Affection?

Or had they sailed so far off the edge they were in uncharted territory? He certainly felt as if he was somewhere he'd never been before, in some strange, uncertain hinterland where they weren't quite enemies, nor lovers, nor friends. Where did that leave them? Floundering around in the Swamp of Bloody-God-Knows-Where.

She should put *that* on her map.

A glint of silver on the corner of the desk caught his attention and his eyes widened in sudden recognition. "Isn't that the—"

"—pencil you threw in the stream when we were younger?" she finished, seeing the direction of his gaze. "The one my mother gave me? Yes. It is."

She picked it up and stroked her thumb over her own inscribed initials.

Morgan feigned shock. "How did you get it back?"

He waited for her to tell him how it had been miraculously caught in Tom Evans's fishing net, but instead she sent him an odd, sideways smile. Her lips twitched in the way they always did when she was about to do something to annoy him, and a flash of heat washed over him.

"You know how I got it back," she said softly.

Chapter Twenty-Four

Morgan's heart stuttered. "What?"

"You waded into the stream the morning after you'd thrown it in, and got it." Harriet said.

"I don't know what you mean."

"Liar. I *know* that's what you did, because I went there myself, with exactly the same idea." She lifted her brows. "But you were already in the water. I hid in the bushes and watched you dive down to get it."

Morgan felt an unaccustomed heat stain his cheeks. God, he *never* blushed. But she'd caught him out in a lie, and—even worse—she must have guessed that his studied indifference toward her then had been little more than an act.

Shit. He thought he'd hidden it so well.

Flustered, for possibly the first time in his life, he tried to deflect the conversation.

"You saw me in the stream? I was probably going for an early-morning swim. You should be ashamed of yourself, spying on innocent bathers." He sent her a sly, sideways smile. "Was I naked?"

"You were shirtless."

"Did you like what you saw?"

He'd been a scrawny lad of sixteen back then. Now he

was a man, muscled and toned from years of strenuous physical activity. He'd give anything to have her look on his naked body now.

Her cheeks had become a little pink. "I barely saw you before you dived beneath the surface."

He was sure she was lying; the thought cheered him immensely. "You should have joined me."

"You'd have tried to drown me."

"I wouldn't have bothered. Davies tradition says Montgomery women are impossible to drown. Plenty have tried, over the years, but witches always bob back up to the surface. Water, being a sacred element, rejects them, apparently."

"Are you saying I'm a witch?"

As he'd done so many times before, he hid the truth by making it sound like a joke. "Of course. You've bewitched me for years. I'm completely under your spell."

She snorted.

Unbidden, his brain produced an image of what she would have looked like in that stream, a soaking wet shift clinging to her body. The material, obligingly, would have been transparent: he would have seen the tight buds of her nipples, seen every wonderful feminine curve.

He'd have put his hands on her and pulled her weightless body to him in the water, would have pressed his cold lips to hers. And then he would have dragged her over to the riverbank, stripped off their clothes, and warmed them both up by—

His body hardened and he cursed his overactive imagination. He really needed to make such fantasies a reality.

"We should make another bet," he said. "Loser has to take a swim in the river at Trellech."

She shook her head. "No. No more bets. I heard what you said to the Aunts the other day."

"What was that?"

"You declared, publicly, that you were looking for a wife. Which means it's high time you stopped making inappropriate bets with me and started considering who you think is suitable wife material."

You're suitable wife material.

He bit back the impulsive words. She wasn't ready to hear them, not yet. Her body might be half-convinced, but she was inherently stubborn, and her intellect was still coming round to the idea.

"I like making inappropriate bets with you," he said instead. "*Especially* when you win."

As he'd intended, she flushed at the reminder that she'd been the one to insist on kiss number three. Unfortunately, the only thing he could do now was to hope she came to want more of the same. From him, and only him.

"No more bets," she repeated sternly.

He was about to argue when a carriage clattered to a stop outside. Her father emerged, helped down by a footman, and Harriet rushed to open the door. Morgan moved quietly to one side of the shop so as not to interrupt their reunion.

The easy affection between Harriet and her father had always been a source of wonder to him. His own sire, the late Earl of Powys, had been an undemonstrative parent who'd paid little heed to his children unless he thought they needed scolding. He'd sent all four of them, Carys included, off to boarding school, and rarely bothered conversing with them during the holidays. Unfilial he might be, but Morgan really didn't miss the old bugger.

"Father, you're back!" Harriet bustled to help him out of his coat and scarf. Taking him by the arm, she guided him gently around the various furniture obstacles in his path and settled him in his customary chair in the back room.

Henry Montgomery made a big show of shooing her away, but it was clear he enjoyed the attention. "Yes, yes, I'm back. No need to fuss."

"How did your visit with Mister Bronte go?"

The older man drew his rug more firmly over his lap. "Well, as to that, I've come to a decision. Doctor Saunders is going to perform the same surgery on me."

Harriet's gasp was audible, even from where Morgan stood. "He is? But that's wonderful! What made you change your mind?"

"I've been selfish," Henry admitted gruffly. "I've let my own fears turn me into a burden. An unnecessary one, as it happens."

"You could never be a burden!" Harriet protested.

"Pfft. You're a young woman, Harriet, with your whole life ahead of you. You shouldn't have to consider me whenever you make a decision. You've always wanted to visit Paris, Rome. With Bonaparte defeated, and the windfall from the gold, you can do that. As long as you're not looking after me."

Harriet gave him a fond hug. "I don't blame you in the slightest for being reluctant to have the operation. Anyone would be."

"Well, Mister Bronte explained the process and his own recovery very well. He didn't make exaggerated claims about it being a miracle cure, but he did put my fears to rest. No surgery is without risk, but he made me see that the potential benefits by far outweigh it. *Nothing ventured, nothing gained*, as they say."

"Have you set a date? Where do you have to go?" Harriet sounded a little dazed.

"Once I realized there was no point putting it off any longer, I asked Doctor Saunders when he could see me. I'm going to his surgery on Harley Street tomorrow morning."

"Tomorrow!"

Harriet's father smiled at her obvious shock. "Might as well get it over and done with. I'll only sit and fret about it, otherwise."

Morgan crossed the shop on silent feet, determined to leave without interrupting them. Harriet, however, turned and caught his eye.

"I suppose we have that dreadful Captain Davies to thank for this change of heart," she said loudly, addressing him, as well as her father. "Since he was the one who introduced you to Doctor Saunders."

The older Montgomery chuckled. "True. At least you know who to blame if the operation isn't a success."

"*Of course* it's going to be a success," Harriet countered firmly. "I have every confidence in Doctor Saunders." She sent a threatening glare back at Morgan. "If anything *does* go wrong, I'll wring Captain Davies's neck."

Morgan threw her a mock-terrified look as her father laughed.

"I doubt you'd have much luck strangling the man. He's twice your size, Harriet. Might as well try strangling a tree. You'd be better to shoot him."

Henry was clearly joking, but Harriet's teeth flashed white in a smile. "Oh, I will definitely consider it."

Morgan deemed that the perfect time to take his leave. With a silent wave at Harriet, he opened the shop door and slipped out into the street.

A ripple of anxiety caught him as he walked toward his carriage. Despite Harriet's teasing, he *was* responsible for prompting her father to undergo this operation. He'd feel dreadful if anything went wrong. Not merely for the older Montgomery's discomfort and disappointment, but for subjecting Harriet to such stress and worry.

And what if the operation *was* a success? If her father regained his sight—and therefore a large part of his independence—Harriet would indeed be free to start having all those adventures she'd been putting off for years.

What if she had them without him? What if she had them with someone else?

It didn't bear thinking about.

He supposed he should want her to be happy, even if it wasn't with him, but he wasn't *that* noble. He hadn't wanted her for so long, hadn't sailed halfway around the world, to watch her marry someone else.

He didn't deserve her, of course, but that was beside the point. No other man deserved her either. They'd had their chance to charm her while he was away. None had succeeded, and he was arrogant enough to think it was because Harriet harbored feelings for him that she didn't feel for anyone else.

He was still humbled by the fact that she'd allowed him to show her pleasure, but he had a sneaking suspicion she'd used him as some kind of sexual adventure. Not that he was complaining—he'd happily participate in every debauched and scandalous thing she could dream up—but she needed to see him as less of a temporary experiment and more of a permanent solution.

He would have to wait until tomorrow night to see her again. They'd both been invited to Lady Scarborough's, and he planned to do exactly what Harriet had told him to do, namely, set about selecting his ideal fiancée.

How long would it take for Harriet to realize it was *her*?

Chapter Twenty-Five

Harriet hadn't been sure whether to attend Lady Scarborough's gathering. She'd barely slept; her mind kept flitting between worry over her father's impending surgery and amazement at the wicked things Morgan had done to her for kiss number three.

I've dreamed of tasting you for fucking years.

The impassioned words echoed in her brain. Had he *really* said that? Or had she just imagined it in her lust-addled delirium?

No, she was sure he'd said it.

Maybe men always said things like that to women at the height of passion? And yet there had been nothing practiced or suave about it; the guttural growl seemed to have been ripped from his throat, unbidden.

Dare she believe it? She'd always thought her attraction was one-sided, that Morgan saw her as an amusement to torment and then forget the moment she was out of his sight. He flirted with her, true, but he'd flirted with plenty of other women over the years and he was certainly no virgin. She'd been jealous whenever she'd heard rumors that he was seeing someone.

But what if all those years of superficial teasing had been hiding an attraction as dark and as burning as her own? What if he'd stayed away because he thought she wasn't interested?

Her skin tingled. He must know she was interested *now*. What they'd done yesterday had changed everything. How would she ever look at his lips without knowing they'd tasted her most private, feminine parts? How could she see his beautiful hands and not dream of having them back on her skin?

She had no idea how she should act when she saw him next. At his house she'd hardly been able to look at him for mortification, but Morgan had done a remarkable job of coaxing her back toward their usual state of pointed bickering before he'd left.

A liveried carriage pulled up outside the shop, and she took a deep breath to fortify herself.

She'd sent Maddie a note that morning, just after Doctor Saunders's carriage had collected her father, telling her of his sudden change of heart. Maddie had insisted on coming to escort her to Lady Scarborough's so she wouldn't sit around worrying all night on her own.

Gryff had accompanied his wife. "Good evening, Harriet. You look lovely."

Harriet flushed as he handed her into the carriage. "Thank you." She glanced over at her cousin. "Maddie convinced me to buy this dress last time we were at Madame Cerise's."

"Maddie is *excellent* at convincing people to do things she wants them to do," Gryff teased. "Whether *they* want to do them or not."

His wife gave him a playful punch on the arm. "And I'm usually right. As in this case. That color is exquisite on you, Harriet."

Harriet smiled. The turquoise silk was more flamboyant than the tones she usually chose, but she trusted

Maddie's judgment, and when she'd glanced at herself in the mirror she'd been struck by how different she looked. How sophisticated. The artful tailoring created curves she never knew she possessed, and her skin seemed to glow from within.

Was it the satisfied glow of a woman who'd finally discovered the pleasures of the flesh? Would people be able to tell, just by looking at her?

God, she hoped not. The last thing she wanted was to be inundated by lecherous gentlemen who somehow perceived the change in her.

"Any news about Uncle Henry?" Maddie asked.

Harriet shook herself from her introspection. "Yes. I just had a note from Doctor Saunders. The operation went without a hitch."

Maddie sank back on the seat with a sigh of relief. "Oh, that *is* good news. Have you been to see him? When will he be allowed home?"

"Doctor Saunders doesn't allow visitors. Father's been sedated to relieve his pain, so he likely wouldn't be aware of me anyway. He'll be kept under strict observation for the next twelve hours, but as long as he has a full night's rest, he'll be allowed home tomorrow so he can continue to recuperate with me."

"See, I *told* you not to worry," Maddie said.

"How long until you can remove the bandages?" Gryff asked.

"A few days, to give the eyes time to heal."

Gryff shook his head in wonder. "Modern medicine never ceases to amaze me. Is there anything more incredible than giving a blind man back his sight?"

"A Montgomery marrying a Davies?" Maddie suggested, her brows raised in humor.

Gryff sent his wife a loving scowl and Harriet gave

an envious sigh. The love between those two former enemies was something to behold.

What were she and Morgan, now she'd allowed him
such shameful liberties with her body? Were they lovers?
They weren't exactly friends. But they'd never truly been
enemies either, not in the purest sense of the word. She
didn't want his demise. Far from it. She wanted to continue their flirtatious rivalry forever.

Which was impossible. Morgan would be selecting
a wife very soon, probably by the end of the season—
maybe by the end of *tonight*—and they couldn't continue
their sparring once he was wed.

Harriet's chest constricted, as if she could already
sense the hole in her life that his absence would bring. It
would be worse than if he simply sailed away again. If he
was physically gone, she could fool herself into thinking
that he might come back for her. It would be torture of
a different kind to see him across the room with another
woman on his arm, laughing and looking at her with the
same wicked, knowing smile he'd always given her.

She bit her lip, swamped by a feeling of helplessness.
Everything was changing, and she wasn't sure she was
ready. Perhaps, if Father's operation really was a success,
she'd remove herself from temptation and plan some adventures of her own.

"I can't wait to see Morgan tonight." Maddie chuckled.

Harriet's heart gave a guilty leap. "Why is that?"

"Because I'm going to tell everyone who will listen
about you winning that fabulous race. One should never
let slip an opportunity to brag when a Montgomery bests
a Davies."

"Traitor," Gryff muttered. "You're a Davies now."

Maddie sent him a superior smile. "Legally, perhaps.
But in my heart, I'm still half Montgomery. Harriet did

us proud. She beat him with both brains and brawn. It was magnificent."

Harriet nodded regal acceptance of the compliment.

Gryff settled back into his seat. "I have to say, you and Morgan have provided us with some epic entertainment over the years."

Maddie nodded. "It's true, watching the two of you devise new and exciting ways to each annoy the other is one of my favorite pastimes."

"We're not that bad!" Harriet protested.

Maddie and Gryff shared a laughing glance. "You really are."

"I have a confession to make," Gryff said. "Do you remember that time we were all playing hide-and-seek in the woods back at Trellech? We were back for the school holidays and you must have been around fifteen or sixteen."

"*I* remember," Maddie said. "I hid in a holly bush and ruined my favorite pair of gloves."

Harriet was sure her cheeks were heating. "Yes."

"Well," Gryff said, "I saw you and Morgan both hide in the folly. And since it was obvious to anyone with eyes that the two of you fancied each other, I pretended I couldn't see you."

"You didn't!" Harriet gasped, scandalized. "Why would you do that?"

"Because I thought Morgan would take the chance to kiss you and get it out of his system," Gryff said, "and I knew he would kill me if I interrupted him."

Maddie's eyes were wide with fascination. "You, Gryffud Davies, are an *agitator*. You just love to stir the pot and create a little mischief."

Gryff shrugged, utterly unrepentant. "All's fair in love and war. Constance and Prudence would have been proud of me. It's exactly the kind of thing they would have done."

Maddie turned to Harriet. "So *did* he? Kiss you, I mean?"

Harriet shook her head, beyond embarrassed. "In the folly? He did not."

Maddie's shoulders slumped, and even Gryff looked a little disappointed.

"How vexing of him," Maddie said. "I thought he had more initiative."

"You Montgomery women can be an intimidating bunch," Gryff muttered.

Maddie whacked him playfully on the arm.

"I think he might have kissed me," Harriet admitted, "but I left before he had the chance. But if he *had*, it would only have been to embarrass me, or to have something to blackmail me with later."

Gryff snorted. "You're as blind as your father. Morgan's always been attracted to you."

"Ha! Then how come he's shown such an interest in other women?" Harriet countered. "It's not as if he's remained celibate all these years, pining away for me."

"Maybe he wasn't ready to settle down and commit to a single woman before now?" Gryff said. "We men are slow learners. It takes us a while to recognize the one woman we're actually happy with."

Maddie rolled her eyes at his reasoning. "Or perhaps he didn't think *you* were interested in *him*? You did pull away, after all. And despite their *many* other failings"— Maddie shot a taunting glance at her husband—"the Davies men are extremely honorable when it comes to treating women with respect. Morgan would never have forced a kiss on an unwilling recipient. You probably dented his pride."

Harriet shrugged, desperate to get off the subject. If she and Maddie had been alone, she might have admitted to still pining after Morgan and asked her opinion, but there was no way she was discussing such a thing in front of his brother. Even if Gryff, surprisingly, didn't seem to disapprove of the two of them as a couple. "Who knows what goes on in the male brain? It's a source of endless mystery."

"We're really not that complex," Gryff chuckled. "We like to pretend we are, but we're usually just thinking about food, women, sports, or business. And nine times out of ten, it's women. Just so you know."

Maddie shook her head but couldn't hide her smile. "And I thought you were all such complicated creatures."

"Sorry to disappoint."

The look Maddie sent Gryff made Harriet blush even more. "Oh, you never disappoint me, Husband," she purred.

Harriet laughed at their innuendo-laden banter. In truth she was envious of the playful relationship they had. It just went to show that despite hundreds of years of feuding, a happy union between a Davies and a Montgomery *was* possible. Tristan and Carys had proved the same thing.

But a permanent union between herself and Morgan? Impossible. Even if he did, by some miracle, consider her for a wife, he was still going to sail away and have adventures without her. And that just wouldn't do.

The flickering torches of Lady Scarborough's Belgrave Square mansion illuminated the carriage interior, and they rocked to a stop.

"Ah, here we are."

Chapter Twenty-Six

Harriet followed Gryff and Maddie up the front steps and handed her shawl to one of the waiting footmen. The three of them drifted into one of the many anterooms that were already overflowing with guests, and her heart seized as she caught sight of Morgan's dark head and broad shoulders among the throng.

As ever, he was surrounded by an admiring group of women, mainly matrons with eligible daughters in tow. A shaft of jealousy pierced her as he laughed at something one of them said, effortlessly extricated himself from the lady clinging to his arm, and led another onto the dance floor.

Any one of those girls would make him a suitable wife. Millicent Connors had a fortune for a dowry. Emily Goodford looked like a fairy princess, with silken blond hair and limpid blue eyes. And Elizabeth De Vere could trace her family back to before the Norman Conquest.

Not that Morgan would care for an illustrious name, particularly. He was the brother of an earl; he didn't need a titled wife to add to his consequence.

He might need a *rich* wife, though. Harriet had no idea how much a captain in the Royal Navy was paid, but she doubted it was much, and Morgan was only a younger son. His father had undoubtedly left him something in his will, but it was a rare man who refused a wife who came with an influx of cash.

Millicent Connors was laughing up at him in a cloying way that made Harriet feel slightly nauseous. Morgan really shouldn't marry her, even if he did need the money. Her only interests were fashion and gossip: Morgan would strangle her before the week was out. He needed someone to challenge him, to keep him on his toes, not a simpering ninny who agreed with every word he said.

"That man is a menace to the female half of the population."

Harriet gave a guilty start and looked down to find Aunt Prudence's diminutive form seated to her right. "Oh! Hello, Aunt Pru. I didn't see you there. Who are you talking about?"

Prudence sent her a shrewd, twinkling smile. "Why, Captain Davies, of course. That *is* who you were looking at so intently, isn't it?"

Harriet felt heat rush to her face but she was saved from lying by Aunt Constance's bawdy chuckle.

"A very *attractive* menace, though. I do love a rogue. He reminds me of that highwayman we once encountered on Hampstead Heath. Do you remember, Pru?"

Prudence rolled her eyes. "The one you *gave* your amethyst ring to, you mean?"

Constance shrugged. "He'd already taken the matching earrings. No point in separating the set. And it was worth it for the kiss he gave me in thanks."

Harriet laughed. She'd never heard *that* particular story from the Aunts before. Despite the fact that neither of them had ever married, they'd clearly lived lives far more exciting than hers.

"I see he's busy finding the next Mrs. Davies," Prudence said, eyeing Morgan and Millicent as they swirled past in a waltz. "I do hope he doesn't choose that Connors girl, though. The chit hasn't a thought in her head. Do you know she once asked me if they had the same moon in France as we do here in England?"

Harriet let out an involuntary snort. *Dear God.* Morgan would strangle her in three days, never mind a full week.

"Now Harriet, it's your turn to make yourself agreeable. Look who's coming our way!"

Harriet forced herself not to swing around. "Who?"

Prudence sent her a congratulatory look. "Why, young De Montfort. The Duke of Evesham's heir. He's been staring at you ever since you got here."

"Almost heir," Constance corrected softly. "He's the duke's nephew. His father is the heir presumptive, since the duke doesn't have any children of his own."

"So he could be duke himself one day," Prudence insisted. "And he's handsome too. He would be an excellent catch, Harriet."

Harriet, still with her back to the man, frowned. "He's not a trout, for heaven's sake. And I don't think I've ever met him."

"That's because he's been away at sea ever since he turned eighteen."

"Who needs Debrett's when they have you two?" Harriet muttered.

Both Prudence and Constance preened at the compliment.

"I *believe*," Constance said, with the air of someone about to impart a vital pearl of gossip, "that he was on the same ship as our Captain Davies—"

Harriet swirled around, suddenly interested, and bumped into the man who'd come up behind her. "Oh, I beg your pardon!"

The man laughed, blue eyes twinkling. "The fault was mine. I was so eager to make your acquaintance, Miss Montgomery, I've practically run you down." He sketched her an easy bow. "Oliver De Montfort, at your service."

Harriet blinked. Prudence had been right to call him handsome. Guinea-gold curls fell in an artless style around a face that could have graced a young Adonis, and his smile was so open, so contagious, she found herself smiling back at him.

He offered his hand. "Shall we dance?"

"Why not?" Harriet allowed him to lead her onto the dance floor where a waltz had just begun.

"Why would you want to make my acquaintance?" she asked as they came together.

De Montfort smiled. "I wanted to meet the only woman I've ever been threatened with."

Harriet missed a step. "What do you mean, *threatened with*? By whom?"

De Montfort laughed, but not in a malicious way. "By my captain, of course. I was a midshipman on the *Briseis*. Whenever someone had done something wrong, Captain Davies used to say, *And be thankful I'm only making you scrub the decks, and not having you flayed alive by Harriet Montgomery.*"

Harriet's mouth went slack. She snapped it closed with a jolt that jarred her teeth.

"He said that? Out loud? In everyone's hearing?"

De Montfort's eyes twinkled with humor. "Oh, many times. But please don't take it the wrong way. He always said your name with such reverence, such *awe*. We all imagined you as some glorious, vengeful goddess."

"Dear Lord."

"Once, when we'd struggled all night through a particularly horrible squall, he stood on the foredeck and shouted at the waves, *Is that all you've got? I've had worse tongue-lashings from Harriet Montgomery!*"

Harriet shook her head, torn between fury and mortification. "Oh, no."

"Of course, after *that*, every man on board vowed to meet the woman who could cut our fearless captain down to size. You achieved near-mythic status on board."

Harriet hardly knew what to say. The young man clearly hero-worshiped Morgan. And, rather oddly, *herself*.

"I take it he was a good captain? Aside from making you scrub the decks, I mean."

"The *best*, ma'am." De Montfort's blue eyes were sincere.

"But weren't you held prisoner with him too?"

"Oh, yes. But that wasn't the captain's fault. His map was wrong. Could've happened to anyone."

Harriet's cheeks warmed with a guilty flush. "Quite."

"The fact is, I owe Captain Davies my life."

Harriet raised her brows at that fervent declaration. "How so?"

"He took a flogging on my behalf. On Martinique. We were kept in the most awful conditions, you can't imagine. We were locked in our cells most of the time, but twice a day we were exercised in the fields beside the fort. De Caen—that was the commander of the place—rode up one day and accused me of stealing a loaf of bread." His golden brows lowered in indignation. "I'd done no such thing! I denied it, but he started to whip me with his riding crop."

"That's dreadful," Harriet murmured.

"I honestly think he would have beaten me to death if Captain Davies hadn't intervened. He tackled De Caen off his horse and started pummeling him in the road. Even with both of his hands bound, he managed to land a few good kicks before he was pulled off by De Caen's men."

"Good heavens."

"The commander was furious. He had the captain flogged—six lashes—then had him thrown into solitary confinement for two weeks. They only fed him once a day."

Harriet swallowed. She'd always known Morgan was a decent man beneath his provoking Davies exterior, but hearing a firsthand account of his heroics was something else. Her heart ached for his suffering, even as she felt a flash of anger at how he'd endangered himself. She'd *known* he'd do something stupidly noble like that when they made their bet two years ago. What if he'd been killed? Her blood ran cold.

"So *that's* why the Frenchman walks with a limp," she murmured.

De Montfort sent her an odd look. "You know him?"

"What? Oh," Harriet prevaricated, suddenly realizing that De Caen's presence in London wasn't common knowledge. "No. I . . . heard Captain Davies mention him. In passing."

They completed another graceful turn.

"You know what the captain said when they brought him out of solitary?"

Harriet raised her brows. "Something along the lines of, *At least I wasn't stuck in there with Harriet Montgomery*?"

De Montfort chuckled. "Something like that. But you mustn't think of it as an insult. You were our talisman—fierce and fearless, so we had to be the same. Captain Davies told us never to lose hope, never to give up, because one day all our hardships would be just a memory. We'd be safe, and free, and dancing in some glittering ballroom with a beautiful, vexing woman in our arms." He sent a droll glance at their surroundings. "I can't tell you how glad I am that he was right."

Harriet's heart was pounding. Morgan had said that about *her*?

"You're quite the poet, sir. You make me sound like some kind of saint. Except for the vexing part."

His laughter made the couples next to them stare. "Oh, most definitely *not* a saint. To hear the captain tell it, you'd make the devil himself cry."

"I suppose I should take that as a compliment too?"

"Absolutely. And please, call me Oliver."

Harriet laughed, amused despite herself. "Very well, Oliver. I'm glad to have been of service."

He let out a theatrical sigh. "It really is a shame, you know. You're just as I imagined you'd be. Beautiful. Witty. Clever."

"Why is that a shame?"

"Because I'd very much like to get to know you better."

Harriet flushed. De Montfort was handsome and charming, but at two years younger than herself, he was still a puppy. A boy, not a man. Adorable, but just not . . . wicked enough for her.

Not *Davies* enough for her, curse it.

Still, she raised her brows. "And you can't get to know me better because—?"

He flashed a glance at something over her shoulder and grinned as he leaned closer to whisper in her ear, "Because you're the captain's woman."

Her stomach somersaulted, even as her intellect rebelled at being labeled any man's possession. "I most certainly am *not*—"

"Evening, Captain," Oliver said jauntily, spinning her into one final whirl.

Harriet turned, and came face-to-face with Morgan,

standing at the edge of the dance floor. Her feet skidded to a stop. "Oh!"

Morgan looked both amused and forbidding, handsome as sin in dark evening clothes, snowy-white shirt, and cravat. If anyone was a devil it was *him*.

"Good evening, De Montfort. I see you've already made Miss Montgomery's acquaintance."

The younger man bowed. "I have indeed. And might I say, she's everything I expected and more." He raked her with an openly appreciative look, which Harriet ignored. She glared accusingly at Morgan instead.

"You made me sound like shrewish harpy! To your *entire crew*."

Morgan's lips curled at the corners, even as he raised his brows. "I hope you haven't been telling tales, De Montfort," he drawled. "We might be ashore, but I can still find decks that need scrubbing for cheeky midshipmen."

Oliver grinned. "Not at all, Captain, sir. I was merely telling Miss Montgomery how dear she was to everyone on the *Briseis*. It's an honor to finally meet her in person."

Morgan narrowed his eyes, as if he planned to say more, then clearly changed his mind. He turned to Harriet and pulled her arm through his in a proprietary gesture that made her pulse flutter.

Oliver shot her an amused *I told you so* smile.

"De Montfort might know something of the house you mentioned the other day," Morgan said. "The one in Grosvenor Square. It belongs to his uncle."

De Montfort accepted the change in topic with ease. "What of it?"

"I wondered why it was always shut up," Harriet said.

"Oh, Uncle Harold won that place years ago, in a game of cards. He keeps it ready for a visit, but he never comes to town. He hasn't left his estate in Cornwall for the past twenty years. He's offered to let me use it, but to tell you the truth, it's too big for my taste. I keep bachelor lodgings at the Albany instead."

Morgan nodded. "I hear you're about to take your examination for the rank of lieutenant, in front of the Navy Board?"

"Yes. Next week."

"You'll get your commission, I'm sure of it."

Harriet glanced up and was surprised by the proud, paternal look on Morgan's face. He clearly held deep affection for the younger man, an affection that was returned tenfold.

Oliver's cheeks reddened. "Thank you, sir. I was taught by the best."

Morgan flicked his hand in a dismissive gesture. "Very well, off you go. Stop monopolizing Miss Montgomery's time and filling her ears with gossip. Go and dance with Miss Connors over there."

"Aye aye, sir." Oliver sent him a jaunty salute, then raised Harriet's hand to his lips for a kiss surely designed just to irritate Morgan. "Miss Montgomery, it has been a pleasure. I hope to dance with you again soon."

Morgan let out a growl of warning and Oliver retreated with a laugh.

"Cheeky pup," Morgan muttered. "Dance with me."

Harriet raised her brows. "Do you mean, *Please, Harriet, do me the honor of granting me this waltz?*"

Morgan's eyes met hers and her stomach flipped.

"No," he murmured, "I mean, *Dance with me, Harriet, or I'll take you somewhere private and show you something better than dancing.*"

"You wouldn't dare!" she gasped, before she realized that was the *last* thing a Montgomery should ever say to a Davies.

He raised his brows. "Did you just—?"

"No!" she sputtered. "You'll cause a scandal!"

"Don't tempt me." He caught her right hand and raised it to shoulder level, then slid his left hand around her waist to settle low on the curve of her back. He pulled her in toward him with a brutal little tug.

Chapter Twenty-Seven

Harriet's breath caught.

Waltzing with Morgan was completely different from waltzing with Oliver. De Montfort had held himself at a respectable distance; she'd barely been aware of his body at all. Morgan somehow managed to monopolize every square inch of space. His chest was too close to hers, his thigh insinuated itself between her legs, and his palm burned through the layers of her dress like a brand.

"I like this dress," he said as they drifted into the first swirl. "It's the color of the sea near Martinique."

Harriet tried to catch her breath. "That's the first time you've ever said something complimentary about my clothing. At Trellech you said my dress looked like sea-weed."

"It did. And it's not that I hate your dresses, per se. It's just that I'd rather see you out of them."

She missed a step, but his arms tightened to hide her stumble and keep her upright. His chuckle did something funny to her insides.

"Stop it," she admonished.

He sent her a mock-innocent look from beneath his lashes. "Stop what?"

"Flirting."

"Is that what I'm doing?"

"I don't know *what* you're doing," she admitted crossly. "You're the most confusing creature I ever met. Oliver said you cursed me on a daily basis when you were at sea. You used me as a *threat*."

"No," he corrected softly. "I used you as a way to bring the crew together. You were a shared joke, a rallying cry. A reminder of every female back in Britain we were fighting to protect. You were their sweetheart, their mother, their mistress, their wife—not some perfect goddess, but a real, flawed human being. Someone they could identify with. Someone worth living for."

Her lips parted in surprise. She'd never heard of herself described in such a way. And yet his words echoed what De Montfort had said. Clearly the tactic had been successful in motivating his men.

Had it motivated him too?

His arm tightened at her back. "You were also a way of reminding the men that I was human. That while I was their captain, I was also a man—a man completely under the thumb of a sharp-tongued devil woman."

Harriet rolled her eyes. "You're not under my thumb. Nor under my heel, more's the pity."

"No? I thought of you every single day I was in prison."

"Wishing I was there instead of you, I expect," she said drily.

He shrugged, but didn't deny it, and she laughed. "Poor Morgan. Did you *miss* me? Did you get tired of everyone following your orders? I bet you were longing for a little insubordination."

"It's possible," he said. "Obedience gets extremely tiresome after a while."

He guided her into another effortless turn and her senses reeled. Why did he have to smell so good? And why did she have to be aware of every flex of his shoulder muscle beneath her palm as he moved? Those gorgeous lips of his were so close she could kiss him if she went up on tiptoe.

She wanted to.

He was the vexing one.

He glanced down. "I forgot to ask. How is your father?"

"Doctor Saunders says the operation went well."

"But you're still worried about him?"

"Of course. We won't know how well his sight has improved until he can take off the bandages. And there's always the risk of him developing an infection before he's fully healed." Harriet shook her head. "He was so brave to go ahead with it. I'm not sure I would have been that courageous."

"Perhaps he realized he didn't have much to lose? His sight was almost gone. He'll be no worse off if it doesn't improve."

"That's true." She tightened her fingers on his shoulder. "I really do want to thank you. Whatever happens, at least now there's a chance he'll have a better life."

His cheeks flushed, as if he was awkward with her praise, but his lips curled up at the corners as they always did. "Anything for you, my sweet. I'd raze cities to the ground if only you asked me to."

She snorted.

"Men always say things like that. But I'd rather have someone *build* me a city, not burn one down. Destroying something is the work of a moment. Creating something that will stand the test of time takes much more effort."

"True." His smile faded as a new thought struck him. "Surely you didn't leave your father alone this evening?"

"Of course not. He's staying with Doctor Saunders until tomorrow."

"So you're spending the night with Maddie and Gryff? Tristan and Carys?"

She shook her head. "I don't want to put them to any trouble. It's only for one night."

"But who will be at the house with you?"

"Our cook, Mrs. Jennings, was going to stay with me, but her daughter took ill this morning, so I told her to go home and tend to her."

His frown intensified. "You can't stay alone."

"Yes, I can."

"No, you can't. De Caen might still be a threat."

Harriet rolled her eyes. "To you, perhaps, but not to me."

Morgan didn't look convinced. "What about Heron, then? I *think* we scared him off, but I wouldn't stake my life on it. Or your life, for that matter. Men can get funny when it comes to retaliation." His face grew grim. "And they can do terrible things. Believe me, I've seen the worst of people."

"Pfft. I'll be fine."

His hand squeezed hers. "I'm not willing to take the chance. You're alone because of me. I convinced your father to get this operation. I have an obligation to make sure you're safe until he returns."

"I'm not your responsibility. Nor a *duty*. I'm perfectly fine on my own."

"Don't be a fool. Your safety means a great deal to me."

Her heart gave an odd thump at his fervency, but she tried to make light of it. "I know that. Who would you fight with if I wasn't here?"

A muscle ticked in the side of his jaw and his pupils flared as he leaned closer. "Fighting's not the only thing we do well, Harriet. We weren't fighting yesterday, when my tongue was between your—"

"Shhh!" She glanced around, terrified someone would

overhear. Heat scalded her cheeks. "Don't say another word, Morgan Davies!"

He chuckled, a low vibration that made her stomach swoop in agonized delight. *Oh, he was wicked.*

She took a fortifying breath. "So what are you suggesting? You want to send a strapping footman to guard me overnight? Find a bunch of rowdy sailors to keep watch?"

He lifted his brows but kept his lips pressed firmly together, and she let out an exasperated huff as she remembered she'd forbidden him to speak. "Oh, you can talk, you idiot."

He grinned. "Thank you. And no, that wasn't what I was thinking at all. It wouldn't be proper for you to be alone with strangers."

"What, then?"

"I'll stay with you."

Her heart stopped, then pounded back to life with renewed vigor. "You will not! That's even more improper."

"I'm not trying to seduce you, I swear. I'm trying to be gentlemanly." He shook his head. "I know that's hard for you to believe of a Davies, but we don't *always* have an ulterior motive."

She lifted one brow in blatant skepticism, but he pressed on.

"I won't be able to sleep if I know you're there alone. You don't even need to provide me with a bed. I can sleep in a chair or on the floor. I've slept in worse places. Have you seen the size of the captain's cabin on board a ship? It's tiny. Smaller than a shoe box. And that was a luxury compared to my cell on Martinique."

Harriet bit her lip, wracked with indecision. She didn't truly suspect him of having a nefarious plan. Morgan was so shameless he'd just tell her outright if he was planning to seduce her. He wouldn't bother with subterfuge.

He was also a decent man. He might be overestimating the potential danger, but she trusted him to protect her with his life. *How odd.*

The thought of being alone with him *all night* was both exciting and terrifying. He wouldn't so much as kiss her hand if she didn't ask for it, but how was she supposed to resist him?

Don't.

The unbidden thought made her catch her breath, even as it settled with undeniable *rightness* in her chest.

Don't resist him.

Her startled gaze clashed with his, as if the answer lay in the mossy green depths of his eyes. The ballroom, the dancers, the candles, all blurred together in a dizzying kaleidoscope of color and left her with the one, inescapable conclusion:

She loved Morgan Davies. She'd been in love with him for years. And she wanted him, however she could get him.

"Yes!" she breathed.

Morgan's eyes narrowed. "Yes what?"

"Yes, I accept your offer. Stay the night with me."

Chapter Twenty-Eight

Morgan's heart stuttered, even though Harriet had merely agreed to let him guard her. Still, it felt like a victory.

"A miracle," he murmured. "A Montgomery being sensible for once."

She deliberately stood on his toe.

Luckily, he barely felt her satin-shod weight through his leather boots. He quashed a laugh of triumph and tried not to notice the delicious scent of her hair or the way she felt so blessedly perfect in his arms.

God, what had he let himself in for? Spending the night under the same roof as her and not being able to touch her was going to be torture, but he couldn't take advantage of the situation and seduce her, however much he wanted to. Years of training in the gentlemanly arts had ingrained that into him.

His father's words, delivered at regular intervals to himself, Rhys, and Gryff throughout their adolescence, echoed in his head:

There are two types of women, boys. Women you can dally with, and women you must wed. Actresses, courtesans, barmaids, and the like—they're all very well for a quick tumble, but seduce a lady of the ton *and you'll be caught in the parson's mousetrap before you can blink.*

Be sure you know precisely which type you're dealing with before you do something you regret.

Privately Morgan had always disagreed with his father's logic. In his mind there were *three* types of women: women you bedded, women you married, and *Harriet Montgomery.* She alone was the outlier, the single female of his acquaintance who didn't fit neatly into either box. At age sixteen he'd definitely wanted to bed her, but the thought of wedding her had been enough to make him break out in hives.

Funny how age and experience changed a man. Now he wanted to bed her *and* marry her, but Harriet was a law unto herself. Despite what she'd allowed him to do at his house, she wouldn't surrender her virginity to a scoundrel like him.

Still, staying at her house and keeping her safe was better than nothing.

Even if he expired of unfulfilled lust in the process.

The waltz came to an end and they twirled to a stop. Harriet's eyes were sparkling with excitement, her cheeks pink with either embarrassment or exertion, and it took everything he had not to pull her into his arms, right here in the middle of the dance floor, and kiss her.

Thereby creating precisely the kind of scandal they were trying to avoid.

He placed her hand on his arm instead, and drew her to the edge of the room, heading for where Gryff, Maddie, and Rhys stood chatting together.

"Did you come in a hackney?" he murmured.

She glanced up at him. "No. Gryff and Maddie collected me. I was going to get a ride home with them too."

"I walked," he said. "But that doesn't matter, because we couldn't be seen leaving together in my carriage anyway. You get a lift home, as arranged. I'll go to my house, get a horse, and ride over to yours later."

Harriet's jaw tightened a little. "You seem well-versed in planning illicit rendezvous."

"Just accustomed to solving logistical problems." He shrugged, trying to conceal his delight that she might be jealous. "That's half the work for a captain on a ship; figuring out who goes where, when."

"Hmm."

Gryff smiled in welcome as they drew near. "Evening."

Morgan tried not to scowl as Harriet pulled her arm from his.

Maddie turned to her. "Harry, I hope you don't mind, but I promised to take you to meet Lord Elmswood and Sir Roger Hargrave. They've both been pestering me for an introduction."

"Oh."

Harriet looked surprised, yet pleased, and Morgan quelled a growl. Why the hell was she always surprised that men wanted to meet her? Didn't she own a mirror? She was beautiful. And not only that, she was witty and clever too.

For every man in the room who'd settle for marrying a pretty, brainless featherhead, there were an equal number who'd realized that having a bride with a modicum of intelligence would make life far more bearable in the long run. Not to mention increasing the odds of having children who weren't complete idiots.

Elmswood and Hargrave both fell into the latter category, and Morgan quashed the urge to grab Harriet's gown and pull her back. He watched, brooding silently, as the two women disappeared into the crowd, leaving him with his brothers.

Rhys jabbed him in the ribs to regain his attention. "Dancing with Harriet Montgomery again? Did you lose a bet?"

"No."

"Interesting." Rhys pursed his lips.

"What do you mean, *interesting*? I've danced with a dozen women tonight."

"And looked as if you'd rather be anywhere else," Rhys said.

"I didn't look like that with Harriet?"

"Oh, no." Rhys lowered his voice to a whisper. "With Harriet, you looked the same as you've always done. As if you can't decide whether to fight her, or *fuck* her."

Gryff snorted, then tried to disguise it as a cough.

Morgan scowled at him. "Got something to add, Gryffud?"

Gryff shrugged. "It's a crude way of putting it, but he's right. That *is* the way you look at her."

"Do you deny you want to bed her?" Rhys demanded.

"No," Morgan said, irritated by their teasing. "I don't deny it. I'm just saying that I won't."

Rhys didn't look convinced. He raised his brows at Gryff. "He could charm a Mother Superior. You know how persuasive he can be. Remember that time he convinced me to shave off just one eyebrow?"

Morgan snorted. "Oh, please. If anyone's proved she can resist me, it's Harriet. You know how stubborn she is. She can't be talked into doing anything she doesn't want to do."

"But what if she *does* want to?" Rhys pressed. "What if she looks at you in the same way?"

Morgan's heart gave an extra thump at the thought that Harriet might reciprocate his feelings, but he kept his tone level. "I would still never do anything to ruin her reputation."

Gryff sent him a penetrating look. "You've let it be known you're looking for a wife, and you've spent more time with her than with any other woman in the *ton*. People are beginning to gossip. You need to decide what you're going to do about her."

Morgan bit his lip. Did his brothers suspect his feelings for Harriet ran deeper than mere lust? Should he confess his plan to marry her? They might frown on yet another Davies-Montgomery alliance. Then again, Gryff had already crossed party lines by marrying Maddie, so he must know the infuriating appeal of the Montgomery female. Rhys, however, would probably be appalled at him for falling for the enemy's wiles.

Gryff took a meditative sip of his wine. "I know the two of you love to goad each other, but Harriet's not some demimondaine you can trifle with and then leave. As head of this family, it falls on me to remind you—"

"God, you sound just like Father, about to launch into one of his sermons." Rhys feigned a yawn. "Spare us."

"I know what I'm doing," Morgan said testily. "And the only thing I'm leaving is the navy."

Rhys's brows rose. "You're resigning your commission? But you love the sea."

"I do. But I don't like taking orders, or having to spend months away from home."

"What will you do instead?"

Morgan glanced at Gryff. "The Admiralty is selling off some ships, now that Bonaparte's no longer a threat. They're decommissioning the *Briseis*. I thought I'd buy her and refit her as a trading vessel."

"And do what?"

"We currently pay other firms to transport our coal from Wales to London and beyond. I'll do it instead. It'll be cheaper. And it means I can choose which routes I take and how long I'm away."

"Good idea." Gryff nodded. "I hate being at the mercy of captains who increase their prices at a moment's notice."

Rhys rocked back on his heels. "I don't suppose this decision has anything to do with the fact that Harriet said she wouldn't marry a sailor who spent months at sea?"

Morgan shrugged. "Maybe."

Both brothers scowled at him for refusing to give a straight answer, and Morgan grinned. Annoying them never got old. "And since we're on the subject of Harriet, I should tell you that I'll be staying at her house tonight."

Gryff and Rhys adopted identical *you must be joking* expressions.

"Why?"

"Because her father won't be there and I don't want her staying on her own."

"She can stay with Maddie and I," Gryff offered immediately.

"That's what I suggested, but she wouldn't hear of it. She wants her own bed."

"And you're staying with her purely out of the goodness of your heart?" Gryff's tone was deeply sardonic.

"Yes, actually. I'm not a complete barbarian. Despite what you two think about those of us who joined the navy, instead of the fusiliers."

Rhys wrinkled his nose. "Even if you *don't* sleep with her, if anyone finds out you've stayed in the same house together, alone and unchaperoned, she'll be ruined."

"Nobody's going to find out. But if they did, then I'd do the honorable thing and marry her, of course."

Gryff opened his mouth to say something, but Rhys beat him to it.

"I don't think she'd have you," he said, with brutal simplicity. "I think she'd prefer ruination."

Morgan tried not to wince. "Yes, well, since I have no intention of finding out, it's a moot point." He turned to Gryff. "You and Maddie can escort her home as planned. I'll ride over to Bury Street later."

Rhys gave a fatalistic shrug. "It's your funeral."

Morgan turned on his heel and went in search of a drink. God knows, he was going to need every ounce of fortitude he could get.

Chapter Twenty-Nine

Harriet tried not to fidget as she waited for Morgan to arrive. The house seemed unnaturally quiet. The streets were rarely this deserted, even at past midnight; the night teemed with watchmen and thieves, revelers and whores. But tonight the world seemed to be holding its breath, right along with her.

She forced herself to exhale.

Gryff and Maddie had deposited her at her front door half an hour ago, and she'd bustled through the shop and up into the apartment, hurriedly lighting a fire in the drawing room grate, and another in her bedroom.

As agitated as she was, it was hard not to look at everything with a critical eye, as if seeing it for the first time. The rooms were elegant, but small compared to the rambling medieval chambers of Trellech, where Morgan had grown up. Still, it was nothing to be ashamed of. The furniture might not be the most fashionable, and some of the upholstery had certainly seen better days, but it was comfortable enough.

A sharp rap on the back door made her stomach somersault. She opened it to find Morgan on the step, his broad shoulders made even broader by a heavy greatcoat, his face shadowed by a tricorn hat. When she moved aside to let him enter, she had the oddest thought that in crossing the physical threshold he was also crossing another, more intangible line. The point of no return.

Stop being so dramatic.

"Good evening. Again." He swept past her, tugging the hat from his head and introducing a delicious waft of cold air, leather, and man.

"Good evening." Her tongue felt too big for her mouth. Alarmed by his size, his overwhelming *maleness* in the narrow hall, she stepped back, holding her arms out automatically to take his coat.

He shrugged out of it, revealing the same evening clothes he'd worn earlier, and she hung it on a peg and beat a hasty retreat into the back room.

She hadn't bothered to light a fire in here. A single oil lamp cast a warm puddle of light in one corner and she bustled over to it, trying to quell her nerves.

Any other night she would have been exhausted, desperate to fall into bed, but instead she felt energized, aware of every breath she took, every swish of her ball gown beneath the shawl she'd thrown around her shoulders.

Morgan, it seemed, shared none of her nervousness. He glanced around, completely at ease, then tilted his head to study her face.

"So, do you want to go straight to bed?"

He must have heard her indrawn gasp, because his mouth curved into that wicked smile she knew so well.

"What I mean," he clarified, clearly trying not to laugh, "is that you must be tired. If you'll just show me where you want me to sleep, you can go."

Be brave. You want this. Take control.

Harriet met his gaze. "I'm not tired yet. Would you like a drink?"

She needed a little Dutch courage for what she was about to do. She'd never propositioned a man before.

A flash of surprise and confusion crossed his face, but he inclined his head in assent.

"That would be nice. It's cold out there."

"There's a fire upstairs in the parlor. Come along."

Harriet picked up the lamp and led the way up the stairs, conscious at every step of his big body following behind her. Her pulse gave an erratic flutter at the thump of his boots on the treads.

When she showed him into the parlor he crossed to the fireplace and stretched his hands to the blaze, and for a moment she just stared at him, appreciating the way the fire glow caressed his features.

She could hardly reconcile the image before her. It was so strange to see him here, in such a domestic environment. She'd always thought of him as a force of nature, too large to be contained by four walls and a roof. He ought to be on the prow of a ship, glaring out at the vast horizon, or chopping his way through some impenetrable forest with a fierce-looking blade.

Even in a ballroom he gave the impression of being not quite tame, like the sleek jungle cats she'd seen at the Royal Exchange: well-behaved for now, but prone to unexpected attacks.

She deposited the lamp on the sideboard and poured two tumblers of her father's favorite brandy from the decanter, proud that her shaking hands didn't rattle the lip on the glass.

Morgan took his with a smile of thanks, and tapped the rim against hers in a toast.

"To damsels in distress," he said with a smile.

She rolled her eyes, and a little of her nervousness fell away with his teasing.

"I know, I know," he said, before she could reply. "You're far too capable to need my assistance, but let a man pretend. Heroes like myself need to think of ourselves as indispensable."

She took a sip of brandy, enjoying the way it burned down her throat and settled in a hot, glowing puddle in her belly, and her skin prickled as she realized he was watching her. His dark gaze lingered on her mouth. Self-conscious, she licked her top lip to make sure she hadn't left a droplet of the liquid there.

His eyes narrowed, and he made a low sound that was nearly a groan.

"God, Harriet, you'd try the patience of a saint."

She wasn't sure that he meant it as a warning or an admonishment, but for some reason it warmed her as much as the brandy. He wasn't impervious to her. She had a power of her own.

He threw back his head and took a large swig of his own drink. The muscles of his throat worked as he swallowed, and Harriet couldn't seem to look away.

He glanced at her again, then shook his head, as if trying to dislodge a persistent thought, and downed the rest of the brandy in another gulp. His knuckles showed white where he gripped the glass, and it landed with an uncharacteristically heavy thump on the sideboard as he placed it down.

"There. Time for bed."

He sounded gruff, desperate. As if he couldn't wait to escape.

She drained the rest of her brandy and placed the tumbler on the side. Her hand was remarkably steady.

"I need your assistance."

"In what way?"

She slipped the shawl from her shoulders and placed

it on the sideboard, then turned, presenting him with her back and the row of tiny buttons that held her ball gown closed. She glanced at him over her shoulder.

"Would you mind? I can't undo them myself."

His long exhale suggested he was struggling for patience, or possibly counting to ten, and she bit her lip to quell a smile.

He cleared his throat. "Yes. Of course."

The satin of her ball gown rustled as he stepped close and his knees pressed into the back of her skirts. She sucked in a breath as he lifted a tendril of hair from her nape and repositioned it over her shoulder to give him clear access.

His knuckles brushed the bare skin between her shoulder blades as he opened the first button; her bodice tightened across her breasts as he pulled the fabric before it released with a tiny pop.

She suppressed a shiver.

He moved lower, to the second button, and her senses swam at the feel of his body behind her. The scent of him teased her nose and she pressed the front of her dress in mingled fright and anticipation.

She wasn't wearing stays, nor a chemise. The bodice of her gown was designed with a built-in corset: All she had on beneath was a petticoat, stockings, and garters.

She knew the exact moment Morgan realized it too; he paused at button number five and his breathing hitched. His fingers slipped beneath the edge of the fabric, brushing the bumps of her spine in a tiny caress, as if he couldn't help himself.

"Will that do?" he rasped. "Can you manage the rest?"

His nearness was glorious, almost suffocating. Her heart was pounding against her ribs, but she managed to shake her head.

"I don't think so. Keep going."

He *definitely* muttered a curse that time.

She lowered her chin, exposing the back of her neck as he continued: his large fingers made light work of the tiny buttons and her skin pebbled as he worked his way downward. The rasp of his breathing and the crackle of the fire were the only sounds. Cool air rushed into the sliver of bare skin he'd exposed, and when he finally reached the last button, right at the base of her spine, she sucked in a deep breath.

The sides of the dress sagged open. Harriet slipped her arms from the tiny puff sleeves and pressed her hands to the front of the bodice to prevent it from falling to her waist. She turned, just as Morgan stepped back, his hands raised as if he'd surprised a venomous snake and didn't want to make any sudden moves.

His gaze flicked helplessly from her face to her throat, then down to her hands holding up her dress, and he shook his head, as if in answer to a silent question.

"Harriet, I—"

She didn't wait to hear what he had to say. "Shall we make another bet?"

His gaze snapped back up to hers. "What kind of bet?"

"I bet you can't kiss me until I say stop."

"What?" His confusion was obvious.

"*I bet you can't kiss me until I say stop*," she repeated, enunciating each word so there was no mistaking the challenge.

His eyes narrowed in suspicion, and she almost laughed. He was clearly trying to identify the trick she was playing on him. He lowered his hands slowly to his sides.

"You want me to kiss you?"

"On the mouth," she clarified.

"Until you say stop?" He was convinced she was trying to con him. Which she was, of course, but not in the way he imagined.

"It's not that difficult a concept." She infused her tone with just the right amount of scorn to suggest she was questioning his intelligence. "I'm sure you've kissed a hundred women before. And stopped when they said stop."

"They rarely ask me to stop!" he growled. "Is this a trick?"

"No."

"Ah!" His expression cleared, as if he'd just received enlightenment. "I see what you're doing. You're punishing me. For making fun of you on board ship. You're going to let me kiss you—just for a moment, just long enough for it to start getting *interesting*—and then you're going to tell me no."

She allowed a little smile to curve her lips. "Maybe."
Or maybe not.

He lowered his brows and glared at her. At any other time, she might have found it alarming, but for some reason she found his irritation adorable. Power, lust, and restrained aggression was a winning combination.

"You want to torture me," he said slowly. Accusingly. "You want to get me all worked up into a lather, make me think there's a chance you might make love with me, then dash my hopes."

She raised her brows. "Kissing me gets you all worked up into a lather?"

He ignored her delighted amusement. "You seem very certain that I'll be able to control myself. Aren't you worried I'll get so carried away I won't heed your order to stop?"

"Oh, no. I'm not afraid of that," she said with perfect truthfulness. "You might be a dastardly Davies, but you have a code of honor. And extraordinary control. I can't imagine you being so overcome with lust for a vexing virgin like myself that you'll abandon it."

A muscle ticked in his jaw and she stifled the urge to smile. How could she be both amused and terrified at the same time?

He leaned in, looming over her, using his size to deliberately intimidate: all glorious threat and empty bluster. Her heart pounded in delicious anticipation.

"You, Miss Montgomery, are what they call a *tease*."

She batted her eyelashes at him. "Well, if you're worried you might lose—"

"I'm not going to lose." His eyes bored into hers. "I'll take your bet. And I'll kiss you so stupid you won't even *remember* to say stop."

Harriet tried not to let her delight show on her face.

Perfect.

Chapter Thirty

God, she was infuriating.

Morgan had no idea what game Harriet was playing, but whatever it was, if it involved letting him kiss her, anywhere at all, then it had his full support.

He was equal parts frustration and shimmering lust. Only she would blithely remind him of his honor and—in the very same breath—tempt him to abandon it.

He didn't know whether to curse her or kiss her to within an inch of her life.

Fight her, or fuck her. Rhys's sly comment echoed in his head.

No. There would be no fucking. They would stop long before that point. Harriet was just punishing him for making her the butt of the jokes on the *Briseis*. She would tell him to stop the moment she'd brought him to his knees.

Well, two could play at that game. He liked kissing. He *loved* kissing *her*. He'd kiss her so thoroughly she'd forget her own bloody name.

He would remain in control.

He'd stop when she said so.

And he would win.

Even if winning—stopping—would feel very much like losing.

Ugh. She made him want to bash his head against the wall.

He wasn't entirely sure what prize they'd agreed on, but since he'd been given permission to kiss her, he didn't much care what it was. The kissing was a prize in itself. However long it lasted.

She was staring up at him, her gray eyes wide, her cheeks a faint pink in the firelight, and his stomach tightened in longing as his eyes dropped to her cheeky, damnable mouth.

He hadn't kissed that mouth since Gryff's garden—kiss number one—and the taste of her, the luscious feel of those pillowy lips, had plagued him ever since.

Bloody woman, to make him dream of her.

She wasn't as confident as she was trying to appear. He could see the rapid rise and fall of her chest beneath the hands splayed over her breasts. She was as much bravado as challenge, and the combination of innocent girl and provocative vixen was almost more than he could bear.

She wanted kissing? While she was half-undressed?

Fine.

It would be his pleasure.

Holding her stare in blatant challenge, he stepped forward, caught the back of her head in his palm, and tilted her face to his. She didn't resist one bit. Her hands, still clutching the front of her gown, were crushed between them, trapped against his chest. He shot her a taunting smile.

"Don't forget to say stop, Harriet."

He kissed her. Not softly, not sweetly. He kissed her the way he'd dreamed of doing for years: open-mouthed and hungry, claiming her in a way that was utterly, unashamedly carnal. He kissed her with all the pent-up longing in

his soul, making up for all the nights he'd lain awake in
his bunk, or in his prison cell, fantasizing about doing exactly this. Without restraint. As if this was the last kiss he'd
ever receive.

His tongue delved deep, drawing her into a wicked
dance of advance and retreat, shaping his lips to hers.
Coaxing her to feel it too, the rising heat, the madness.

Breathing ceased to matter. He couldn't get enough of
the brandy-laced taste of her, the warm perfume of her
skin seeping into his pores. He brought his other hand up
and drew her toward him, and the soft hum of pleasure
she made against his mouth was the sweetest sound he'd
ever heard.

Her hands slid to his shoulders, stroking up his neck
to tangle in his hair, and it took his dazed brain a moment to realize that she must have released the front of
her dress. The fabric was crushed between them, held up
only by his chest.

The thought made him go weak at the knees.

He pulled back just a fraction, keeping his lips on hers,
and felt the bodice slip to her waist. He smoothed his hand
down the bare skin of her back—so soft—and brought
it around her ribs. Her breast fit his palm so perfectly he
couldn't stop the groan that escaped him.

She gasped his name. He rolled her nipple between his
finger and thumb, teasing her there as he devoured her
with his mouth, dizzy with lust. A crashing wave of emotions enveloped him: urgency and tenderness, frustration
and desire.

With an effort he dragged his lips from hers and rubbed
his cheek across hers to growl in her ear, "Want me to
stop, Harry?"

They were both panting. Her fingers tightened in the

hair at the back of his head, and she pressed her own lips to the side of his neck, beneath his jaw. His pulse was thundering beneath the skin, his body as tight as a drum.

"Not yet."

She pressed her nose into his throat, inhaling his skin, and he nearly exploded when he felt her take a tiny bite, followed by a kiss, right over the scar she'd given him.

Bloody woman. She'd be the death of him.

His blood was pounding in his veins, his body hardened to the point of pain. With a growl of pure frustration, he caught her bottom and dragged her to him with a force that made them both stagger. His backside hit the sideboard, rattling the glassware on the top.

Chest to chest, thigh to thigh. He pulled her closer, pressing his throbbing erection against her stomach so there was no way she could mistake the effect she was having on him.

"Want me to stop?" he repeated hoarsely.

She laughed—*laughed!*—against his skin. "No."

He pressed his mouth into her shoulder, giving her a gentle bite, but the bloody woman only tilted her head back to grant him better access. If he'd thought to scare her away with the violence of his response, he'd badly miscalculated.

This was madness. Utter madness.

He didn't care.

Eyes closed, he trailed a line of feverish kisses down her throat, her breast. Her hands gripped his hair as he captured her nipple in his mouth and she arched her back, offering herself wordlessly.

Pleasure roared in his ears. He feasted on her, long, lascivious pulls and licks, with a hunger that bordered on insanity. He felt unhinged. Utterly wild.

Every pulse of his body pounded in longing, a thick, heavy *mine, mine, mine*. He *wanted*. Craved more than simply entry into her body. He craved full possession.

He dragged his mouth from her and pressed his forehead to her breastbone, struggling for air. He was feverish, burning up. It took three tries to make his throat work.

"Tell me to stop, Harry."

Was that a demand or a plea? His voice was pure gravel, dragged from his chest.

In answer she pulled his head up and fastened her mouth to his, kissing him with unprincipled abandon. It was inexpert, it was untutored, and it was the most erotic thing he'd ever experienced in his life.

He grasped her hips, hard, and gave her a little shake.

"Tell me to stop!" he growled.

She shook her head.

Stubborn chit! She had no idea what she was dealing with. What she was inviting.

Enflamed, dangerously close to losing his fabled control, he spun them both around and pressed her up against the wall. She gasped as her bare back came into contact with the cool wallpaper, then groaned as he tightened his grip on her hips and slowly, deliberately, ground himself against her. The solid ridge of his cock pushed against her mound through the material of her skirts.

"Say stop!" he panted. Begged, really. She had greater belief in his willpower than he did. He'd wanted her too badly, for too long. He was hanging by a thread.

He slid his hands behind her and gripped her bottom, dragging her closer still. He rested his forehead on the wall behind her shoulder, praying for the coolness to clear his fevered brain.

"Witch," he groaned. His hips rocked against her. His

entire body was taut, shaking. "*Say it*. Say it, or so help me, I'm going to fuck you up against this wall right now."

He dragged his head back and glared at her, determined to frighten some sense into her, but his heart stuttered at the expression on her face.

She looked as feverish as he felt. Her hair had come loose from its upswept style and hung in glorious disarray around her face. Her cheeks were flushed, and her lips—God, her lips—were pink and swollen from his kisses.

Every muscle tensed as he waited for her to put an end to this insanity, but instead a wicked twinkle sparkled in her eyes.

"Go on then. I *dare* you."

Chapter Thirty-One

Dear God, she'd said it!

Harriet's heart felt like it might give out, it was pounding so hard. The feel of Morgan pressing against her was extraordinary, overwhelming in the most wonderful way.

She wanted him so much she felt faint. Desire thrummed in her blood and pooled in a heavy, aching pulse between her legs, in the tips of her breasts.

Please, she prayed silently. *Play with me. Make love to me. Finish this.*

She had to know. Just once, before he slipped from her grasp forever. One night to do everything she'd dreamed.

She didn't want a slow, choreographed seduction, the same thing he'd done with other women. She wanted the passion their teasing had always promised, that wicked spark, that burning conflagration she'd glimpsed in his eyes the few times he'd let his polite mask slip.

Their relationship had never been predictable. Making love with him shouldn't be predictable either.

He seemed to have stopped breathing. His green eyes had darkened to black and for a moment he looked almost frightening. He shook his head, and her stomach dropped with the thought that he was about to refuse her, but then he leaned in until his nose brushed hers. His fingers tightened on her backside.

"You want this?" His tone was belligerent. "Truly want this?"

"Yes." She moistened her lips.

"We shouldn't. I'll ruin you."

She couldn't look away from his face. "Not if I ruin you first."

That made no sense, but his eyes narrowed, his lips parted, and she saw the precise moment he gave in. He bent and took her mouth with a groan that sounded like surrender.

Elation almost made her crumple at his feet. She closed her eyes and allowed herself to be swept away. His intention was clear: to stoke the fire in her with the answering flame in himself. She ought to be ashamed, to have invited such wickedness, but she couldn't regret it for one moment.

With a groan, he shrugged out of his jacket and threw it aside, his mouth barely leaving hers.

His shirt was next, and she sighed in delight. She flattened her palms on his chest, desperate to touch, to feel the heat and texture of his skin.

God, he was beautiful. His skin was tawny in the firelight, his pectorals broad and flat. Breathless, incredulous, she slid her hands down, tracing the ridges of muscle on his abdomen down to the top of his breeches.

With a warning growl he caught her arm and spun her around to face the wall. His arms came around her, pulling her back into the hot curve of his body and she let out a ragged gasp as his bare chest made contact with her back.

So hot. So hard.

One of his hands slipped between her and the wall to

caress her breast while the other unhooked her skirts. The entire dress, petticoat and all, collapsed in a whisper of satin at her feet.

She sucked in a ragged breath and pressed her palms to the wall in hot mortification as the cooler air teased her skin. She was naked, completely bare, save for her stockings.

But he was right behind her, his body full against hers, a heavy masculine weight that was both crushing and welcome.

His free hand caressed her hip, strong fingers clasping her as he moved in a rhythm as instinctive as breathing. The hard rod of his erection pressed the top of her buttocks through his breeches.

Excitement coiled in her belly and throbbed between her legs as she tried to process the extraordinary sensation. She tilted her head back against his shoulder, desperate for a kiss, and he obliged, consuming her with an urgency that made her light-headed.

She was vaguely aware of him fumbling with his falls, and then the hot flesh of his cock was between them, pressed against her bottom.

She could barely suck in enough air. The hand on her breast moved down, over her stomach until he encountered the hair at the juncture of her thighs. And then he slid lower, between her legs, playing in the wetness of her body as he'd done before.

She rocked back, shamelessly encouraging him, and with a groan he changed the angle of his hips and slid his cock between her legs, rubbing in the furrow between her thighs.

"Oh, God." His groan was a hot rasp against her temple. "God, you feel so good."

Harriet was on fire, even though she shivered. Her

lungs burned; her skin felt like it was glowing. *Good* didn't even begin to describe it. Bare skin sliding between her legs, a tease and a promise, a plea and a demand. It was immoderate and wonderful, the most indecent torture imaginable.

Unable to help herself, she arched her back, loving the friction right at the heart of her. His finger slid *into* her, as his tongue had done, smoothly in and out. Pleasure shimmered behind her eyelids even as a great tension began to build in her limbs. He made her clench, and burn. She wanted more.

"More!" She must have gasped it aloud. "You."

He withdrew his hand and she tilted her hips, instinctively trying to position him exactly where she longed to be filled. The slick head of him pressed against her as he leaned in, just the smallest amount, and she moaned at the incredible sensation.

He stilled and hissed out a curse, then dropped his forehead to her shoulder.

"Fuck. Not like this."

Alarm flashed through her. Was he refusing her? Was he *stopping*? Now?

As soon as the thought materialized, it was banished. He caught her arms and turned her, claiming her mouth in a fierce, possessive kiss.

"Where's your bedroom?" he panted between kisses.

"That way." Light-headed with lust, she waved vaguely toward the corridor, then gasped as he bent and swept her up into his arms. She hardly had time to protest as he strode out of the parlor and unerringly located her bedroom just down the hall. Familiar paintings and curtains blurred in a flash of color as he dropped her in the center of her bed, then followed her down, covering her with his body.

Harriet let out a surprised little wheeze.

He loomed over her, hands planted on either side of her head, and she stared up in wonder at the glorious sight he presented. Beautiful tawny skin, smooth muscular curves. Her heart gave a funny little thump. She might not have him forever, but tonight he was completely hers.

"Last chance." He sounded strained. Tortured, like a man on the rack. "Do you want me to stop?"

"Don't you *dare*," she countered fiercely. She widened her legs, letting him drop farther into the lee of her body.

"Fine." He held her gaze captive as he reached between them and fitted himself at the entrance to her body again. "Just remember, you *asked* for this."

It sounded so much like a threat that she almost laughed, but her humor faded as he pressed forward, still staring deep into her eyes. She fought not to blink at the sweet, strange ache as he entered her. Not pain, precisely, but discomfort. He was bigger than his finger. Much bigger.

She must have flinched, or grimaced, because he stilled, barely inside her.

"Stop?" His voice was hoarse, as if he'd been shouting.

She shook her head, even though tears threatened at the corners of her eyes. What could she say? *It's too much. It's perfect.*

It's you.

A slight tremor ran through him. "Breathe. Give it a minute."

She nodded, willing her body to relax, and to her amazement it did. Her tension seeped away and she sank deeper into the bed, just as he slid deeper into *her.*

They both groaned. A shiver of pleasure ran through her, a ghost of what she'd found before, and she wiggled her hips, trying to find it again. He dropped to his elbows and made an impassioned sound into her neck.

"Harriet, I'm *dying*. Please, let me move."

He lifted his head, so close she could see the gray flecks in his green eyes, and she raised her hand to his face. His jaw was scratchy with late-night stubble.

"Yes."

He closed his eyes as if he'd received a benediction. And then he rocked his hips, joining them more fully, and withdrew. He did it again, and the abrasive friction gave way to a wicked, pervasive slickness that made her blood thrum in her veins.

Harriet closed her eyes in delight.

So this was what it was all about. Shuddering darkness and aching need. Desperate, glorious possession.

She clasped his shoulders as he drove deeper, loving the weight of him, the sheer animal strength. He was so much larger than her, surging and pulling at her body like a tide, but she felt sheltered in his arms. He was both the port and the storm, the safe haven and the treacherous deep.

And God, she was drowning.

"Never. Going to. Stop." He punctuated each word with a roll of his hips, and each time he hit a spot somewhere inside her that promised the heaven he'd shown her with his tongue.

She arched her hips, urging him on, and the pleasure built like a bank of great billowing clouds on the horizon, rolling in with a speed to take her breath away.

She wrapped her arms around his neck and buried her face in the muscled curve of his shoulder, straining upward, taking his every thrust with a feeling of pure joy.

Close! So close! So—

She tensed, straining for the peak like a ship at the very crest of a wave, teetering on the edge. And then the wave broke. Pleasure crashed over her like surf, wringing her soul and squeezing her heart so she could hardly breathe for pleasure. Ripples of release radiated outward, flooding her with warmth.

Morgan cursed, still moving within her, and then, with one final thrust, he withdrew from her body and pressed himself hard against her stomach. He stiffened, then let out a tortured groan as great shudders wracked his body.

He collapsed on top of her, full weight, as if all the life had been drained out of him. And then he gave a sigh that seemed to come from the very depths of his lungs.

"Bloody hell, Harriet. What a dare!"

He rolled off her, onto his side. The weight of him depressed the mattress so she rolled onto her side too, toward him. He pushed a strand of her hair away from her flushed cheek and pressed a gentle kiss to her eyebrow, then another to the top of her nose.

Such unexpected sweetness after the near violence of before clutched at her heart. He pressed another feather-light kiss to her lips, his thumb stroking her jaw in the lightest of caresses, then one to her chin.

Her lips curved upward. She felt breathless, shaky, as if she'd run a race. The sheen of sweat on her back was cooling rapidly in the night air, but the heat of Morgan's body at her front was keeping her warm.

She stared up at him, still dazed by the magnitude of what they'd just done.

"Stop," she whispered, half laughing. "Now you can stop."

Chapter Thirty-Two

Morgan's mouth curved, and he gave her that crooked smile of his, that pirate smile, secret and swift. He propped himself up on his bent arm, his biceps curling most impressively, and sent a leisurely glance down her front.

Harriet tensed, still a little anxious for his verdict. She hadn't felt truly naked until now. Before, it had all been a blur of limbs and heat and passion.

"Beautiful," he growled. "Like the first sight of land after a month at sea." He reached out and traced the curve of her breast and she shivered at its new sensitivity. "You'd make a lovely ship's figurehead."

She snorted. "Do you say that to all the ladies of your acquaintance?"

"Only the ones with spectacular breasts."

She hadn't thought she'd ever blush again, but she was wrong. A pink flush warmed her chest.

It deepened as he gathered a handful of the sheets and gently wiped the wetness he'd left on her stomach. His seed, she realized dazedly. Thank God one of them had retained some semblance of sanity and self-preservation. She hadn't given a thought to the fact that he might make her pregnant.

"So, who won the bet?" He lifted his brows in lazy

challenge. "You didn't tell me to stop. Which means *technically*, I won."

"Ah, but I dared you to make love to me up against the wall, which you failed to do. So *I'm* the winner."

He gave a weary chuckle. "We'll call it a draw. Satisfied?"

She let her lips curl up in a mischievous smile. "Extremely."

He snorted, even as he flopped to his back and threw his forearm across his eyes as if acutely embarrassed. "I swear, I can do better. I wasn't expecting—I mean, you caught me by surprise—God, I still have my *boots on*."

She smiled at his uncharacteristic stuttering. His confusion—and masculine pique—was highly amusing.

"Feel free to take them off."

He growled and sat up, shifting to the edge of the bed, and she was seized with another bout of embarrassment. She was only wearing her stockings.

While he caught the heel of his boot and tugged it off, letting it drop to the carpet with a thud, she retrieved her nightgown from beneath her pillow. She dived into it, glad to have the thin cotton to shield her nakedness.

He removed his other boot and glanced at her over his shoulder, then stilled when he saw she'd registered the faint lattice of pale scars on the beautiful musculature of his back. She couldn't contain her gasp of dismay.

"Dear God, was that from when you were flogged? By De Caen?"

"Yes. Not a pretty sight, is it?"

She reached out and touched him without thought. He didn't flinch. Instead, he watched her warily as she smoothed her palm across his skin and felt the raised bumps where the flesh had knitted itself back together. It was hard and knotted, like the bark of a tree.

Her heart squeezed in sympathy. How that must have hurt. And the fact that he'd taken the punishment for another, for his brother in arms, a weaker, younger man? How could she not love him?

He half turned toward her, but she shuffled forward on her knees and pressed her lips to the stripe that curved below his shoulder blade.

"I'm so sorry you were hurt," she whispered.

He gave a little shrug. "It wasn't the most fun I've ever had. But it healed quickly enough. I was lucky it wasn't worse."

"De Montfort told me you diverted attention away from him."

"De Montford should keep his mouth shut," he growled.

She gave him a little shove, as she had so often when they were children. "I *knew* you'd do something stupidly noble. I was right."

"You're insufferable."

He made it sound like the sweetest compliment, so she answered in kind.

"So are you."

He shook his head, but she saw his lips curl before he turned away and made a big show of inspecting their surroundings. "Do you know how many times I've dreamed of seeing your bedroom?" The cheeky twinkle in his eye was back. "Too many to count."

"Yours is nicer," she said, a little defensively.

"It's not."

"It's bigger, more luxurious."

"But it doesn't have you in it," he said simply.

Her heart gave a funny jolt. Oh, he was so good at saying things like that. Such practiced charm.

"So . . . what do we do now?"

He gave a lazy stretch, all effortless grace. "We go

to sleep, of course." He sent her a sideways look. "Do you still want me to sleep in the drawing room? I can, if you wish."

"It seems a little pointless, doesn't it? Like closing the stable door after the horse has bolted." She made a wry, self-mocking face. "You might as well stay here. If you want to, that is."

"Of course I want to. Get under the covers."

He stood and she tried not to stare at the glorious sight of his muscled chest and ridged abdomen in the lamplight. He really was a splendid specimen. Was he going to remove his breeches?

She scrambled up the bed and plunged beneath the covers. He leaned over and extinguished the lamp and she bit back a huff of disappointment as the room was plunged into shadow. She hadn't even seen him naked!

His large shape was barely visible in the darkness, but she listened with bated breath to the intriguing rustle of fabric as he presumably removed his breeches and stockings.

The intimacy of the moment struck her forcefully. How many times had she imagined waking in the night to find Morgan in her room? She'd spun countless girlhood fantasies that were variations of this exact scene: Morgan climbing the trellis outside her window in Wales, sneaking into her moonlit bedroom to make love to her in secret.

Reality was so much better.

She stiffened as he pulled back the sheets and slid into bed next to her, but he gave her no chance to shift away.

"Come here, Harry."

In one smooth movement he rolled her to her side, her back to his chest, and tugged her into the hot curve of his body. Her bottom fit snugly into the lee of his groin, his long limbs curled around hers perfectly. She could feel the heat of his skin, his nakedness, burning through her thin cotton nightdress. Her senses reeled.

His left arm burrowed beneath her pillow, supporting her head, while his right arm draped over her waist and cupped her breast. One of his thighs insinuated itself between hers and she tried not to giggle at the unexpected tickly texture of the hair on his leg.

It was overwhelming, almost suffocating, but in the best possible way. She was surrounded by hard, male body, but instead of feeling threatened, caged, she felt . . . wonderful. Protected in the most basic way. Cocooned and cherished like some precious treasure.

Morgan pressed his face to the nape of her neck and let out a deep sigh of appreciation.

"This is *much* better than the drawing room." He yawned and pulled her closer as if it was the most natural thing in the world for them to be lying here like this. As if they'd done it a thousand times.

Harriet stared blindly into the darkness, her thoughts a jumbled mess. Her heart squeezed a little at how *right* it felt to be in Morgan's arms. She felt like a ship that had braved the fiercest storm and now lay safe and sheltered in the harbor.

Every muscle in her body was sated and heavy. Her eyelids fought to close, but she resisted the exhaustion claiming her. She wanted to stay awake, to savor this incredible—temporary—feeling of being exactly where she wanted to be. She wanted to engrave every detail into her memory: the rise and fall of his chest against her back, the mind-fogging scent of his naked skin, the warm brush of his breath against her hair.

Happiness was such a tenuous emotion. She hugged it to herself, soaked it in, just as Morgan was hugging her body to his.

By morning this incredible dream would be over. Harsh daylight would interrupt the beauty of the night, and this quiet harmony between them would vanish.

How would he act tomorrow? How would she? They'd sailed completely off the map tonight, gone so far there would be no going back.

Her muddled brain couldn't provide an answer. The pull of sleep was too great to fight. Harriet snuggled deeper into Morgan's embrace and simply surrendered.

Morgan knew the exact moment Harriet finally fell asleep. He'd practically been able to hear her busy mind trying to sort through all the implications of what they'd just done, but eventually her body softened and relaxed against his. Her breathing deepened and she let out a tiny sigh of contentment, like a satisfied kitten.

His chest tightened as he cataloged the sensation of finally—*finally*—holding her in his arms.

Part of him was afraid to trust the feeling. He'd dreamed of this so many times, imagined this soul-deep feeling of peace, only to find himself roughly shaken awake, or roused with a bucket of cold water to the face by a surly prison guard.

No, this was real. As wicked and wonderful as the woman in his arms.

He allowed himself a soft, incredulous exhale, and tried to sort through his emotions. Amazement at how incredible it had been to finally join his body to hers. Chagrin, for acting little better than a rutting animal. At least he'd managed to stumble them to a bed for her first time and not sated himself against the wall like some lust-crazed idiot.

God, he'd never been so impetuous, nor so desperate. But Harriet had seemed to *like* his desperation. She'd encouraged it, goading him on, daring him. Matching him kiss for kiss, fire for fire. Her flame had burned as brightly as his own.

He'd always known they'd be a perfect match.

The feel of her curled up next to him, so small and yet so womanly, was everything he'd ever dreamed. Sleep had stripped her of her defenses, rounding her sharp corners, muting her sharp tongue and sparkling animosity.

A great surge of tenderness hit him as she made a soft little snuffle in her sleep. Awake she was bristly and formidable, but now he was reminded of how vulnerable she'd allowed herself to be. He felt honored by her gift, awed and gratified that she'd entrusted him with her body. And incredibly glad that he'd come to visit her tonight.

He honestly hadn't expected to do anything other than sleep on some uncomfortable sofa or overstuffed armchair in her parlor, but despite Gryff's and Rhys's dire warnings, and his own fervent denials, he couldn't regret what they'd done.

How Harriet would feel about it, of course, was anyone's guess. Every time he thought he knew how she'd react to something she managed to surprise him, and he had no idea what she'd think of waking up pressed to his naked body in the morning.

Had this been enough to convince her they should be together? They were perfectly compatible: different enough never to grow bored of one other, similar enough to share the same humor and interests.

His love for her glowed inside him like banked embers. She'd accused him of laughing at her, of making her the butt of his jokes, and he *had*, but that was only half the story. She'd also been the shore to which he'd navigated. The X on the map that marked treasure. His star. His guiding light, the one fixed point by which he'd set his course.

Home.

Morgan inhaled, filling his lungs with the sleepy-warm, womanly scent of her. Of them.

He would not lose sight of her now.

Not when he was so close to his final destination.

Chapter Thirty-Three

Harriet woke to a profound feeling of warmth and contentment, and her first thought was that Mrs. Jennings must have come in and started the fire.

She cracked her eyes open and squinted at the still-dead hearth. The faint gray light of early morning slid through the curtains and the lively calls of tradesmen echoed up from the street below as the great beating heart of London stirred: grocers and bakers, brewers and sweeps.

And then her dazed brain registered the heavy weight beside her and her eyes popped fully open. Morgan's arm was slung casually over her chest, his much-larger body pressed down her entire right side. Hot. Hard.

Startled, she turned her head and encountered his face, and the sight of his laughing eyes so unexpectedly close to her own caused a full-body flush. She reared back in alarm.

"Morning, Miss Montgomery, I trust you slept well?"

His voice was gravelly from disuse and it made her stomach quiver.

Oh, she'd done it now.

"Good morning." Why on earth was she trying to sound so prim when he was *naked in bed beside her*?

She sat up and tried to gather her scattered wits, determined to take control of the situation. Unfortunately, her brusque movement revealed the mouthwatering expanse of his chest as the bedspread dipped. Unconcerned, he rolled onto his back and tucked his hands behind his head in a supremely masculine stretch of contentment.

She swallowed and clenched her hands into the bedspread to stop herself from falling on him like a ravenous beast. She wanted to touch him *everywhere*.

Morgan was clearly used to this terrible awkwardness of waking up next to a member of the opposite sex—a member whose body had been intimately acquainted with one's own. She, however, felt heat rush to her cheeks.

No doubt he was wondering how he was going to politely extricate himself from her bedroom and make his escape. Well, she wouldn't be one of those dreadful, clinging females he usually encountered. She would be sensible. Mature. *Sophisticated*.

She cleared her throat. "Morgan."

"Harriet." He answered with equal gravity, mocking her businesslike tone. His eyes crinkled at the corners.

"Last night was lovely, but . . . it can't happen again."

His eyes widened in comical shock. He hadn't been expecting *that*.

"What? Why not?"

Because you'll break my heart.

"Come, we're both adults. I think we can both agree that one night was enough to assuage our curiosity."

"But—"

She pressed on, pleating the fabric in her fingers to quell her nervous jitters. "I've always wanted to know what it would be like to make love, and you've shown me how pleasant it is. I'll be forever grateful to you."

"Grateful!" he growled, his eyes narrowing to furious slits. "*Pleasant*?"

He sat up and she hastily averted her eyes as the covers dropped to his lap. Acres of tawny skin beckoned and her eyes seemed transfixed by the intriguing line of dark hair that arrowed from his navel down below the sheets. She clutched the covers tighter.

"Bloody hell, Harriet. *You* might not have the experience to know it, but last night was amazing. Incredible."

That gave her pause. *She'd* thought it was wonderful, but what did she know? She would have thought anything he did to her was wonderful. He was the one with all the experience. If he said it was amazing then he must know what he was talking about. He wasn't one to flatter.

She cleared her throat.

"I don't deny that, physically, we're an interesting combination. But you and I both know there can be no *future* for the two of us. You're about to go sailing off around the world again. Best to stop now, when we've had one wonderful night to remember."

Morgan stared at her, dumbstruck. How many times had a man given this exact speech to dismiss a woman? How many times had *he* given it?

Thank you, and goodbye.

It would have been amusing if his chest didn't hurt so much. If his heart wasn't starting a panicked thump at the realization that she was slipping away from him.

This should have been a moment of triumph. They were supposed to wake in each other's arms and make love again—slowly, taking time to learn each other's secrets. Drawing out the pleasure into the most exquisite kind of torture.

Instead, it was . . . all going wrong.

Why? She'd enjoyed herself last night; he was sure of it. He'd felt her body shudder with pleasure, felt her soften and surrender in his arms.

"Are you regretting what we did?" he asked cautiously.

"No, of course not."

"Well, you can't think I'll tell anyone about this. I'd never blacken your reputation."

"I know that."

"There's no chance you could be pregnant," he said bluntly. "I made sure of that."

She flushed scarlet. "And I thank you for that."

He tried very hard not to glower at her, and probably failed. "Then what's the problem?"

She bit her lip and he prayed for strength. God, she looked delectable, all mussed from sleep. He wanted to strip that prim cotton nightgown off her and make love to her all over again. His lazy morning erection stiffened even more at the thought. Bloody thing. It couldn't tell the difference between fighting and foreplay.

Then again, with Harriet, fighting usually *was* foreplay.

Not in this case, however.

"Did you just use me for sex?" he growled.

Her sudden flush suggested he'd hit the nail on the head. "No! Not exactly, I—"

"You did!" he accused. "You wanted to see what the marriage bed would hold. Or to see what you'll be missing if you never marry."

"Morgan! That's—"

Inexplicably annoyed, he flung back the covers and stood, enjoying her scandalized gasp as he granted her the glory of his naked backside. He should turn around and let her see the iron rod that was his erection, he thought savagely. That would *really* give her something to gasp about.

No. Showing her how much she affected him would put him at a distinct disadvantage. He couldn't think straight when he was naked with her.

He grabbed his breeches from where they lay on the floor and pulled them on, and from the frantic rustling behind him he deduced that she'd also left the bed and was scrambling into some clothing of her own.

He turned and found her hastily belting the sash of a pretty aqua silk dressing robe. The sight almost robbed him of his anger. The fabric flowed over her lithe form, clearly outlining the peaks of her nipples below the flow of her unbound hair. His cock twitched, as if furious at having been constrained by his breeches. He took a deep, calming breath.

The bed had become an unexpected battlefield between them; they faced each other across the vast expanse of its rumpled sheets.

"I'm just being realistic." Her tone was both irritated and resigned. "You're going to find a wife who doesn't mind being left behind, and that's definitely not me. I feel like my own life's just *beginning*. For the first time in years, I'm excited about my future. If Father's eyesight improves, I can make plans I never dared to consider before. I can start having adventures of my own."

Her eyes were soft, begging him to understand, and his gut tightened in reluctant sympathy. He knew that yearning feeling precisely.

"One night wasn't enough," he said, trying to keep his voice level.

She swallowed, clearly digesting that idea, and his spirits rose, but then she tilted her head and sent him a scornful look.

"So what do you suggest? That we keep doing this for another few weeks until you're married? Because I won't be any man's mistress, Morgan. I won't sleep with another woman's husband."

"You don't have to," he said crossly. "You can marry me."

Chapter Thirty-Four

Marry me.

Morgan could have kicked himself for such a graceless proposal. *Idiot!* A woman wanted to be asked, not told.

Harriet's expression was one of utter shock. He held his breath, waiting for her reaction. It was the same sensation of weightless dread as hearing the boom of an enemy cannon, of seeing the puff of smoke, and then waiting for the whistle of an incoming cannonball that might or might not kill you.

As always, Harriet did the unexpected. She placed her hands on her slim, silk-clad hips and frowned at him.

"Marry you? Are you *mad*?" She shook her head as if to dislodge a cobweb from her hair. "You're not serious."

Bollocks. He was cocking this up. He should be down on one knee, begging, not blurting it out across a messy counterpane in only his breeches. He held her stare, silently willing her to believe him.

"I'm perfectly serious. I want to marry you. I love you."

Those magic words did not have the effect he'd intended. Her brows lowered in furious disbelief.

"No, you *desire* me. It's not the same at all. It's a temporary aberration from which you'll recover very soon."

He flexed his fingers in frustration.

"That's not true. I won't deny that I desire you physically." He gestured angrily at the still-hard rod in the front of his breeches and gained a moment's satisfaction from the way her eyes widened in belated realization of his state. "I've wanted you since I was sixteen years old. But there's more to it than that. We *suit*, Harriet. In all the ways that count."

"Is this some kind of joke? To tease me because I won the race?"

"Of course not! I love you."

"Stop saying that!" She was almost shouting. "You don't love me. You love *tormenting* me. You love beating me in our stupid games and this is just another game to you. Well, I don't want to play anymore. You win. You wanted me in your bed, as a conquest? You've had me. You wanted me to want *you*? I do! Against my better judgment. Against all good sense."

She stopped, panting, her cheeks flaming as she realized how much she'd admitted. But the bed stretched like a gulf between them. The ridges of the fabric might as well have been an actual mountain range, such was the distance.

"Then what's the problem?" he growled. "I want you, and you want me. Why shouldn't we get married? And don't give me that 'Davieses and Montgomerys are sworn enemies' rubbish, because we both know that has nothing to do with it."

"You're in the navy," she said, as if it was the most obvious thing in the world.

"So?"

"So I want someone to share my life with, a partner, a friend. Someone who's there to hold me in his arms at night and tease me beyond reason during the day."

"I'm leaving the navy. Resigning my commission."

"That's a terrible idea. I *know* you, Morgan. You need constant challenges, new worlds to conquer. You'll be bored within weeks."

"I'll never get bored with you. I love you. How can I prove it?"

She sent him a sad, almost pitying sigh. "You can't prove something that doesn't exist. Your 'love' for me is as fictional as my Paradise Court."

His chest felt like the time he broke three ribs falling from his horse, but it was clear that there would be no persuading Harriet now.

He was no stranger to military tactics: sometimes the best course of action was to withdraw, regroup, and live to fight another day. That's how he'd captured the *Brilliant*, after all. He'd let the French think he was beaten, dispirited, outgunned—and then he'd launched an unexpected counterattack.

"Fine," he said diffidently.

He bent and retrieved his shirt from the floor and tugged it over his head, taking heart from the slight pout of disappointment on Harriet's face as his chest disappeared from view.

He bit back a smile, suddenly glad she hadn't had time to see him naked. She hadn't explored his body the way he'd explored hers. His physique was still a mystery to her—and uncharted territory to Harriet was a terrible temptation. She'd be plagued by the unknown, desperate to know what was lacking from her store of worldly knowledge. That could definitely work to his advantage.

He sent her a challenging stare. "One week."

Her brows drew together. "What?"

"Give me one week to prove that I love you."

She let out an exasperated sigh. "I don't know what on earth you think you can do, but fine. Whatever you want. One week."

His sprits soared, but he nodded as solemnly as if they'd sealed the bargain in blood, even as a small, amused corner of his brain appreciated how inevitable it was that he and Harriet were bargaining *yet again.*

The stakes, however, had never been higher.

He bent and retrieved his boots and stockings from the floor and resisted the urge to round the bed and kiss her. "In that case, I'll bid you goodbye. You don't need to show me out. I'll make my own way to the stables."

She opened her mouth to say something, but he held up his hand to forestall her. "I'll make sure nobody sees me leave. One week, Harriet."

Harriet sank gratefully onto the bed as Morgan strode out of the room. Her hands were shaking, her chest tight. She let out an incredulous huff of air, as if she'd been winded.

Dear God!

She'd never thought she'd hear Morgan actually say *I love you. Marry me* was more than she'd ever dared to dream. She'd have wagered the entire contents of the shop that he'd never say those particular words to her.

If only he really meant them.

She didn't doubt that he desired her. Even a near virgin like herself could discern that, but lust was temporary.

Three years ago the papers had been full of the salacious affair between Lady Caroline Lamb and Lord Byron, and the disastrous outcome to that had seemed to Harriet both tragic and completely predictable. She'd been at the ball in honor of the Duke of Wellington when Byron, tired of his lover, had publicly spurned her. Lady

Caroline had smashed a wineglass and threatened to cut her own wrists, and although the gesture had been merely for dramatic effect, it had been the start of Lady Caroline's eventual blackballing from society. Harriet had vowed then and there *never* to make such a fool of herself over a man.

A marriage needed more than lust to make it survive. Her parents had shown her that. And while she and Morgan undoubtedly shared the same sense of humor and an irresistible urge to goad each other, the gulf between what they wanted from life was unbridgeable.

She could never be content to stay at home while her husband had all the adventures. And while the thought of bearing Morgan's children caused an ache of pure longing in her chest, she wouldn't want any offspring of hers to grow up without a father for long periods of time.

Tears threatened, but she fought them back.

A month ago, if Morgan had asked her to marry him, she would have assumed it was some kind of evil Davies trick to humiliate her. That she'd say yes—revealing her love for him—only to have him laugh and expose it as a cruel joke.

She didn't think that now. Morgan had somehow convinced himself he was in love with her, but she didn't dare believe his proposal was anything other than a last-ditch attempt to convince her to come back to bed.

She'd been tempted. His sly reminder that there was more to discover from lovemaking had gnawed at her resolve and the thought that she'd just turned down the chance to see him completely naked, to explore all those incredible muscles and sinews at her leisure, was enough to have her question her sanity.

She buried her face in the pillow and let out a groan of frustration.

Was she the greatest idiot in England? A man she was irreversibly in love with had offered to make her his wife. The same man had a near-magical ability to give her unreasonable amounts of pleasure. True, he might not love her as ardently as she loved him, but surely that would have been a small price to pay? Half the weddings in the *ton* were based on practical things like money and power, not love.

She punched the pillow and sat up.

No. She'd made the right decision. Accepting him would only have led to heartache, as would agreeing to an affair. He would tire of her and move on to someone new. It was far better to be the one doing the leaving.

She wanted *all* of him, or nothing at all.

Chapter Thirty-Five

Harriet had little opportunity to wonder what Morgan planned to do to "prove his love." Mrs. Jennings bustled in only a short while later and the two of them busied themselves getting the house ready for her father's return.

Knowing it would be difficult for him to navigate the stairs with bandages covering the top half of his head, Harriet borrowed a folding campaign bed from Jem Cooper and set it up in the back room next to father's armchair so he could move easily between the two. She arranged a small tilt-top table next to the chair so he would have somewhere to put his food, and ensured his favorite lap rug was ready and waiting.

He arrived home as she was finishing her lunch. Doctor Saunders escorted him down from the carriage, and the two of them guided him slowly into the shop.

It was a little alarming to see Father so helpless, and her heart gave an odd twist at the short gray stubble that covered his chin and cheeks—she'd never seen him anything other than clean-shaven, and the tiny lapse seemed to underscore how frail and vulnerable he was.

"Father, it's so good to see you!" She stroked his hand and spoke a little louder than usual so he could hear her through the layers of bandages over his ears.

His mouth turned up in a smile. "I wish I could say the same, Harry my girl! Can't see a thing with this blasted mushroom on m'head."

His jovial response reassured her no end. "Don't worry that his speech is a little slurred," Doctor Saunders said quietly as they lowered him to lie on the bed. "It's a common side effect of the laudanum he's been given."

He pulled a piece of paper from his coat along with a small blue glass bottle. "Here, I've written precise instructions on how to care for him, and when to readminister the laudanum. His dose will gradually decrease over the next few days to ensure he's in the least amount of discomfort."

Harriet nodded, pleased to see that Father had already started to doze.

"Don't let him remove the bandages for at least two days. Many patients report being able to see almost immediately after surgery, but I prefer to keep the eyes covered for a little while to prevent infection." He sent her a friendly nod. "I'll come back to check up on him in a couple of days if that suits you, Miss Montgomery?"

"That would be wonderful. Thank you."

The doctor tipped his hat. "Glad to help a friend of Captain Davies."

Harriet's stomach flipped at the mention of Morgan, but she managed a serene smile. "Well, I wouldn't exactly call Captain Davies a *friend*, exactly. More of an acquaintance." Her conscience gave her a guilty little stab for that patent falsehood. "His brother married my cousin Madeline. And his sister married my *other* cousin, Tristan."

The doctor raised his brows and chuckled. "My, what a tangled web! It sounds as if you and Captain Davies are inextricably linked—whether you wish to be or not."

She tried not to wince at the terrible accuracy of that

statement. Fate had certainly conspired to bring them into each other's orbit. Whether there was any way to *escape* was another matter entirely.

After the doctor had left, she spent the rest of the day caring for her father, even though he spent a great deal of the time asleep. Still, making endless cups of tea was a welcome distraction that prevented her from dwelling on Morgan and the wonderful, sinful things they'd done.

The following day passed uneventfully, apart from a brief visit from Maddie to check on Father's progress.

"Morgan arrived just as I was leaving," she said blithely. "And Rhys had already invited himself over for breakfast, so I probably had a lucky escape. All three Davies brothers in the same room is playing with fire. One never knows quite how things will progress. They're just as likely to throw punches at one another as they are to have a sensible conversation." She gave a wicked chuckle. "Sometimes they're completely uncivilized."

Harriet felt her cheeks heat with betraying color and Maddie raised her brows in avid fascination. She took a demure sip of tea, but Harriet's heart began to pound at the speculative twinkle in her cousin's eye. Maddie had always been fiendishly good at ferreting out her secrets.

"Gryff let slip that Morgan came to guard you the other night while Uncle Henry was away."

Harriet took a desperate gulp of her own tea, but it was too hot and she began to cough. Maddie put down her cup and gave her a helpful whack between the shoulder blades.

"Thank you," Harriet wheezed, mopping the front of her dress with a napkin. "I wasn't expecting it to be so hot."

"Morgan's visit, or the tea?" Maddie lifted her brows. Harriet choked again. "Maddie!"

"Harriet!" Maddie countered, laughing. "Don't you

dare try to tell me that nothing happened between the two of you because I shan't believe it."

"Nothing happened," Harriet said desperately. "He came, he slept on the chaise in the drawing room, and he left in the morning satisfied that no mad Frenchmen or mapmakers with a grudge had tried to kill me in the night."

Maddie gave a disbelieving snort. "I bet that wasn't the only reason he left *satisfied*. You seem to be forgetting that I'm *married* to one of those devilish Davieses, Harry. I know precisely how irresistible they can be. *I* bet he came, he saw, and he conquered. Just like Julius Caesar."

"I resisted!"

Maddie gave her a hard stare and Harriet crumpled like an unstarched collar. She'd always been terrible at lying, and her pink cheeks had probably given the game away ages ago.

"I *tried*," she protested weakly.

Maddie lifted her brows.

"Oh, fine. I didn't resist at all," she confessed testily. "Not even a little bit. In fact, I was utterly shameless."

Maddie squealed and clapped her hands in delight. "I knew it! How marvelous. Tell me everything."

Harriet sighed, and resigned herself to her fate. "Oh, Maddie, I was terrible. I goaded him into kissing me. And then I dared him to keep going until I said stop."

Maddie's eyes grew round with awe. "You dared him? Oh, Harriet. Daring a Davies is like waving a red rag at a bull."

"I know."

"I assume you didn't tell him to stop?"

Harriet shook her head.

Maddie beamed. "Well, I can't honestly say I'm surprised. You two have been at each other's throats for years, but the attraction has been obvious to anyone with eyes. Did you enjoy it?"

"Very much. Enough not to care that I'm ruined."

"Pfft. You're not ruined. You're only 'ruined' if people find out about it. That's what makes the *ton* so fickle. Truth rarely comes into it. Reputation and appearances are everything." Maddie leaned forward conspiratorially. "And to be perfectly honest, I doubt many men could even *tell* if a girl's a virgin or not. I bet half the 'virgins' in London went to their wedding night knowing what to expect. You can still make a brilliant match if you want one."

"Well, as to that, Morgan proposed."

It was Maddie's turn to choke on her tea. "Pardon?"

"He said we could get married, and I said no."

"God in heaven! Why?"

"Why did he propose, or why did I say no?" Harriet teased, even though her heart felt like lead.

"Why did you say *no*, you goose? I know why he would have proposed—because he's been in love with you forever."

Harriet's stomach somersaulted at Maddie's absolute conviction, even as she shook her head. "He doesn't love me. He lusts after me. And enjoys teasing me. But that's not enough. I want what you have with Gryff: a husband who's there for you, who shares your life. Morgan isn't ready to give me those things."

"But you love him." It was a statement, not a question, and Harriet frowned.

"I do. But one has to be practical. Sometimes love isn't enough. Sometimes you have to stop playing games and start facing reality."

Maddie shook her head, as if Harriet were a strange

artifact she'd unearthed during one of her archaeological digs. "Hmm."

"What does that mean, *hmm*?"

"It means I'm reserving judgment. Life has a funny way of messing up the best-laid plans. And you have to give Morgan a little credit. If nobody knows about the two of you, then he didn't propose out of a sense of duty, did he? He could have asked any single woman in the *ton* to be his wife and expected the answer to be yes."

"He asked for a week to prove he loves me."

Maddie's brows shot toward her hairline. "Good Lord. What do you think he's going to do?"

"I have no idea, but it had better not be some mortifying public declaration. If he *truly* loves me, he'll know that's precisely the kind of thing I hate."

"Morgan has no problem being the center of attention." Maddie chuckled. "I think that's why he became captain of his own ship, you know."

She leaned over and helped herself to a slice of cake. "Four hundred years ago he would have set off to kill a dragon for you, or entered the lists to joust for your hand. It's much harder for men nowadays. Even dueling's frowned upon."

Harriet took her own mouthful of cake. "Dueling is stupid," she mumbled. "And love isn't about grand gestures. It's all the tiny, everyday, seemingly insignificant things that all add up to something big."

"But Harriet—" Maddie's expression was almost pitying. "Morgan's been showing you *those* for years."

Harriet's heart gave an irregular little thump as the truth of that struck her with the force of a blow. Maddie was right. He'd dived into an icy stream to get her pencil. Taken her on his travels by describing her to an entire ship full of sailors. He'd introduced her father to Doctor

Saunders, and stood at her side to confront Heron, and cared enough about her safety to stay overnight.

She swallowed her cake with difficulty, as if she had a lump in her throat. Morgan *had* already proved his love in a thousand different ways. She'd just been too blind to notice.

Harriet resisted the urge to slap herself on the forehead. Father wasn't the only one in this house who couldn't see what was right in front of him. She was a fool.

She glanced at Maddie and found her cousin watching her with a knowing smile on her lips. "Have you realized it yet?"

"I . . . may have been a bit hasty," Harriet admitted. "Maybe Morgan *does* love me, but that still doesn't erase all the other reasons we aren't suited."

Maddie drained the last of her tea and stood. "Give him a chance. I, for one, can't wait to see what he comes up with. Considering he's a Davies, I can guarantee it will be something worth waiting for."

Chapter Thirty-Six

"If you're going to the Stevensons' musicale tonight, you'll need to be on your guard."

Morgan raised his brows at Gryff. The two of them, plus Rhys, were enjoying a midafternoon brandy in Gryff's study.

Morgan tried to erase the memory of Harriet, blindfolded, leaning against the very desk Rhys was now lounging upon. It didn't work. He could practically smell her perfume. He took a long sip of his drink.

"Why?" he asked, finally responding to his brother's comment.

"Because the Aunts have been telling anyone who'll listen that you're on the hunt for a wife. You're going to be inundated with simpering debutantes and matchmaking mamas."

"I'm always inundated with simpering debutantes and matchmaking mamas," Morgan said.

"It's your own fault," Rhys said, without a trace of sympathy. "You're the one who said you were looking to wed." He shuddered. "Although God knows why, when you've only just escaped one prison. Why put yourself back in chains? Voluntarily. For the rest of your life."

"Marriage isn't *that* bad," Gryff protested. "If you

find the right woman it can be the best thing that ever happens to you. Maddie's the most amazing—"

Rhys made a retching noise. "Spare us the details of your marital bliss. It's terribly unfashionable to love your *own* wife, you know."

Morgan interrupted them before the argument could spiral out of control.

"Well, the debutantes are going to be disappointed, because I've already proposed."

Gryff raised his brows. "Who?"

Morgan deliberately waited until Rhys had taken a mouthful of his drink.

"Harriet."

Brandy sprayed in a satisfying arc from Rhys's lips.

"Hoi! That's an Aubusson rug, you Neanderthal!" Gryff glared at him. "Maddie paid a fortune for it."

Rhys sputtered as Gryff whacked him hard between the shoulder blades. "Harriet?" he continued between gasps. "Are you out of your mind?"

Morgan grinned. "Funny, that's exactly what *she* said."

Gryff's mouth dropped open. "She refused you?"

"She did indeed."

"The cheek of the woman!" Rhys growled, apparently now annoyed on Morgan's behalf. "Who refuses a Davies? We're perfect husband material. Matrimonial gold."

Morgan snorted. "Not according to Harriet."

"What was her objection? We're rich. Titled. Impossibly good-looking. Well, *I* am," Rhys amended. "You two are only slightly better than average, if we're being honest."

"Modest too," Gryff drawled, laughing. "Don't forget modest."

"She objected," Morgan said, ignoring their byplay, "because she didn't believe me when I said I loved her."

Both brothers blinked as if this was the stupidest thing they'd ever heard.

"Oh, you must have *really* buggered up your proposal," Rhys said with relish. "You've been in love with her for years."

"I knew it the day she whacked you with a sword," Gryff said.

"It was a branch," Morgan corrected. "And I didn't think it was that obvious."

"Was to us. We're your brothers." Gryff shrugged. "I didn't think *you* knew, though."

"What? That I loved her?"

"Yes."

"Well, I didn't really," Morgan confessed. "Not until I was stuck in that stinking French prison and started thinking about all the things I regretted. Not seeing Harriet again was pretty high up on the list. She's the most frustrating woman alive, but I realized I couldn't live without her."

Gryff leaned over and gave him a brotherly whack on the shoulder. "Welcome to the club."

Rhys, however, frowned. "Why are you still smiling if she refused you?" He peered at Morgan closely. His eyes narrowed. "Wait a minute. I know that look. It's the glassy-eyed, satisfied look of a man who's been well and truly pleasured." His tone became accusing. "You slept with her, didn't you?"

"A gentleman never—"

"Bloody hell, Morgan!" Gryff thundered, not even waiting for him to finish.

"I *told* you he would, didn't I?" Rhys groaned. "What did I say?"

Morgan held up his hands. "I'm smiling because Harriet's given me a week to prove to her that I love her."

Rhys wrinkled his nose. "A week? That's not very long. And how the hell do you show a woman you love her? Flowers? Jewels? Coach-and-four?"

Morgan smiled. "I don't know about any woman, but I do know Harriet. She said my love for her is as real as one of the made-up streets on her maps."

"So what are you going to do to prove otherwise?"

"Make it real, of course."

Chapter Thirty-Seven

If Morgan was trying to prove his love, Harriet thought as she glared at him across Lady Bressingham's garden three days later, he was doing a terrible job of it.

She'd seen him at Lady Stevenson's musicale two days ago, and he hadn't even spoken to her. He'd simply sent her a friendly nod across the room and gone back to conversing with Letty Pickworth, a merry widow with a fortune as impressive as her cleavage.

Harriet had told herself she didn't care.

Now she'd been here, wandering around Lady Bressingham's garden for over an hour, and the blasted man hadn't even come over to greet her. He'd caught her eye—once—across the croquet lawn and sent her one of his patented secret smiles that managed to turn her knees to jelly, but he'd made no effort to approach. There he stood, looking unreasonably handsome in a dark gray coat and buff breeches, chatting casually with De Montfort, the two of them as thick as thieves.

Harriet fanned herself, both irked and confused as to why he seemed to be ignoring her. Perhaps he'd changed his mind, and decided that proving his love was too great a task?

Or perhaps he didn't love her at all.

Her heart gave an unpleasant little squeeze.

She turned away and pretended to listen to their hostess, Lady Bressingham, as she described the many ailments afflicting her long-suffering Pekinese dog Fluffy-Woo.

The animal was as overstuffed as the red velvet cushion on which he reclined. Harriet bit her lip and refrained from suggesting that most of Fluffy-Woo's problems could be solved by feeding him less and exercising him more.

She gulped down her half glass of lemonade and tried to look regretful. "Oh dear! I seem to be out of lemonade. I'm quite parched this afternoon—must be the heat. Do excuse me, Lady Bressingham."

The older woman nodded regally. "Yes, you're quite right. It is unseasonably warm."

Harriet was about to make her escape when Lady Bressingham caught her arm.

"Oh, Miss Montgomery. Before I forget! Anne Melville showed me the most amusing map you'd drawn for her when I went for tea the other day. The *Map of Love* or some such thing? I don't suppose you have any more copies, do you? I'd love to send one to my sister, down in Kent."

Harriet's smile was more genuine this time. "It's titled *A Map of the Heart*, and yes, I was planning to do a limited print run. I can reserve you one. Do send someone or call into the shop yourself whenever you have the time."

Lady Bressingham was the third person who'd asked for a copy in two days. *A Map of the Heart* seemed to have universal appeal, at least with the female half of the population.

Harriet started toward the house with an inward shake of the head. Everyone, in a sense, was a mapmaker. True, not many of them physically drew the maps they created, as she did, but every human made a mental map of their own, dotted with personal points of interest. Significant events were forever associated with certain physical locations: *Here's where I lost my shoe. Here's where we cried. Here's where we fell in love.*

That was why Maddie's garden was no longer just a neat black rectangle in Grosvenor Square. It was the place where Morgan had first kissed her, in a tunnel dripping with blooms. She'd never see Squeeze Gut Alley without recalling the way her heart had pounded at the hungry look on Morgan's face when she'd demanded kiss number three.

And she'd never be able to look at Paradise Court without a crushing sense of sadness and loss.

Unable to help it, she glanced back to search for Morgan in the crowd, but he was gone. She turned back and skirted an oak tree, irritated at her uncharacteristic melancholy, only to come face-to-face with the man himself.

She skidded to a stop with a startled, "Oh!"

His lips twitched at her obvious surprise.

She tried to think of something witty and cutting to say, but her brain refused to cooperate. Instead, she simply stared at him, her chest aching with longing.

A million words hovered on her tongue.

I was wrong to refuse you.

Ask me again.

I love you too.

Morgan, though, didn't seem to require conversation. He simply caught her wrist, unfurled her fingers, and pressed a folded piece of paper into her palm. Her treacherous heart leapt at even this simplest of touches, and her skin burned where he'd brushed it with his own.

She opened her mouth to say something, but he merely flashed her another of his cheeky, utterly confident grins, bowed, and strode away.

Harriet unfolded the paper and frowned down at it in confusion. It was a copy of her own map of central London. A particular area had been circled in pencil—in very much the same manner as she'd circled Squeeze Gut Alley when she'd sent her challenge to Morgan.

Her pulse began to thump with renewed excitement.

Was this a *challenge*?

She brought the map closer to see where, exactly, he'd chosen as their field of battle, and her brows drew together as she saw the location. Mystified, she turned the paper over, and found Morgan's unmistakably masculine handwriting scrawled across the back in ink the same deep blue as his naval uniform jacket.

Paradise Court.

Tomorrow. 7pm.

I'll send a carriage for you.

M.

What did he mean by this? How could she attend a rendezvous at a place that only existed in her imagination? Did he mean to show her the wall at the bottom of the Duke of Evesham's garden?

Oh, the man was infuriating!

But her heart was suddenly fluttering with the faintest stirrings of hope. Perhaps he hadn't given up on her after all.

Chapter Thirty-Eight

The following day Harriet could scarcely hide her nerves. She busied herself with printing another ten copies of *A Map of the Heart* and used her watercolors to tint the various points of interest. A bilious, envious yellow-green for Jealousy Isle. Deep red for the heart on the hanging sign of Tenderness Tavern. And the beautiful Prussian blue of Morgan's uniform for the water bubbling up from the Spring of Eternal Hope.

Her stomach clenched in anticipation. What *did* he have planned for tonight?

She pushed away the thought.

She'd sold six more copies of the map since she'd displayed one in the shopwindow yesterday; a constant crowd hovered outside, all of them peering through the glass and engaging in good-natured discussion as to its accuracy and omissions.

Harriet smiled. Word of mouth was good for business, and it seemed she'd inadvertently stumbled upon an extremely profitable new sideline. Few members of the general public ever required geographical maps, but there were plenty of people who appreciated a humorous commentary on love.

She might never be bold enough to start engraving satirical prints or erotic sketches to appeal to the masses, as Rowlandson and Hogarth had done so successfully, but there was clearly profit to be made in amusing projects like this. Every shilling that went into the cashbox was another step toward adventure and independence.

Father had almost completely recovered from his surgery; he'd stopped needing the laudanum and his increasing impatience to be up and about was a clear sign he was on the mend. He'd already bumped into the side table and knocked over his cup of tea this morning. Harriet had taken him for a short walk around their courtyard garden, leading him gently by the arm, and finally resorted to reading *Robinson Crusoe* aloud to him in an effort to get him to stay put.

Doctor Saunders paid them a visit. He removed Father's outer bandages and inspected his eyes, but despite Father's claims that he was ready to be done with them altogether, the doctor suggested waiting one more day until they discarded the dressings completely. Father had acceded to this decree with grouchy acceptance.

Harriet got more and more nervous as the afternoon progressed. She generally closed the shop at five, but since the evening was fair and there was still a smattering of potential customers gathered around the bay window, she left the door open for another hour. It was just starting to get dark when she locked the door, turned the sign to Closed, and stepped into the back room.

"I'm going out for a little while this evening, Father. Do you think you'll be all right on your own? Mrs. Jennings has just left, but I can ask Jem Cooper to come and sit with you for an hour or so if you want company."

Father, seated in his armchair by the fire, made a shooing gesture with his hands, barely missing *Robinson Crusoe* on the table.

"I'll be fine. No need to bother Jem. Where are you off to, Harry?"

Harriet was glad he couldn't see the guilty pink flush that heated her cheeks. She tried to think of something that wasn't an out-and-out lie.

"I'm going to Grosvenor Square. To Maddie's house." That was nearly true. Paradise Court theoretically bordered Maddie's garden. They even shared an adjoining wall. Or they *would* do, she amended silently, if Paradise Court actually existed.

Father nodded. "Oh, good. If you happen to see that Morgan Davies, tell him I can't wait to *see* him in person to thank him."

Harriet rolled her eyes fondly as he chuckled at his own joke, even as the mention of Morgan sent her pulse to pounding in her throat.

"I will. But I'm not certain he'll be there." That, too, wasn't completely untrue. Morgan had said he'd send a carriage for her at seven, but there'd been no indication that he would be in it. Surely he planned to be present if he meant to prove his love?

Harriet shook her head and went upstairs to change.

It was impossible to step into her bedroom and not think of Morgan. Every time she looked at her bed she imagined him there, but that entire evening had already taken on the aspect of a dream. She could hardly believe it had actually happened, that she'd *made love with Morgan Davies*. Right there. Sometimes she was convinced she could still smell his cologne on her pillow.

She wanted to make love to him again. Maybe tonight she'd pluck up the courage to tell him that.

Since she had no idea what kind of activity Morgan had planned, she donned a relatively simple dress of midnight blue and a matching spencer edged with velvet trim. Both were new additions to her wardrobe from the excellent Madame de Tourville, and she was pleased with the way the color brought out the gray of her eyes.

The fact that it was the exact color of Morgan's navy jacket was neither here nor there.

Her cheeks, when she glanced in the mirror, were flushed and her eyes sparkled with devilish excitement. Morgan did this to her. He brought her to life. He made her glow.

She snatched up a pair of gloves and a shawl, and descended the stairs just in time to hear a strange thump from the back room. Worried that Father had knocked his book dangerously close to the fire, she rushed forward, only to stop dead in the doorway.

The Frenchman De Caen stood by her father's chair, a wicked-looking pistol aimed at his head.

"Ah! Here she is! The little whore who lied to my face."

Harriet gasped. His tone was loud and jovial, a complete contrast to the insulting words and the terrifying threat of that pistol.

"Harriet?" Father wavered uncertainly. "What's going on?"

Harriet laid her gloves on the sideboard, keeping her eyes fixed on De Caen. She wasn't sure if her father knew there was a gun pointing at his head or not.

"We have an unexpected visitor," she said levelly, trying to keep the rising panic out of her voice. "I believe General De Caen wishes to speak to us."

De Caen gave a sarcastic congratulatory nod. The sheen of madness glittered in his eyes.

"So you know who I am. I'm honored, mademoiselle. Did your friend Captain Davies tell you about me?"

The venomous way he spat Morgan's name shot a chill of foreboding up Harriet's spine and she fought to divert his mind from the memory.

"How may we help you, sir?"

"You know how you can help me," De Caen sneered. "Your father is the mapmaker known as Crusoe. Is he not?"

Father's head jerked round and Harriet's stomach somersaulted at how vulnerable he appeared. With the two circular cotton bandages covering his eyes and his hair standing up in all directions, he looked like a tiny fledgling bird whose eyes had yet to open.

"How did you know that?" Father rasped.

De Caen's smile was not reassuring. "One of the junior officers at the Admiralty was *persuaded* to tell me."

Harriet's blood ran cold. The emphasis he put on the word *persuaded* made her certain the poor young man, whoever he was, was either dead or severely injured. She suddenly recalled Morgan's conviction that De Caen had killed his deputy: He would stop at nothing to get what he wanted. Her throat began to constrict with fear.

His gaze narrowed on her. "But now I see that your father is blind, mademoiselle, and I wonder whether *you* are not the cause of all my problems, hmm?"

There was little point in evading the truth now, so Harriet drew herself up tall. "You're quite right. I drew the Crusoe maps. And if I inconvenienced you in any way, then I'm glad."

De Caen's eyes glittered malevolently at her bravado. "Oho. Now I see why Captain Davies is so enamored." His lips stretched into a sickly smile. "Even in Martinique we heard tales of that sharp tongue of yours, mademoiselle. He cried your name after I had him whipped for his insolence."

His satisfied sneer turned her stomach, even as her heart clenched at the depth of Morgan's feelings for her. God, she'd been such an idiot. And now she might not even get to tell him how much she loved him.

"You know what I want," De Caen said softly. "A Crusoe map of the Caribbean. Martinique, to be precise. The last time I was here you swore you didn't have one." He used his thumb to cock the pistol, and her father's shoulders stiffened as he registered the implicit threat of the sound.

De Caen raised his brows. "Perhaps you'd like to reconsider?"

"Very well." There was only the tiniest tremor in her voice. "We do have a copy." She tilted her head toward the front room. "Through there. In the shop."

De Caen waved the pistol to indicate that she should move. "Get it for me."

She'd hoped he might come with her and put some distance between Father and the gun, but he stayed where he was.

Damn.

A glimpse through the bay window revealed that it was nearly dark: No potential ally—or witness—lingered outside on the street. Her own pistol, primed and loaded, sat on a shelf beneath the main counter. She hadn't been lying to Morgan when she'd told him about it. But De Caen had a direct view of that part of the shop and she didn't dare try to get it, not with Father so exposed.

Since there was nothing for it, she dragged the set of library steps across the room and unhooked the map of Martinique from the wall.

"Hurry!" De Caen ordered impatiently.

There was no large table in the back room, so she brought the frame to the counter, making sure she stood on the side usually reserved for the customers. As she'd hoped, the move drew De Caen away from her father's side. He brought the lamp from the back room and placed it on the counter, then leaned over the opposite side as she turned the accurate chart over to reveal the second map pinned to the reverse.

De Caen hissed out a breath of satisfaction. "Is that it? The map I need?"

"Yes."

He uncocked the pistol and placed it flat on the counter with a warning glance at her not to try anything stupid, then pulled a paper from his coat. He unfolded it and flattened it next to the Crusoe map. Harriet glanced at the engraver's cartouche: It was a map drawn by a French contemporary, Lionel Pascale. Ironically, famed for his accuracy.

De Caen slid his hand to a group of islands circled in pencil on his map, then glanced across to find the same islands on the Crusoe version. Harriet tried not to gag at the dirt embedded beneath his fingernails.

He stabbed an accusing finger down onto the cream paper. "I knew it! The Crusoe map is different!" He glared up at her, his sallow skin waxy in the lamplight. "Why this is so?"

She cleared her throat. "I assume you're referring to that archipelago there?"

He'd circled the southernmost island of the chain.

"Yes. Why does my map show two when your map shows five little islands?"

"Because I added some," she said defiantly. "And I moved them all six miles to the east, for good measure."

De Caen's eyelid twitched. "And why would you do that, mademoiselle?"

His tone was so lethally quiet that Harriet's rebelliousness quavered.

"Because that's what the Admiralty paid me to do. We created false maps to lead you and your countrymen astray."

De Caen's cheeks grew mottled with suppressed anger. "Little bitch! Do you know how long I wasted, looking for—" He stopped abruptly, biting off his impulsive words, but Harriet raised her brows.

"For Napoleon's gold?" she asked sweetly.

He glanced up, startled, and she enjoyed a brief moment of satisfaction at having surprised him, but when he grinned her stomach swooped in dread.

"Yes indeed. How do you know about that?"

She feigned a bravado she certainly didn't feel. "The Admiralty knows all about it. As does your own government. I expect both of them have men out there looking for it already."

De Caen's lip curled. "They won't find it. Only I know where to look."

She sent a pointed glance down at his map, then met his eyes.

"Not anymore."

Chapter Thirty-Nine

Harriet's heart was pounding in her throat. Why on earth was she taunting him? She should be placating him, feigning ignorance, trying to get him to leave.

But a coldly logical part of her knew De Caen had no intention of letting them go. Like his deputy, Garonne, they knew too much. Panic started to trickle through her veins.

De Caen began to chuckle, even as he picked up the pistol from the counter. He wiped the corner of his eye as if genuinely amused.

"Ah, *chérie*. You have such fire. I regret that I must put it out."

A flicker of movement from the back room snagged her attention and Harriet froze, as much in shock as by instinct; Father had pulled the dressings from his eyes. Over De Caen's shoulder she saw him blink several times, as if growing accustomed to the light. He swung his head around to glare at De Caen's back and rose silently from his chair, like some mythical sea monster rising from the deep.

Harriet's stomach somersaulted. Convinced De Caen would notice the direction of her gaze, she whipped her head back around to look at him.

"Don't shoot me!" Her voice was reedy with panic. "Please. I won't tell anyone, I swear."

De Caen pulled the hammer back with his thumb to cock the weapon. His eyes hardened as he pointed it at her chest. "I cannot take that risk."

Harriet stared at the black hole at the end of the pistol. Should she push the barrel away? Dive behind the counter?

"Wait!" she shrieked, bringing her hands up in front of her as if they could, miraculously, stop the bullet. "You're forgetting one thing."

De Caen paused, momentarily diverted. "And what's that?"

"My father!"

Harriet let her gaze flick behind him. De Caen half turned—just as Father swung the leather-bound copy of *Robinson Crusoe* at his head.

The thick book connected with a terrible sound against the Frenchman's ear. De Caen cursed and Harriet took full advantage—she grabbed the barrel of the pistol, thrusting it aside just as he pulled the trigger. It fired with a deafening roar and a flash; the bullet missed her head by a fraction of an inch and shattered one of the panes of glass in the bay window behind her.

The Frenchman staggered, and Father hit him again, then again.

"Get off my daughter, you cur!"

De Caen slumped against the counter, then crumpled to the floor, toppling the oil lamp as he fell. The glass globe shattered. Oil spattered the carpet and instantly caught alight.

Father let out a shout of dismay and leapt backward: The hem of his banyan robe was in flames.

Harriet rounded the counter and leapt over De Caen's

prone body. For a split second she couldn't think of what to do. She tried to beat the flames out with her bare hands, but that just spread the fire upward, toward Father's waist, fanned by her efforts.

"Harry!" Father grunted in alarm.

Harriet lunged into the back room and grabbed a vase of flowers from the sideboard. She dashed the contents at the front of Father's robe, daisies and all, but the splash of water only extinguished half the flames.

Father was twirling this way and that in agitation. She snatched his lap rug from the chair and tried to wrap it around his waist, but he wouldn't stand still.

An earsplitting crash interrupted her frantic efforts, and she glanced up to see Morgan come stumbling through the shop's glass front door, shoulder first.

Harriet blinked in astonishment. Shards of broken glass glittered like raindrops on the shoulders of his coat and in his hair. "Morgan!" she panted. "Help!"

He raced across the room, pulled the blanket from her hands, and tackled her father to the floor. Harriet gasped at such rough handling, but Morgan rolled her father over and over, smothering the flames with the rug.

Within a few moments the fire had been completely extinguished. Harriet stamped out the last remaining spots of oil that still flickered on the carpet, and both Morgan and Father sat up with a series of groans.

"Holy hell!" Morgan panted, draping his forearm over his bent knees and dropping his head in an attitude of weary exhaustion. "What in God's name happened here?"

Harriet gingerly helped her father to his feet and inspected him for damage. The thick cotton material of the banyan had, mercifully, been slow to burn where it hadn't been splashed with oil. His hands and face had not been damaged.

"Father, are you hurt?" she demanded shakily.

He shook his head. His hair was sticking out at all angles, like a haystack.

"Just a little shaken." He caught her shoulders in his hands and held her at arm's length, then let out an incredulous laugh. "And dear God, I can *see* you, Harry! Really see you, not just a blurry shape!"

He blinked, studying her features with such a look of wonder and affection that a lump formed in her throat. His thumb brushed her chin fondly.

Harriet stared into his eyes. The cloudy white lenses that had obscured his pupils for the past few years had gone.

She let out an unsteady breath and turned to Morgan. "Thank heavens you came."

Morgan clambered to his feet and gestured to the broken lamp on the floor. "What happened?"

A noise from behind the counter made all three of them turn and Harriet let out a groan of dismay. She'd forgotten about De Caen in all the excitement.

"Morgan, it's—"

She didn't have time to complete the sentence. The Frenchman emerged from behind the counter and her heart seized as she saw her own pistol in his hand; he must have found it on the shelf when he was down there on the floor.

Bloody hell.

His brows shot toward his hairline as he recognized Morgan, and an incredulous wheeze escaped him. "You! Even here you plague me."

Morgan had stilled, but he sent the Frenchman one of his most sarcastic smiles. Harriet had been the recipient of that particular look a dozen times: She knew just how infuriating it could be.

"Commander De Caen! What a pleasure to see you

again." His voice oozed insincerity. "I trust you're enjoying our famous English hospitality?"

De Caen cocked the weapon with a snarl. "A curse on this country!"

"You've only got one shot," Morgan said softly. He sidestepped, positioning himself squarely in front of Harriet. "And you'll have to kill me before you get near her again."

De Caen's lips curved in a mocking smile. "Oh, don't worry, Captain Davies. Killing you will be a pleasure."

Morgan lunged without warning. He swept his leg out and his boot connected with De Caen's knee with a horrible cracking sound. The Frenchman let out a scream of agony as his leg buckled beneath him.

"*Bâtard! Non!*" He collapsed on the floor, clutching his leg, as Morgan reached down and twisted the pistol from his grip with ruthless efficiency.

"Oh dear, not that knee again. How clumsy of me."

De Caen was screaming a litany of invectives at him now. His face was mottled with fury. He reached out and tried to grab Morgan's ankle, to pull him down, then tried to bite Morgan's calf, but Morgan evaded him with ease.

"That was for the flogging." Morgan caught his collar in his fist and hauled him partly off the floor. "And *this* is for threatening Harriet." He pulled back his fist and punched the Frenchman squarely in the jaw. De Caen's eyes rolled back in his head.

Harriet let out a squeal of dismay, but Morgan just made a disgusted sound as he released the other man's collar. De Caen slumped to the carpet, clearly unconscious.

"He's not dead, more's the pity. The bastard deserves it, but I'll be damned if I'll be court-martialed and hanged for murder." He glanced over at Harriet. "Do you have any rope? We'll tie him up and send for Melville. The Admiralty can deal with him."

"Here." Father untied the sash from his banyan robe and held it out.

"Thank you." Morgan rolled De Caen's limp body over none too gently, and made quick work of binding his hands and his feet behind him. Harriet couldn't help but be impressed at the speed with which he achieved it.

"I expect you learned all those complicated knots in the navy," she said faintly.

Morgan smiled. "Always comes in useful."

He stood, smoothing down his jacket, and Harriet reached over and brushed some broken glass from his shoulder. The urge to throw herself into his arms was almost overwhelming, but she bit her lip and forced herself to take a step backward instead.

"That was a very welcome rescue, Davies," Father said. He put his hands on his hips and gazed around the shop, taking in the chaos. The front door swung drunkenly on its hinges, the central pane of glass in ruins.

"Sorry about the door," Morgan said belatedly. "I'll pay for it, of course."

Father waved the offer away with a hearty chuckle. "Dear Lord. If you hadn't arrived, I dread to think what that scoundrel would have done. Shot us both, most likely. You saved our lives."

He turned in a full circle, his eyes scanning the proliferation of prints on the walls. "And as if that wasn't miracle enough for one night, I can *see* again." He let out an amazed sigh and turned back to Harriet. "What a gift! I never thought it would be possible." His voice quavered with emotion and Harriet felt tears gather in her own eyes.

Now that the danger was truly past, she felt sick and

shaky. The thought of what *could* have happened was terrifying.

Luckily, Morgan seemed quite accustomed to such stressful situations. He crossed to her worktable, picked up her silver pencil—the one he'd rescued all those years ago—and scrawled a hasty note. He stepped through the remnants of the front door and hailed his carriage, which must have been driving slowly around so as not to keep the horses waiting.

"This needs to go to Lord Melville immediately." He handed the folded note to his coachman. "Deliver it and come back here for me."

The man tipped his hat. "Aye, sir."

When the carriage had left, Morgan turned. "Harriet, why don't you get your father settled and make a cup of tea? I'll make sure this door is secure so you're not robbed in the night."

"I think we all need something a little stronger than tea after tonight's adventure." Father beamed. "You might as well go get the brandy, Harriet, and we'll toast our victory in style."

Harriet flicked a glance at Morgan, remembering the last time they'd drunk brandy together, and just knew her cheeks were coloring. The mischievous heat in his eyes convinced her he was recalling it, too, and her stomach somersaulted.

"Yes, of course." She glanced down as De Caen groaned and stirred. "What about him?"

Morgan's lips quirked. "Oh, he does *not* get any brandy. He's been a naughty boy."

Chapter Forty

It took less than an hour for Lord Melville to arrive with two uniformed sailors. De Caen had regained consciousness and was busy shouting his displeasure to anyone who would listen, and Harriet watched in satisfaction as he was bundled roughly into Melville's carriage.

"Did you find the man he used for information?" she asked, dreading the answer.

Melville nodded, his expression grim. "Yes. We stopped at the Admiralty on the way here and found one of our clerks had been ambushed in the lane behind the mews. De Caen beat him badly with his cane. The chap's got a few broken ribs, but he'll live."

"Thank goodness. When he said he'd 'persuaded' someone to reveal who Crusoe was, I thought he might have killed him."

"I should have hit him harder." Morgan glowered. "And wrecked his *other* knee."

"He'll look back on your beating with fondness, I expect, when his countrymen get hold of him," Melville said darkly. "I doubt he'll have much fun in a French prison."

"It'll be a taste of his own medicine," Morgan said with satisfaction. "He'll be lucky if nobody flogs him and throws him into solitary."

Harriet winced at the reminder of how Morgan himself had suffered. She crossed to the counter and gathered up the map De Caen had annotated.

"I believe this, if used in conjunction with a Crusoe map, will show where he buried the gold meant for Bonaparte."

Melville folded the paper and slipped it into his coat. His eyes twinkled mischievously. "No need to tell the French about this particular development, hmm?"

Morgan chuckled. "Not until we've made a copy, and got a head start, at least."

"We're not at war with France anymore, gentlemen." Harriet shook her head, not sure whether to disapprove of or condone such shameless maneuvering.

Neither of them looked the least bit abashed.

"Of course we're not," Melville said smoothly. "Which is why His Majesty's government will be extremely sympathetic if the gold *happens* to have disappeared by the time the French arrive."

"Amazing how many pirates there are in those waters," Morgan echoed drily. "All manner of disreputable characters."

"Precisely." Melville beamed.

Harriet shook her head.

"It seems your country owes you another debt, Davies," Melville said. "And you, too, Harriet. Rest assured, I'll let Prinny know who to thank for putting De Caen behind bars."

"Thank you, sir."

An outraged bellow sounded from the carriage as De Caen made his displeasure known, and Melville sighed. "Well, must be off. I trust you're both coming to Anne's little gathering next week?"

Harriet nodded. Melville climbed into the carriage and the two of them watched in silence as it rumbled away down the street.

Finally, Morgan turned to her. "I assume, since you're a Montgomery—and therefore incredibly stubborn—that a man has to do more than simply bash down a door, extinguish a burning man, and shield you from a bullet in order to prove his love."

Harriet met his eyes. "Well, as to that, I—"

"No." Morgan raised his hands as if to ward her off, even though a smile lingered at the corners of his mouth. "I know you and your ridiculously high standards. *Normal* heroism isn't enough. You need something extraordinary."

"I really don't—"

"You really do."

Her heart turned over at the look in his eye. It was amused and loving, wicked and sexy, all at the same time.

"Mister Montgomery?" He raised his voice so it carried to her father in the next room. "Before all this excitement, I'd planned to take your daughter on an outing. There's something I wanted to show her. Something I hope she'll like."

Father appeared in the doorway and sent Morgan a level stare. The fact that he could *see* them, from right across the room, was a miracle Harriet hadn't yet fully accepted.

"I thought you were going to Maddie's house?" Father frowned.

"It's next door," Morgan said.

"But it will just be the two of you? Unchaperoned?"

Harriet felt heat warming her cheeks, but Morgan seemed as at ease as ever.

"If that's acceptable to you, sir?"

The subtext behind the words made Harriet's stomach twist. Morgan wasn't just asking permission for a carriage ride alone. He was asking if Father agreed to them courting in general. To them being a couple.

Father sent them both a long look. And then his face broke out into a smile as he opened his arms wide for Harriet to come and hug him. "If it would make Harriet happy, then you have my blessing."

Harriet crossed the room and hugged him tightly. "I think it would make me very happy," she murmured into his shoulder.

Father pressed a kiss to the top of her head. "Oh, Harry. I know the sacrifices you've made for me these past few years. You're the best daughter a man could have. Thank you." His arms tightened as he bent and whispered in her ear, "Go. Take something for yourself. Even if it *must* be one of those devilish Davieses."

He pulled back and shooed her away, but not before she saw the betraying sheen of tears in his eyes. He cleared his throat. "Well, off you go then. And Davies?"

"Yes, sir?"

"Take good care of my daughter."

Morgan nodded, and sent Harriet a simmering look from beneath his lashes. "Yes, sir. I intend to." He offered her his arm, elbow bent. "Come along, Miss Montgomery. Adventure awaits."

When they were safely ensconced in the carriage and rattling down Bury Street, Harriet sent Morgan a questioning look. She'd expected him to sit next to her on the seat, but instead he'd kept his distance and settled his long, elegant frame on the bench across from hers.

"Well, what a night!" she breathed.

Morgan made a wry face. "Not exactly the evening I

had planned, but no matter. One should never complain about a bit of excitement. Makes one appreciate the quiet times all the more."

"I didn't think you adventurous types liked quiet times?"

Her tone was teasing, but Morgan answered her with perfect seriousness.

"Of course we do. I can't tell you how often I've *longed* for quiet times. Especially after weeks at sea on a boat with thirty other men, all shouting and laughing, singing and quarreling."

Harriet smiled.

"There's a lot to be said for being alone," Morgan said quietly.

"Don't you get lonely?"

He shrugged. "Being alone isn't the same as being lonely. It's possible to be lonely in a room full of people." His gaze snagged on hers. "Do you ever get lonely, Harriet? Because I do."

Harriet blinked at this unexpected admission. She'd never imagined Morgan would tell her something so personal, or make himself so vulnerable. "You? But you're the *ton*'s golden boy. Invited everywhere. Always surrounded by people."

By women, she added silently.

His mouth made a cynical little quirk. "Yes, I have friends. Plenty of people I can go to the opera with, or drink with at the club. People I can converse with for an hour or so."

Ladies to warm my bed at the click of my fingers.

"But that's not the problem."

"Then what is?"

His eyes bored into hers. "It's finding someone to do *nothing* with, that's the real test. Someone with whom to just sit and read by the fire. Someone to eat dinner with. To converse with, or *not* converse, as the mood takes us."

Harriet's heart was hammering against her ribs.

I want to be that person. I want to do nothing and everything with you.

She didn't say it. Instead, she reached into the pocket of her cloak and brought out the map he'd pressed into her hand in Lady Bressingham's garden.

"All right, out with it. Where are you taking me? Because we both know there's no such place as Paradise Court."

The smile he sent her was full of mischief, as if he knew the last line of a joke and could barely wait to deliver it. But being the irritating, enigmatic brute that he was, he ignored her question entirely.

"Have you ever considered that mapmakers like you *need* sailors like me?"

She raised her brows at his cocky, self-congratulatory tone. "Oh, really? How so?

"Because we're the ones who fill in all your empty spaces."

Her pulse stuttered at the double meaning in those words, and she wondered if he'd used them deliberately. Knowing Morgan, the answer was undoubtedly yes. He rarely did things without purpose.

And it was true. He filled her. Not just from a crude, physical standpoint, but emotionally too.

He leaned forward and rested his forearms on his knees, narrowing the gap between them.

"The greatest sailing expeditions have unfurled the edges of the world. Sailors like me have shown what lies in the places where all it said was 'Here Be Dragons.'"

Harriet was determined to match his teasing tone. "So you could say that 'sailors like you' are guilty of ruining the mystery. 'Here Be Dragons' allows people to dream. You, good sir, have killed the romance. You've banished the dragons and replaced them with boring old rivers and hills."

He grinned at her, clearly loving the fact that she was countering him at every turn. "I think you should reserve judgment on how dead romance is until we arrive at our destination." He glanced out of the window and lifted his brows. "Ah, Grosvenor Square. Perfect. I've given the driver directions to go around the back."

Harriet peered through the glass as Maddie's house sped by, then the knockerless black door of the Duke of Evesham's property. Lights shone from Maddie's front room, but the Evesham place was its usual dark shell. The carriage turned the corner and slowed as the driver maneuvered the horses into the narrow lane that led to the mews behind the houses.

The carriage rocked to a stop and Morgan jumped down impatiently, then reached up and helped Harriet down the steps.

She peered around, not entirely certain what she was expecting to see. A few lamps illuminated the stables on one side of the lane, and on the other side the imposing brick walls surrounded the row of gardens attached to each house.

Morgan still hadn't relinquished her hand. He drew her forward until he stopped in front of a narrow wooden door in the wall. From its position Harriet estimated it must lead directly into the Duke of Evesham's garden.

She frowned. The door looked new. The bricks around it had been disturbed, and the mortar was a different color from the rest of the wall.

Morgan squeezed her hand and she turned her attention to him. "You said my love for you was as real as your Paradise Court." He caught the iron door handle, swung the door open, and tried to pull her through.

Harriet resisted. "We can't go in there; we'll be trespassi—"

Her protest was cut off with a gasp of shock as she saw what lay within.

Chapter Forty-One

Harriet stopped short only a few steps through the gate. She'd expected a dark and unkempt garden. What she saw was Paradise Court.

She gazed around, utterly lost for words. The scene was magical, like some fairy-tale dream. A cherry tree had been planted in the center of the courtyard. Its pale blossoms gleamed in the light from scores of lanterns that had been hung from its branches, each one containing a flickering candle. Beneath her feet a gravel path led around the tree on both sides, bypassing the flower beds that had been planted in each corner with pleasing geometric symmetry. Four smaller pathways branched off in the four directions of the compass.

Exactly as she'd drawn on her map.

Her heart started to pound. What a grand, foolish, wonderful gesture.

An iron bench had been placed at the far end of the walk, and more lanterns glowed on either side of it, suspended from metal stakes pushed into the ground.

"Ah, I'm glad the candles are still alight," Morgan said softly. "We took longer than expected at your house."

She could feel his gaze on the side of her face. He still hadn't let go of her hand.

"You've been busy," she managed breathlessly. "How on earth did you convince the duke to let you do this to his garden?"

Morgan's soft chuckle made her stomach swoop. "I didn't have to convince him of anything. It's not his garden anymore."

That made her turn. "What do you mean?"

"I bought it. Not just the garden. The house too."

Her mouth dropped open. "What? How? I thought you said he'd never sell."

"Oh, Oliver put in a good word for me. He reminded the duke I'd saved his life on Martinique. Evesham gave me a very good deal." A satisfied smile curved his mouth.

Harriet shook her head, still amazed. "You'll live next door to Gryff and Maddie."

Morgan squeezed her hand. "*We'll* live next door to Gryff and Maddie . . . if you'll reconsider my proposal."

He turned more fully toward her and his free hand came up to tuck a wayward strand of hair behind her ear.

"I love you. I've *always* loved you. Even when I hated you." His lips quirked and he shook his head at that wonderful contradiction. "You're etched into me like one of your maps. Engraved upon my heart. You're a fire in my brain that I never want to put out."

The walls surrounding them gave the garden a magical feel, like a fairy bower, and Harriet blinked several times to make absolutely certain she wasn't dreaming. She opened her mouth to say something, but her throat felt hot and scratchy, and to her utter mortification she felt tears sting her eyes. She gulped and tried to blink them back, but one treacherous teardrop slipped out and ran down her cheek.

Morgan saw it, of course. His lips curved in that smile

she loved so well and her heart almost stopped as he tenderly cupped her jaw and rubbed his thumb across her cheekbone, as if polishing the wetness into her skin.

"Don't cry," he murmured. "This was supposed to make you happy, not sad."

Another tear slid down her nose and gathered at the corner of her mouth. Morgan bent and pressed his lips to the tiny drop. His tongue flicked out to taste it, and when he straightened he gazed deep into her eyes.

"You're salty. Like all the important things in life. Tears. Sweat. The sea."

Harriet finally found her voice. "*Am* I important to you? Truly?"

"You're indispensable," he said solemnly. "My love for you is as deep and as dark as the ocean."

"But will you *leave* me for the sea?" she pressed.

He raised his brows, and the humor returned to his face. "Well, as to that, I should probably tell you that I'm no longer Captain Morgan Davies of His Majesty's Royal Navy. I've resigned my commission."

"But you love sailing!"

"I love you more. And if I have to choose between the two of you, then I choose you." He gave an elegant shrug. "I was going to do it anyway. Now that the war's over the navy has far more captains than it needs."

"But isn't there a chance Bonaparte might escape again? He managed it from Elba, after all."

"He's being sent to St. Helena this time. He'll never escape from there. It's an island right in the middle of the Atlantic, miles from anywhere."

Harriet sent him a chiding smile. "I know where it is."

He grinned. "Of course you do, Madame Map."

"But what will you do if you're not in the navy?"

"I still plan to sail. The coal from our mine needs transporting from place to place. I'm going to buy my own ship and do that."

"Will you be away for long stretches of time?"

"Not at all. I told Gryff you were going to be my wife and you wouldn't like it."

Harriet's eyes grew wide and heat stung her cheeks. "You told him that? Oh, God! That was a little presumptuous, wasn't it?"

"Maybe. But I had hope. Even when you turned me down." Morgan smiled. "Rhys said I must have really buggered up my proposal, and for once he was right. I'll do it properly this time."

Before Harriet could protest, he bent down on one knee, reached into his coat, and pulled out a small leather-covered box.

Her heart was pounding so hard she could hear it in her ears, and when he opened the box to reveal a ring comprised of a huge blue sapphire surrounded by diamonds she couldn't hold back her gasp of delight.

"Harriet Jane Montgomery, will you marry me? I promise to show you adventures and tease you every day for the rest of your natural life."

Harriet caught his hand and tugged him to his feet as joy warmed her from the inside out. "Yes, I'd love that. Yes!"

She threw herself into his arms and he gathered her to him with a crow of triumph.

Oh, he was going to be unbearable now.

But at least he was going to be hers.

Their lips met in a kiss that started out desperate but quickly gentled into something closer to worshipful. Morgan kissed her like a man who'd been starved of sensation. As if she was something sweet, his first taste of sorbet, and he was savoring the taste.

Harriet tasted him back, delighting in the sybaritic pleasure of discovery, loving the low growl that rumbled from his chest as she stroked her hands through his hair and along the back of his neck.

Time flowed around them like treacle. Harriet's knees almost buckled at the way he teased her, deliberately refusing to rush, creating a wicked pleasure-pain of longing.

Minutes or perhaps hours later, he tore his mouth from hers and glanced toward the house in front of them. "I forgot to ask. Will you live in this stupidly big house with me? Your father can have an entire floor of his own, if you want him here with us."

Harriet took a much-needed gasp of breath. "I'll ask him. He might prefer to stay at the shop, now that he has his sight back. At least for a while."

Morgan nodded and took a cooling step back from her. "Do you want to look inside?"

"Why not?" Her euphoric mood made everything seem light.

He threaded his fingers through hers and together they rounded the cherry tree and stepped through a second door in the back wall that Harriet hadn't noticed before.

It opened on to the traditional garden she'd been expecting. The courtyard only took up a third of the total plot, and, just like Maddie's garden next door, the rest seemed to be a grassy, tree-lined oasis. It was hard to see in the moonlight, but it appeared to be relatively well-maintained.

Morgan led her across the shadowed grass and up the shallow steps of a terrace, edged with a stone balustrade. He produced an iron key from his pocket and fitted it to the lock on the back door, which opened with the easy glide of well-oiled hinges. No dusty, haunted-house cobwebs greeted them, and Harriet let out a silent exhale of relief.

Morgan seemed to read her mind. "The duke kept this place ready to live in at a moment's notice, even though he never came. He had servants clean it every few weeks."

They stepped into a high-ceilinged hallway and Harriet was surprised to see the shrouded shapes of dust-sheet-covered furniture all around.

"The whole house is furnished," Morgan said. "I bought the entire contents, lock, stock, and barrel. The only things he wanted were a couple of paintings, portraits of his ancestors, which I gladly agreed to. I certainly don't want people who resemble Oliver De Montfort staring at me while I eat my breakfast."

Harriet bit back a smile. "That's a shame. He's very pleasing on the eye."

Morgan squeezed her hand.

"But not nearly as pleasing as you," she finished dutifully, biting back a laugh.

"That's right," Morgan grunted. "Good answer."

He picked a candle and tinderbox from a side table and lit it, and Harriet followed him around the rooms in a state of awed wonder.

"You can sell anything you don't like," Morgan said. "Do whatever you want to the place. Paper every inch of wall with maps, floor to ceiling. I don't care, as long as you live here with me."

Harriet shook her head, still a little dazed at the enormity of his gesture. "How did you get all that work done in the garden without Maddie noticing?"

Morgan snorted. "Oh, she noticed. I had to swear her to secrecy on pain of death. Gryff too. In fact, they were instrumental in helping oversee the planting when I couldn't be here."

"You Davieses are so sneaky!"

"You'll be a Davies soon."

Harriet chuckled. "I think I finally see your nefarious plan. If every Davies male marries a Montgomery female, there will be none of us left. You'll claim victory for wiping us out."

"Damn," Morgan groused, with faux annoyance. "You've seen through our dastardly plot. Unfortunately, Tristan got his own back by turning Carys from a Davies to a Montgomery, but if you marry me, we'll be one bride ahead."

"And I suppose if we ever have children," Harriet said softly, "I'll be responsible for creating even more dastardly Davieses."

He turned to her. "Do you want children?"

Harriet considered this for only a moment. "Well, yes, I'd like to have some eventually, if possible. But I want you to myself for a little while first, if you don't mind? I want some adventures with just the two of us."

Morgan nodded. "That's fine with me."

Harriet sent him a naughty glance from under her lashes. "Speaking of adventures . . . I assume there are some beds in this ridiculously large house?"

His brows rose in wicked interest. "Why, Miss Montgomery. Surely you're not suggesting we make use of them?"

She took the candle from his hand and started up the imposing staircase. He followed with flattering alacrity.

"As a matter of fact, I am."

Chapter Forty-Two

The first bedroom Harriet found sported an imposing four-poster bed, and she sent Morgan an accusing look when she saw it had already been dressed with fresh linens, pillows, and a luxurious-looking counterpane.

"You, Morgan Davies, are extremely presumptuous."

"*Hopeful*," he amended with a chuckle. "I was hopeful. As a captain I learned to plan for all eventualities."

He took the candle from her hand and went around the room, lighting an assortment of lamps and bending to kindle the fire that had been laid in the grate. When he finished, he came to stand in front of her, and the hungry look in his eyes made her heart pound in earnest.

His gaze dropped to her lips; they tingled in response.

"When I was alone, locked in my cell, I closed my eyes and imagined you there with me."

His voice was serious, but she couldn't resist teasing him, just a little. "You wanted me to suffer too? To share in your punishment?"

He shook his head. "If you'd been there, neither of us would have suffered. I would have passed the time by kissing you. Making love with you. Hours would have stretched to infinity. Time would have ceased to exist. I could have stayed in there forever. All I need is you."

Her heart felt like it was opening like a flower. "Perhaps you should demonstrate?"

His gaze flashed back to hers and her heart somersaulted at the wicked promise she read there. "My pleasure."

His fingers, when he slid them around the nape of her neck, were warm and ever so slightly rough, and when he kissed her she felt time slip away, just as he'd promised.

"Wait!" she panted breathlessly. "This time, I want to see you naked."

His face was a picture of surprise, which quickly changed to a look of arrogant amusement. "I *knew* you'd hate not seeing everything. An incomplete map drives you insane."

Harriet scowled at how well he knew her. "It's only fair. You've seen *me* naked."

"Very well." He gestured to one of the large wing armchairs that flanked the fire. "Take a seat."

Bemused, and enchanted by his playfulness, she sank into the chair, and watched with unashamed enthusiasm as he made quick work of stripping off his jacket and cravat. He toed off his boots, then pulled the tails of his shirt out of his breeches and sent her a teasing, questioning glance.

She made a regal motion with her hand. "Off with it, Davies."

"Aye aye, ma'am."

Her mouth grew dry as he tossed the linen aside to reveal the glorious expanse of tawny chest and a ridged abdomen sprinkled with hair.

Dear Lord, he was beautiful. His arms rippled with muscle and her fingers itched to touch him, to feel the astonishing topography of those dips and curves. He was an entire continent: flat planes and mountain ridges, blue-veined rivers and shadowed clefts just begging to be explored.

She meant to tell him this. But all that emerged from her mouth was a strangled wheeze: "Huhhhh."

Morgan sent her a laughing, knowing look. "I'll assume that's not a sound of disgust, and continue?" He slid his hands to the button of his falls, paused, and shot her a provocative look from beneath his lashes. "*Shall* I continue?"

Harriet gripped the arms of the chair and managed to nod. Everything inside her felt hot and restless.

He unbuttoned his falls and stepped out of his breeches. When he straightened, he was fully naked—and fully aroused.

Harriet bit her lip, certain her cheeks were red from more than the heat of the fire. *Good God!* She'd thought the men in the drawings he'd given her were comically exaggerated, but Morgan was equally well-endowed. That part of him, so proudly male, reared up from a thatch of curly dark hair between thighs that were heavy and rippling with muscle.

She'd seen a statue of Neptune once, in the middle of an enormous fountain. He'd been constructed along similar, epic lines, all glorious sinew and rippling muscles as he whipped up a stampede of plunging water horses with his trident. His bottom half had, disappointingly, been shielded by some frothy, rolling waves, but Harriet could only imagine the rest of him would have been as glorious to behold as Morgan.

"Shall I get the smelling salts?" Morgan teased. "You look a little faint, Miss Montgomery."

Harriet finally snapped out of her trance. "Show me what to do," she croaked. "How to touch you. To please you."

"Don't you remember the drawings in that book I gave you?"

She nodded, and he took a step closer.

"Do what they were doing," he said. "Touch me wherever you like."

His knees nudged her own, through her skirts, and despite the fact that he was looming over her she experienced a rush of power at the fact that he was naked while she was still fully clothed. The contrast was unexpectedly thrilling.

In a flash, she recalled the image of a woman's hand wrapped around the man's member. She reached out and gently closed her fingers around his cock. It was warmer than she expected, soft skin over incredibly hard ridged muscle.

Above her, Morgan hissed out a breath. "Bloody hell, Harriet. Harder. Hold me harder."

He reached down and curled his larger fingers around hers, then slid their joined fists up and down, showing her the rhythm. "God, that feels so good."

He bent over her, propping his left arm on the back of the chair for support while his right hand continued to move with hers. When she caught the rhythm he released her, and her heart sang at the sound of his ragged breathing.

Growing bolder, she slowed the pace and leaned forward, and licked the tip of him with her tongue.

He let out a torturous groan and she smiled up at him, seized by a wicked, heady confidence. "Hmm. You taste salty. Like all good things in life."

Her shook his head at her cheekiness, even as he pulled free of her grip. "That's enough of that, or this'll be over before we begin. Your turn."

He stepped back and gestured for her to rise, and

when she did so he retreated, sinking back into his own wing chair and lounging there like some glorious fallen angel.

"Off with it, Montgomery!" he growled. "Remind me of what I've been missing."

Emboldened by the look in his eyes, Harriet removed her dress, and quickly unlaced her stays. He watched, silent, as she let her petticoats drop to the floor, then caught the hem of her shift and pulled it over her head.

He sucked in a breath as she stood there in just her shoes and stockings, her heart thundering as she waited for his verdict. The heat from the fire warmed her left side, but her nipples were tight and her stomach swirled in something akin to panic.

His gaze roved over her in a caress she could *feel*. He focused on the place between her legs, and when he bit his lip, her knees went a little weak.

"Think we should revisit kiss number three?" His voice was a silky purr, rough around the edges. "Are you wet there, Harry? Tell me the truth."

Harriet pressed her knees together and tried to stop the ache that pulsed between her legs. "Maybe."

His chest rose and fell in great uneven breaths. "I want to touch you. Come here."

Nervous, but willing to try whatever he wanted, Harriet stepped up until her stocking-clad knees touched his.

"Widen your legs."

He placed a hand on each of her hips, drawing her forward until she straddled his lap in the chair. Harriet hitched in a breath. The move brought her breasts directly level with his face. She hovered above him, her thighs splayed wide over his, and she'd never felt so open, so exposed, in her life. Scared that she might lose her balance, she grasped his shoulders, and her fingers dug into the muscles there as though he were a life raft in a storm.

His own fingers tightened on her hips and he made a strangled sound of longing in his throat.

"God, Harry."

He leaned forward and pressed his mouth to her throat, a whisper of sensation, and she shuddered with need. Still holding her hips, he rained kisses on her eyelids, her cheeks, her chin, and then dropped his head and drew her nipple into his mouth.

She sucked in a wondrous breath.

His hands slid upward, molding the curve of her waist, testing the bumps of her ribs until they swept round to cup her breasts. Harriet arched her back, wordlessly offering herself, and he teased her with his tongue, swirling and tugging on her nipple until she writhed in frustration.

He cupped her bottom, fingers splaying wide over her skin, and she realized his erection was right there, below her. Achingly close.

But instead of lowering her down, he slid his hand between her legs, and she groaned in need as he played and teased. He reclaimed her mouth, kissing her deeply as his fingers entered her in a slow, decadent slide.

Her blood felt as if it was on fire. She rocked her hips, urging him to continue the delicious torture. He was like a fever, an infection she might never recover from. Never *wanted* to recover from.

The hungry swirls of his tongue matched the movement of his fingers and she writhed, instinctively trying to hit the spot that felt good. Just when she thought she could take it no more, he withdrew his hand and reached between them, positioning his cock at the slick entrance to her body.

They both stilled. Harriet was shaky with need, her heart pounding, as she opened her eyes and met his stare.

"Lower yourself down," he rasped. "Take me. It's up to you."

Chapter Forty-Three

Harriet held Morgan's gaze as she slowly, *slowly*, did as he commanded. The tip of him slid inside her and she hissed out a breath at the absolute miracle of the feeling.

His eyes were completely black, his pupils huge, and she had the strangest sensation of falling, of being sucked down, fathoms deep. She wrapped her arms around his neck and watched a muscle tick in his jaw as she slid an inch lower.

Her own eyes almost rolled back in her head. He'd been inside her before, but the angle of this position was completely different. Here, she could control the depth of his penetration. Her inner muscles squeezed him, fluttering and clenching as if to pull him even deeper, and she sank even lower, drawing a tortured groan from his chest.

"Oh, God, don't stop. You feel so good."

As if he couldn't help himself, he rolled his hips and slid fully home, and Harriet gasped at the utter perfection of the fit. There was none of the discomfort of last time. It was like diving into the ocean and feeling the water conform exactly to her skin. *How* it worked was a mystery, but the astonishing, irrefutable fact was that he was inside her, joined to her, body to body, heart to heart.

Soul to soul.

She'd never felt more connected to anyone in her life.

And then he began to move. Harriet dropped her forehead to his as he guided her along his length and she caught the rhythm, moving up and down with breath-stealing deliberation. Pleasure rippled along her limbs as he rubbed a spot inside her, and she chased the feeling, grinding her hips shamelessly as the sensation wound her tighter and tighter.

She closed her eyes, straining to reach the highest peak, and with a glorious rush the pleasure caught up with her, pitching her off the edge of the world and into throbbing, blood-singing ecstasy.

Morgan thrust once, twice, then pulled out of her. He pressed himself hard against her thigh and she felt his body convulse as he, too, found his climax with her name on his lips.

Utterly spent, as weak and as boneless as if she'd survived a shipwreck, she dropped her head to his shoulder and pressed a kiss to his sweat-slick skin.

It took several minutes for her heart to return to something approximating a normal rhythm, but eventually she lifted her head and sent Morgan a sleepy smile.

"So much for trying out the bed."

Morgan let out a sigh of utter repletion. "Maybe next time. You, Harriet Montgomery, lead a man disastrously off course."

"Like my maps," she teased.

He shook his head and moved her from his lap, gently disengaging their bodies. Her legs were shaky when she stood, and she blushed when he reached down and dealt with the wetness he'd left on her skin with brisk efficiency.

Her heart gave an odd little flip as she realized he hadn't finished inside her. Tonight's adventures wouldn't result in a baby. The thought of bearing Morgan's children made her heart sing, but for purely selfish reasons she wanted him to herself for a little while.

"We'd better get married quickly," she said. "I want to keep on doing that with you without having to sneak around."

Morgan smiled as he ushered her over to the bed and drew back the sheets, gesturing for her to get in. She did so, and he slid in beside her, gathering her into his arms as if it was the most natural thing in the world. Harriet bit back a sigh of utter happiness.

"How about I ask the Archbishop for a special license?" He pressed a kiss to the top of her head. "He gave one to Tristan. And to Gryff, come to think of it. I'll say we have extenuating circumstances."

"And what might those be?"

"That I can't keep my hands off my fiancée for the three weeks necessary for the banns to be read?"

"I'm sure the Archbishop will love that."

"I'm sure he won't. But I'll remind him that I recently sponsored his cousin, one Tom Manners-Sutton, for a promotion, and provided him with a glowing letter of recommendation. That should sweeten him up."

Harriet shook her head in mock disapproval. "You seem to know how to bribe and blackmail practically everyone in the *ton*. First the Duke of Evesham, and now the Archbishop of Canterbury."

"I prefer to think of it as 'calling in favors,'" Morgan murmured. "It's how the *ton* works, by and large. It's just one enormous, tangled net of who knows who. And who knows *what* about who. I have enough ammunition against everyone that matters to ensure we'll never be bothered by gossip."

"I think another Davies marrying another Montgomery will cause its own gossip," she said sleepily. "We're supposed to be sworn enemies. People will be wondering what's become of the feud."

"We'll keep it going." He chuckled. "In our own particular way. I'll keep teasing you to distraction in public, if you like. It's a habit that's going to be hard to break."

Harriet smiled against his chest. She spread her palm over his heart and felt it beating, steady and true within his chest.

"Very well. We can be enemies who just happen to sleep together. We can fight a little, love a lot."

"That sounds like the perfect recipe for a happy marriage. Anything *too* perfect would be dull. I need you to fire a warning shot across my bows every now and then to keep me on my toes."

"I will definitely do that."

"Do you think your father's expecting you home tonight?"

"No. I think he's accepted the inevitable fact that he's about to get a devilish Davies as a son-in-law."

"In that case—" Morgan threaded his fingers through hers and kissed her lips. Harriet kissed him back, and to her amazement she felt him grow hard again against her belly. She laughed up at him, scandalized. "Again, Davies?"

In a lightning move, he rolled her over onto her back and kissed her down into the bed, supporting his weight on his elbows. "Absolutely again. I have years of fantasies to make up for."

She gave a delighted giggle and wrapped her arms and legs around him like a barnacle. "So do I."

They both groaned as he slid into her again. Harriet spread her hands over his shoulders, loving the weight and the feel of him, creating a whole new sensory map in her mind.

"What were you saying about kisses four, five, and six . . . ?"

Epilogue

Harriet Montgomery married Morgan Davies in the breakfast room of their new house on Grosvenor Square, in the presence of a select group of family members.

Harriet's cousins, Maddie and Tristan, were there, with their respective Davies spouses, Gryff and Carys, as well as Morgan's brother Rhys, Harriet's father, and the Aunts, Constance and Prudence.

Contrary to Pru's prediction, no natural disaster occurred on the occasion of yet another Davies-Montgomery union. Lightning did not streak across the sky. Birds failed to fall from the trees in portent. And the river Thames did not suddenly start flowing backward.

All in all, it was generally agreed to be a delightful affair. The bride and groom looked suitably enamored, tears and smiles abounded, and Rhys, as the last unmarried Davies, looked exceptionally relieved to be the last man standing.

Aunt Prudence, however, managed to ruin his mood. She cornered him as he sidled toward the refreshments table.

"I don't know why you're looking so happy, young man."

Rhys frowned, a sandwich from the wedding breakfast suspended halfway to his mouth. "It's a wedding. Aren't I supposed to be happy?"

Aunt Pru sent him a smug look. "I expect you're thinking you're the lucky one. That you've been spared the terrible fate of falling for a Montgomery."

"And so I have," Rhys said with a grin. "My siblings have very kindly married all the available Montgomerys, so there's no chance of the same thing happening to me."

Aunt Constance, seated to Pru's left, gave a witchy little cackle. "Oh, sweet boy. He's forgotten."

"Forgotten what?" Rhys said warily. He hadn't spent much time around these two batty old spinsters, but his brief experience had taught him that they just loved to meddle.

"Why, the *other* Montgomerys, of course."

Rhys suddenly found it hard to swallow. A nasty, tingling sensation that felt horribly like premonition made the hairs on the back of his neck stand up.

"There are more of you?"

Constance nodded and started another row of her knitting. "Well, of course there are more. It's just that we don't often speak of them." She sent Pru a laughing, sidelong glance. "Not in *polite* society, at any rate."

Rhys's heart began to pound. He absolutely did not believe in fate, or destiny, or any of that rot, but there was something about this conversation that was making him decidedly uneasy.

"Why don't you speak about them?" He was intrigued, despite himself.

"Because they're the *wild* branch of the family." Pru chuckled. "I swear, our Caroline could give your Carys a run for her money. And as for her sisters—"

Constance shook her head sadly. "Well, the less said about those two hoydens the better. Twins." She sent Rhys a meaningful glance that managed to convey both disapproval and reluctant admiration.

Rhys took a deep swig of his champagne. "How come I've never heard of them?"

"Oh, they're the Wessex branch of the family, but they haven't been in England for years. Their father, Rollo, is a famous lepidopterist."

"Investigates moths and butterflies," Constance explained.

Pru frowned at her sister for the interruption. "They've been gadding about the world with him ever since they were old enough to hold a butterfly net. They were in Brazil last year. And somewhere in Africa before that. But I do believe they're finally headed for these shores. Cousin Letty had a letter only recently."

Rhys slid a finger inside his cravat and gave it a tug. The room was decidedly warm. "Well, I'm sure I'll make their acquaintance if they ever decide to reenter polite society."

Pru's beatific smile was disconcerting, to say the least. "Oh, yes, dear. I'm sure you will."

The day after their wedding Harriet and Morgan received an unexpected visit from Lord Melville. The older man presented them with a handsome etched-glass bowl as a belated gift from Anne and himself, but that was only part of his reason for coming to call.

"I have a proposition to put to you, Davies. You too, Harriet."

Harriet glanced at Morgan and raised her brows in interest. "Go on."

"Since you're now a free trader, with a handsome ship of your own, the Admiralty would like to engage your services for a rather sensitive project."

Morgan tilted his head. "What's the destination?"

Melville's eyes took on a laughing twinkle. "We were hoping you'd take a trip over to Martinique. I've heard there are plenty of opportunities for trade. Cocoa, coffee, sugar—"

He reached into his coat and withdrew a folded piece of paper and Harriet's heart jumped as he laid it flat on the table. It was the map De Caen had left in her shop on the night he'd confronted her.

"And while you're there, you might retrieve another valuable cargo," Melville finished.

"You want us to try to find the French gold?" Harriet tried and failed to hide her excitement.

"Who better to head up the expedition than a captain who knows the waters and a mapmaker who knows how to read the charts?"

Harriet stared down at the circle of pencil De Caen had drawn around the tiny island dot far out in the ocean on the other side of the world. Her heart began to thump in anticipation.

She looked up and found Morgan watching her, a wicked smile of understanding on his face. He raised his brows in silent question, even though he must know her answer.

"Sounds like quite the adventure," he said. "What do you say, Mrs. Davies? Think you're up for the job?"

Harriet straightened and sent him a playful scowl. "Of course I am."

"What about your father? A journey like this will take several months."

"He's been talking about going to visit Uncle William at Newstead Park for the summer. I think he'll be fine there until we get back."

"In that case, Lord Melville, we accept. We can be ready to go as soon as the *Briseis* has a crew."

Melville clapped his hands. "Excellent. Time is of

the essence. You will, of course, be paid for your time at your previous rate, Captain Davies, but there's an added incentive: Prinny's offering one-tenth of the value of any French gold recovered to whoever finds it."

Morgan grinned. "In that case, we'd better start packing."

When Melville had left, Harriet couldn't contain her delight. She let out a little shriek of happiness and twirled in a circle in the middle of the drawing room carpet. Morgan caught her in his arms as she staggered giddily, and she looked up into his face.

"Are you sure you're ready for several weeks trapped on board a ship with me?" He smiled.

Harriet went up on tiptoe to kiss him. "Oh, I think I'll manage. I expect we can make your cabin very cozy. Do you think we'll find the treasure?"

"I have no idea. But even if we don't, I don't really care. You'll be getting an adventure. And I have my very own treasure right here in my arms. You're everything I could want. I love you."

"I love you too. I bet we find it."

His lips quirked. "You bet, eh? Well, *I* bet I can make you blissfully happy."

"That's quite a claim. Do you mean right now, or just in general?"

"Both."

Harriet chuckled. She slid her hands around his neck and sent him a wicked look from beneath her lashes. "Go on then, Morgan Davies. I dare you to try."

She shrieked as Morgan bent and swept her off her feet and headed for the stairs. She knew better than to dare a Davies to do anything, of course. But this was one bet she was more than happy to lose.